A Mu
Yule Regret

Books by Winnie Archer

A Murder
Yule Regret

Winnie Archer

KENSINGTON
PUBLISHING CORP.

www.kensingtonbooks.com

For my mom, Marilyn Sears Bourbon, whose family graces the pages and influences the characters in all my books.

Chapter 1

Christmas on the California coast isn't a picturesque greeting card of a snowy scene. Knitted hats and gloves are optional. But our old-fashioned street posts are adorned with wreathes and red ribbons, we have a night dedicated to wassail, and Christmas spirit abounds in storefront windows and holiday parties.

It was present in my Tudor house in the historic district of Santa Sofia, too. Just a little bit, but it was there. I'd just settled down for a long winter's night, a mug of steaming tea cupped between my hands, when my phone rang. Olaya Solis's name flashed on the screen. She was the owner of Yeast of Eden, the artisan bread shop in Santa Sofia, my boss, and a woman I admired. She had become my mentor about a minute after I'd first met her. I glanced at the clock—just after nine, which meant it was her *bedtime*, not *chat on the phone* time. Something was up.

"We must make bread for a holiday party," she announced after I greeted her with a surprised, "Hello?"

"What party?" I asked.

"It is for tomorrow evening."

I was curled up on the couch, wearing red-and-black-plaid pajama pants and a red Henley. Agatha, my little tan and black pug, lay on her side on the couch beside me. She extended her front legs in a long stretch and emitted a squeak. At the words *tomorrow evening*, I sat up from my reclined position. "That's pretty last-minute."

Less than twenty-four hours' notice for a party wasn't something Olaya would normally book. She required at least forty-eight hours to plan an event, and even that was cutting it too close for her comfort. Olaya Solis was a planner. She liked to have all her *I*s dotted and her *T*s crossed.

"It is," Olaya agreed. I could hear how tired she was, so why was she breaking her own rule? Before I could ask her, she said, "It is a high-profile client. I could not say no."

But that wasn't strictly true. Santa Sofia was a touristy coastal destination, even in winter. Business was booming, and while holiday parties during December were the bread and butter, so to speak, of most of the town's businesses, the earnings for the month offsetting any slow months during the town's off-season, that didn't really apply to Yeast of Eden. Stories of the bread's magical properties brought people from far and wide—all year long—to the bread shop. The bread shop was a destination, with people desperate to partake of Olaya's particular loaves and rolls. If they had heartache, the pain lessened. If they sought true passion, they discovered it. If they were lonely, that feeling abated. That kind of magic didn't depend on sunny beach weather. The fact of the matter was, Yeast of Eden didn't really *have* an off-season.

"Are you sure?" I asked, glancing at the wall clock again. "Tomorrow evening is . . . well, tomorrow. That's not a lot of time."

"I am sure, Ivy," she said. "*Pero* I do need your help."

Her Spanish accent always thickened when she was tired or stressed. At the moment, she was both. "Of course," I said, wanting to alleviate her anxiety. "What do you need?"

"Felix and I, we will be here at three thirty."

I couldn't help flinching. She meant three thirty *a.m.* She'd also said *here*, which meant she hadn't actually left the bread shop for the day. And she'd be turning around and going right back in a little more than six hours. No wonder she sounded exhausted.

I worked part-time at Yeast of Eden, mostly to absorb all that Olaya had to teach me, but also for a little extra income as I grew my freelance photography business. Olaya had grown up in Mexico and had learned traditional long-rise bread techniques. When I'd first returned to my hometown, she had helped save me from the grief of losing my mother. I'd become fascinated by the breadth of her skills and the power of her baking. And I'd caught the fever. From making a proof with yeast, sugar, and water, to digging my hands into a mound of soft dough, to shaping and baking, the entire process was cathartic and healing.

Still, the early mornings were not my favorite thing about the job, and usually I didn't have to get up before the roosters.

Felix Macron was Olaya's right-hand man and true apprentice. He and his small crew came in at four thirty every morning, excepting Sundays and Mondays, the shop's days off. That was bad enough, but three thirty was cringe-worthy.

"What are we baking?" I asked, trying not to let my lack of enthusiasm at the early hour creep into my voice.

She rattled off a list of four or five holiday breads, then added a few cookies. "Cookies?" I repeated when she'd finished. Olaya made chocolate croissants and the occasional sweetbread, but other than her ever-present skull cookies, she didn't *do* traditional bakery items.

"The woman hosting the party is . . . mmm . . . private. She wants only a few servers at the event. The person I spoke with—the assistant—she requested cookies, so I agreed."

Just because someone asked for cookies didn't mean Olaya would provide them. The fact that she had agreed showed just how unusual this situation was, but I went with it. "Okay. Cookies it is."

"And anyone involved, we all must sign a paper of some kind."

"What kind of paper?"

"A legal paper."

Something clicked. "Oh, like a nondisclosure agreement?"

"*Precisamente*," she said. "Nondisclosure. That is what she said."

Interesting. "Who's hosting this party?"

"That I will tell you tomorrow, after you sign. Six thirty for you, yes?"

Inside I heaved an enormous sigh of relief at the three extra hours of sleep I'd get. "See you then," I said, and went off to bed, all the while contemplating who this high-profile party host was.

Eighteen hours later, I stood in the festively decorated dining area of Yeast of Eden. Evergreen garlands tied with blue and silver bows hung in swaths around the windows. Delicate snowflakes hung from the ceiling. And Maggie Jewel, a part-time worker, was dressed like an elf, complete with bells on the tips of the curled toes of her green shoes. She stared at me as if I had just granted her a dying wish. "Are you serious?" she asked. "A holiday party?"

I fiddled with the settings on my camera, looked through the eyepiece, and snapped a picture of her, mouth agape. "Dead serious."

I pressed a button to look at the image on the camera's digital screen. Maggie had recently graduated from high school, started at the local community college, and cut her dark hair, taking it from shoulder-blade long to pixie short. She'd added a thin nose ring to her array of ear piercings, each more visible now with her boyish haircut.

She generally kept her small dragonfly tattoo on her collarbone covered, but once in a while, like now, it peeked out for the world to see.

Her hands fluttered frenetically. "But Eliza Fox is a bona-fide movie star!"

The bell on the bread shop's door dinged, and a woman in a red sweater, a young boy in tow, came in. Maggie pulled herself together, put her fingers to her lips, and turned an imaginary key of silence, but her excited grin stayed firmly in place as she greeted the woman, then told the boy to search the display cases for a skull cookie. Olaya baked a batch of her skull-shaped sugar cookies every few days, decorating them and then hiding them like Easter Eggs amidst the loaves of bread, rolls, croissants, and other goodies on display. Kids of all ages begged their parents to come into the bread shop just to search for one. Like all of Olaya's bread, the cookies seemed to hold a magical element, filling the children who found them with giddy joy.

"I see one!" The boy tugged on his mother's sleeve, pointing to a crevice between two loaves of batard.

"You got it!" Maggie pulled a sheet of waxed tissue from a pop-up box and reached into the case to retrieve the cookie.

I laughed as I caught sight of the cookie she handed to the boy. Olaya had decorated it with a red Santa hat, outdoing herself—which was saying a lot. The boy was charmed. He nibbled away at the white pompom as his mother requested a Twisted Star Loaf for an upcoming party. He moved to the red hat as she added a loaf of crusty Italian to her order.

The moment mother and son left the shop, Maggie spun back around to me, bells a-jingling, and jumped right back into our conversation as if we'd never stopped. "I heard Eliza Fox bought a house here, but I didn't think it was true. But it is? Really?"

"True?" I asked. She nodded, wide-eyed, and I said, "Apparently."

"And Olaya's catering the party? O.M.G. This is so exciting! She's better at keeping secrets than Santa Claus!"

"I imagine she didn't mention it because she just got the order last night. It's kind of last-minute."

Understanding clicked behind Maggie's eyes. "So that's why you all have been holed up in the kitchen all day. Santa's workshop, all for Eliza Fox."

"Yep, that's why."

The bell on the bread shop's door dinged again, and a group of twentysomethings came in. "Olaya said you're helping me set up?" I asked Maggie in a low voice before she was pulled away to help the customers.

"I didn't know it was for Eliza Fox, but yes!"

She scurried back behind the counter, her cheeks rosy with excitement.

I had to admit, I was pretty thrilled about meeting a real-life movie star, too. Eliza Fox had risen from obscurity to become *the* Hollywood It Girl as part of the ensemble sitcom *The Beach*. When a reporter asked her why she spent so much time in our little town, she was quoted as saying, "We filmed some of *The Beach* last season in Santa Sofia, and I fell in love."

I could understand her love of our magical piece of heaven. I'd moved back to stay, and Miguel Baptista, my beau, had a place on the other side of town. He'd bought his house as a major fixer-upper. After years of sweat equity and tender love and care, it was now the quaintest bungalow with a million-dollar ocean view. It didn't surprise me that Eliza Fox had bought a place here.

I'd been afraid the early morning call time to help with the baking would leave me needing a midday nap. I'd stifled a few yawns early in the day, but even if I did need a lie down, there was no time. The baking was done, and it was getting close to go time.

"What's with the camera?" Maggie asked after the customers left with armfuls of bread.

"I'm the official photographer for the party tonight," I

said. Eliza Fox's assistant had asked Olaya for a recommendation when they'd talked. Olaya had mentioned me, and just like that, I was hired. My fledgling photography business wasn't exactly booming, but it was steadily growing. Photographing Eliza Fox's party was sure to give it a boost.

Maggie giggled and rubbed her hands together. She was going to wring as much excitement from what would probably be a star-studded Christmas *fiesta* as she possibly could. "So, I'll see you there? Or, no, I'll see you here, right?"

"Right. We'll leave from here in"—I glanced at the wall clock—"one hour."

"Got it," she said, still bouncing on her toes. More customers arrived, and in minutes, a line had formed ten people deep. "Can I help?" I asked, but Maggie waved me away. She managed to put her anticipation aside and served the customers, getting them their bread and moving them out with quick efficiency.

As I passed the display case on my way back into the bread shop's kitchen, my stomach grumbled. I grabbed a sourdough roll to tide me over. I tore off a hunk with my teeth. The crusty outside and pillowy inside instantly satisfied my hunger. All I needed was a healthy slab of butter to slather on the roll. Next time. I pushed through the swinging door between the front of the store and the kitchen and ran smack into Felix Macron. There was an *oomph*, and the roll flew from my hand, straight up toward the ceiling. No!

Before I could react, Felix stepped back and tracked the roll, snagging it with one nitrile-gloved hand as if he were an outfielder easily catching a fly ball.

"Dude, good thing that wasn't your camera," Felix said, handing the roll back to me.

He got that right, but losing the roll would have been terrible, too. "Thank you!" I took another bite and spoke through the chunk in my cheek. "It's so good. Better than the stuff they sell at the wharf in the City."

He looked offended as he said, "God, it had better be," but a dimple etched into his cheek. "Ready for tonight?"

Felix's white chef's shirt with its three-quarter sleeves and buttons running up the right side still looked fresh and light, despite the long hours he'd put in today. His round belly and smiling eyes gave him a Pillsbury Doughboy look. He wore a perpetual grin, and you couldn't help but smile back. The young man was a study in contrasts, his luminescent light eyes looking like pools of glassy water glowing against his rich, dark skin, his easy demeanor belying his immense baking skills. An old soul lived in Felix's mid-twenties body.

I nodded, swallowing the bite of bread I'd taken. "As ready as I can be."

"Have fun. And say hi to the Hollywood stars for me," he said with a wink.

"Hey!" A young woman backhanded him on his arm.

Felix let out a belly laugh, his squinting eyes looking lovingly at his girlfriend, Janae. "Not that she'd ever look my way, but if she did? You have nothing to worry about. Eliza Fox isn't my type."

Janae was petite—five feet on a good day—and had sable skin that was several shades darker than Felix's. Her brown eyes glowed with a rim of gold, and her hair was braided and piled high on her head, giving her another five inches in height, at least. She wore a chef's

shirt similar to her boyfriend's and threaded her arm
through his.

The adoration on Felix's face made it clear that Eliza
Fox, a five-eleven, blond-haired, blue-eyed, pale-skinned
porcelain doll starlet couldn't hold a candle to Janae.

"Get some sleep, you two," I said. They deserved it.

"Can't wait to hear all about it," Janae said. "At least
what you can tell us without breaking the law."

We spent thirty minutes loading everything to go, and
twenty minutes later, we left. Olaya drove to Eliza Fox's
beach house in the Yeast of Eden white van, with Maggie,
no longer dressed as an elf, as her passenger. The shop's
simple logo—"Yeast of Eden" written in a classic font,
"Artisan Bread Shop" in a neat cursive just beneath it,
framed in an oval—adorned both sides of the vehicle. I
followed them in my white Fiat crossover.

A short while later, we arrived at what was less of a
beach house and more of an oceanfront mansion. Olaya
stopped briefly at the open-gated entrance before pro-
ceeding through it and down the driveway. We parked on
the left side of the house, out of the way to allow plenty
of room for the guest's cars.

I couldn't help the nervous pounding of my heart. Ever
since I'd been a child, I'd had occasional celebrity sightings in Santa Sofia. My mother had once pointed out one
of the *Brady Bunch* kids—a show I knew from old re-
runs—now middle-aged, holding court in a diner. An
actor known for his role in a TV medical drama lived here
and had a reputation as a curmudgeonly old coot. And
stars drove up from Los Angeles to experience the quaint
town just like regular people did. Still, being the official
photographer for Eliza Fox's spontaneous holiday party

and meeting the actress herself had butterflies flapping their wings double-time in my stomach.

As I'd rolled up to the house, I'd taken in the details of the home's exterior. It was contemporary, with glass walls in the front that gave an unobstructed view through the interior and straight out the glass walls in the back that overlooked the ocean. The main floor jutted out over a slightly smaller smooth black cement foundation. It was like a transparent box sitting atop a smaller box. Minimalist shrubs dotted the front landscape. Clearly nothing was meant to deter from the main attraction, which was the vast expanse of the Pacific Ocean. I got out and immediately snapped a collection of pictures. I was going to approach the photographs I'd be taking throughout the night as if they were a hamburger. The opening shots of the home's exterior would be the bottom bun, the party itself would be all the fixings, and a parting shot or two of the exterior once night had fallen would be the top bun, completing the set.

I swallowed my nerves, grabbed the rest of my camera equipment, and made my way to the opposite side of the house, which was created from opaque stone walls. The walls formed what looked like cement boxes of varying sizes stacked haphazardly on top of each other. While I'd taken photos, Olaya and Maggie had gotten to work unloading the van. Now I knocked on the side door so I could join them.

The woman who answered the door had a clipboard in one hand and wore glasses attached to a clear crystal beaded lanyard. She took one look at my camera and heaved an enormous sigh of relief. "Ivy Culpepper, I presume? Ms. Solis said you were here, too." She stood back and held the black door open. "Come in. I'm Nicole Leonard, assistant to Eliza Fox. You can put your things over here."

She was all business as she directed me to a tucked-away space with a black bench and a door at the end leading to what I guessed was the garage. Stacks of Yeast of Eden's plastic bins sat just inside the door.

"Ms. Solis and her helper are setting up in the library. Let me show you around," she said, taking her glasses off and letting them dangle around her neck. She was somewhere in her forties, I thought, but I couldn't say on which end. Her dark hair was pulled into an old-fashioned chignon. She would have fit in perfectly in an old Marilyn Monroe film.

I left my camera bag, but brought my Canon and the flash in case there was something I wanted to shoot on my tour of the glass house. "It's beautiful," I said, but I wouldn't have wanted to live here. I'd been inside for a single minute, and I already felt like a fish in a fishbowl. The setting was private enough to feel confident that no one was actually out there watching, but still. I liked the solid walls of my house.

I stole a glance through the glass at the front drive, noting the trees lining the driveway and more low-lying shrubs sprinkled here and there. Plenty of places for paparazzi to hide, though they'd never be able to get past the gate once it closed.

At least I hoped not.

Large windows overlooked a small grassy backyard. With enough money and a good gardener, apparently green grass was accessible all year long. The area was lined with enormous boulders, which created a barrier to the cliff below. A shiver wound through me. I wouldn't want to get too close to the edge. Without a railing, it looked dangerous.

I stared out the massive windows, taking a deep breath as if we were outside and I could inhale the salty sea air. Beyond the green of the yard, the ocean extended as far as the eye could see. If Miguel's bungalow had a million-dollar view of the Pacific, this place skyrocketed into the billion-dollar realm.

"The party will be in the great room, but the food will be in the library," Nicole Leonard said, bringing me back to the here and now.

I managed to say, "Okay," before she continued. "Eliza would like you to take candids of *all* the guests, as well as the Dickens players. Of course, you may not know which is which. People who inhabit Eliza's world tend to go all out at costume events."

I had no idea what she was talking about. It was a Christmas party, not a Halloween haunt, so the costume thing threw me, but I didn't have a chance to ask more about it because we'd reached the library.

I stopped, orienting myself. Walking through the opening that separated the great room from the library felt a bit like driving through the Santa Cruz Mountains from the east bay to the peninsula. It could be clear and sunny east of the mountains, but the second you passed through, a heavy blanket of fog often hid the sky and ringed the mountains like a halo.

I got the same disconcerting feeling here. The great room was large and open and bright from all the windows, even in the fading evening light, but the library was darker and homier. It felt like it belonged in a different house altogether.

Nicole beckoned me forward to the catering tables,

draped in red cloths. Olaya and Maggie had brought in several of the bins, but they'd disappeared again to bring in the rest. The other table held empty serving dishes just waiting to be filled. An artistic stack of books on a corner table formed a unique three-foot Christmas tree, and a fragrant evergreen stood next to the fireplace, decked with tasteful and color-coordinated decorations. A lighted star sat on top.

I quickly adjusted the light settings on my camera and snapped a photo of the two trees. Every shelf in the room was decorated with knickknacks, books, and some of the awards Eliza Fox had won over the years.

"This is one of the rooms Eliza remodeled. It doesn't quite fit with the rest of the house," Nicole said, as if reading my mind, "but it makes her happy."

The two vastly different decorative styles certainly formed a dichotomy.

"You'll need to be in costume, of course," Nicole said. "To blend in."

I lowered the camera and looked at her. "Wait. What?"

"It's a Dickens Christmas party. We will provide the costume, of course." She consulted her clipboard. "You can be a caroler, one of Mrs. Fezziwig's shopgirls, or a flower girl."

"Olaya and Maggie, too?" I asked.

"Ms. Solis will stay behind the table and wear a dark dress and bonnet. I gave the younger girl something. You'll be amongst the guests, so Eliza has other choices for you. She would like you to blend in."

We walked through the library and into the dining room, which was another glass-walled space. Through that was the kitchen. A wall of windows opened to the north side of the house with a clear view of the covered patio with a gray cement outdoor fireplace, a long black table and matching chairs, a lovely sitting area with black-framed outdoor furniture, a standing heater at the ready, and a crystal-clear rectangular pool. Despite the fact that it was December, five black chaise lounges with pristine thick white cushions lined the far side of the pool.

I barely had time to take in the kitchen—one any professional chef would be thrilled to cook in—before Nicole led me back around to the main living area. An open L-shaped flight of stairs led to the second floor. Each stone step had an uneven front edge, an interesting feature in the otherwise minimalistic house—excepting the library, of course. Nicole had a brisk pace, and I hurried to keep up, pausing just long enough at the landing to take in the view from that vantage point.

Even in the gloaming, it was spectacular.

"Hello there," a familiar voice said.

I turned and looked up to the top of the stairs. There, in a short white terry-cloth bathrobe, with tan legs that seemed to go on for miles, stood Eliza Fox.

Chapter 2

It turns out Eliza Fox wasn't the diva I'd half-expected. While Olaya and Maggie continued their setup, the three of us—Nicole, Eliza, and me—chatted in Eliza's dressing room, which had a rose-colored velvet divan, a burgundy sofa, and a floral armchair. None of it fit in the modern house, but it seemed that Eliza carved out certain spaces, making them exactly what she wanted and reflecting a different era than the glass dwelling's inherent style. We chatted about everything from who had the best French fries in Santa Sofia (the Burger Shack) to the craziness of dodging paparazzi (an impossibility) and losing one's anonymity (a sad reality for celebrities).

Eliza, against all odds, was down-to-earth. Unexpectedly, she had plenty of insecurities and doubts about her fame. "I didn't do anything to deserve all"—she gestured wide, encompassing the entire house, her entire world maybe—"this."

I nodded along, listening.

"My start in Hollywood happened just like those old stories about a woman perched on a stool at the soda fountain and being discovered." She made air quotes around the last word. "I was at the right place at the right time. Gunther Hoffman—that's my agent—saw me and said he'd make me a star."

Nicole *tsk*ed. "That's how Hollywood works. You deserve every bit of your success."

"You work for me. You have to say that," Eliza said, flashing her a warm smile.

Nicole waved her off. "No, I don't. If I didn't believe in you, I wouldn't have kept this job. Gunther knows beauty and talent, and you have both. You need to learn to accept it so you can enjoy the life it affords you."

Eliza pushed herself up from the floral armchair and strode across the dressing room to where Nicole stood, leaning against the built-in stack of drawers, and hugged her. "Now. Let's get to know Ivy, shall we?" Eliza said.

She turned and looked at me expectantly. I told her about growing up in Santa Sofia, college in Austin, Texas, and my business and marriage there, both of which fell apart, leaving me free to return to my hometown when my mother unexpectedly died.

"I'm so sorry," she said. "I lost my mother, too, so I know what that's like."

We were silent for a moment before she continued. "When we were filming *The Beach* here, I knew this was where I wanted to live. I left home as soon as I could, but now this"—she spread her arms wide again and glanced around—"this is my home. Second chances. Sometimes they really do work out."

"It's an incredible house," I said.

A sheepish expression appeared on her face. "It's a

little big and not really my style, but the views are great and it's private."

"And privacy is essential," Nicole said. "Eliza has had, shall we say, unwanted attention in the past. The privacy here puts her at ease."

Neither of them elaborated, and I didn't ask for details, but I could imagine. There were crazies in the world, something I'd discovered firsthand with my ex-husband's second wife (who also happened to be the woman he'd cheated on me with). She'd thought Luke still had feelings for me, and jealousy had reared its ugly head. To say it had been disconcerting was an understatement.

I donned the costume Eliza picked out for me—a green velvet robe with white faux fur trim running vertically down the center and around the wide sleeve edges. The robe was belted. I put my hair up in a loose bun, strands framing my face, finishing off the costume with a wreath made of fake holly leaves and berries. It wasn't a caroler or one of Mrs. Fezziwig's girls. It was the Ghost of Christmas Present. Eliza insisted on the green velvet. "It brings out your eyes!"

I took a final look in the mirror, straightening the wreath so it sat squarely on my head. Eliza was right. The emerald robe set off the strawberry tones in my hair and my green eyes. The loose spirals of my hair helped to create a slightly ethereal look. All in all, I thought I looked pretty good for a ghost.

I left Nicole and Eliza, taking a moment to cross through the upstairs loft to gaze out the westward-facing windows. The setting sun lit up the sky like a watercolor painting, splashes of pink and orange and red streaking across the vast expanse of the horizon. It was breathtaking.

Back downstairs, a few Dickens characters had appeared. Several milled about in the great room near the no-host bar, and two others stood on the small grassy area in the backyard—a female caroler and her male counterpart—staring at the last vestiges of the setting sun as I just had. It wasn't the perfect shot, but I took a few pictures of their silhouettes through the glass, the sunset like a kaleidoscope all around them.

Back in the library, Olaya had her back to me. She had changed from the wide-legged jeans and lightweight sweater she'd been wearing into a long-sleeved black dress with a cinched waist and a full skirt. She turned around. Only a bit of her short iron-gray hair showed beneath the black bonnet she wore. She would have fit in perfectly in 1800 London.

"Olaya!" I exclaimed. "It's perfect!"

She favored colorful flowing caftans, palazzo pants, and the like, and kept her short hair spiky and modern, but the period dress and hat looked amazing on her.

She brushed off the compliment and grumbled.

I had to laugh. Olaya didn't watch much television, so I knew she didn't know Eliza Fox from *The Beach*. And she had only recently started going to movies—with my dad. Owen and Olaya. Their dating had given my dad a new lease on life, and Olaya had a happy glow about her, but actors, apparently, didn't impress her. To her, Eliza Fox was just another client, albeit a rich one who required an NDA.

She looked at my outfit, her eyebrows pulling inward. "Who are you?"

"The Ghost of Christmas Present," I said. "This way I can blend in with the party guests and snap their pictures."

"Okay," she said, as if she was giving me permission.

"Okay." I looked at the tables behind her. They were laid out with all the special breads we'd spent the morning baking. Miniature candied sweetbread shaped like candy canes, white icing crisscrossing each one, were neatly lined up on one of the large white trays that had been set out. On another were small reindeer heads with black eyes and red noses. They looked like cookies, but they were made of a crescent roll dough and brushed with an egg wash to give them a shiny finish. Santa bread cookies, done with the same crescent dough, were artfully stacked on another tray. Olaya never took the easy way on anything. She was detail-oriented, even under a strict timeline. She'd used a ricer to create the strands of dough that made up the beards and had taken the time to paint hats and noses on each Santa face.

Finally, she, Felix, Janae, and I had done loaves and loaves of panettone. She'd soaked raisins in rum and had made the dough the night before—the reason she'd stayed so late. She'd begun almost the second she'd found out about the party, because her panettone required two rises.

Each loaf was filled with the raisins and candied orange peel, which added a subtle citrus essence to the brioche-like bread. They had a cupcake shape, only on a much larger scale, with the top puffing up and around the base. Actually, they reminded me a bit of Eliza's contemporary house with the way the main structure sat atop a smaller base.

The panettone loaves were stunning. Olaya would cut them into pieces to serve at the last minute, giving the guests a chance to see them intact.

The rest of the tables were covered with an eclectic variety of heavy appetizers from a different caterer. Rumaki, sticky barbecue meatballs, curry-chicken skewers, sliders, as well as vegetable and fruit trays, would certainly fill up the guests. My stomach growled again.

Olaya raised one eyebrow and handed me a reindeer bread cookie. "It is going to be a long evening. Keep your strength up."

I bit off an antler and felt my eyes roll back. "Mmm. So good." All I'd had since the morning was Yeast of Eden bread. It had been a very carb-heavy day. I'd need something else, but I didn't dare sneak anything off the appetizer table. "I'm going to check out the kitchen," I told Olaya. "Do you need anything?"

"No, *gracias*. I am fine."

As I headed to the kitchen, my velvety robe fluttering behind me, I caught a glimpse of Olaya pulling her cell phone from some hidden pocket in her dress and immediately texting someone.

I arched a brow and grinned. My dad, perhaps?

I'd tucked my own cell phone into my bra—the only option I had. I slung the strap of my camera over my shoulder and pulled my phone out now, bringing up Miguel's name in my Favorites list.

Hey, I typed, hitting Send.

Almost instantaneously, a response came. *Hey.*

I held the phone out in front of me, reversed the camera direction, and snapped a selfie. *Me dressed as the Ghost of Christmas Present*, I typed, then pressed Send.

My Christmas present? A wink emoji followed.

My thumbs flew across the keyboard. A second later, I sent a blushing emoji followed by: *I'll call you as soon as I'm finished here.*

His response came back in a flash. *Can't wait to un-wrap you.*

My heart gave a little flutter. Even though we hadn't had a frank conversation about it, ever since my brother's wedding to my best friend, Emmaline Davis, Miguel and I had both been skirting around the topic of our long-term commitment. After my failed marriage with Luke Holden, I'd told myself that if I ever married again, it would be forever. I wanted Miguel for keeps, and he'd told me he was "all in" with our relationship. We weren't quite at the let's-get-engaged stage, but we were slowly tiptoeing in that direction.

I sent him three beating heart emojis before tucking my phone back into my bra. I liked Eliza Fox and hoped her party was a smashing success, but as soon as I could help Olaya and Maggie pack up and we could skedaddle, I'd be out of there.

From where I stood, I could see the quartz countertop of the rectangular center island covered with food ready to replenish the appetizers already laid out in the library. Circular serving trays were stacked at one end. They'd be filled up and servers would circulate, allowing the party guests to partake.

I started forward, but stopped short at the sound of two men arguing. I trained my ear to follow their voices, placing them in the hallway off the kitchen where I'd stashed my camera bag earlier.

"You ruined my marriage and—"

"And what? Your career? You're still here, man." He gave a mirthless laugh. "You both won. People don't care about affairs anymore. Been there, done that."

The first man—his voice was familiar, but I couldn't

place it—said, "There was no affair. That photo's a fake, and you know it!"

Another laugh, this one dismissive. "That's not what *she* said."

"Then she lied, you son of a bitch. You'd better print a retraction or—"

"Or what?" The man—apparently a reporter—barked.

"I could sue you for everything you're worth."

"Never gonna happen," the reporter mocked.

"You wanna bet?"

"Good luck, man. I'm not seeing the damage, and I've moved on. You're upset about that hot little thing? Wait till you see the *next* piece I'm printing."

"You can't mess with people's lives—"

"Messing with people's lives pays the bills, man."

The next thing I heard was footsteps. I shrank back. All the light, bright open space in the house meant there were no shadows to disappear into, but the man who emerged from the hallway off the garage just marched straight past me without looking left or right. He was dressed from head to toe in grungy black, including a top hat on his head, which looked worse for wear. From where I stood, I could just see into the great room, which was now filling up with more of the early arrivals. From the looks of it, Nicole had been right. Eliza's guests had gone all out with the costumes. The man's retreating figure disappeared into the crowd.

I started into the kitchen, bracing myself for an encounter with the other angry man who'd been part of the argument. Instead, I bumped into one of the caterers balancing a tray on one open palm. "Sorry, ma'am," he said, quickly skirting around me and carrying on.

"Ma'am"? I was only thirty-six. That wasn't "ma'am" territory, was it?

I kept going. Another two steps and I was in the kitchen, free and clear. I glanced down the hallway. My camera bag sat just where I'd left it. No one else was in sight. Whoever had been arguing with the man in black had also disappeared.

"Help you, ma'am?"

I grumbled to myself. Again with the "ma'am."

A young man wearing a neatly pressed, white button-down shirt and black slacks stood at the island filling the trays. He looked at me, his posture stiff, as if he was trying to look authoritative in his task. With their black and white attire, at least it would be easy to tell who the servers were.

My gaze strayed to the array of appetizers. "I'm the photographer," I said, holding up my camera as proof. "I'm starving. Can I sneak a little something?"

"Sure thing." He handed me a small white plate. "Help yourself."

I sagged with relief. Sustenance! Because even I couldn't live on bread alone. "Thank you so much." I picked three stuffed mushrooms, crisps of Parmesan cheese artfully placed on top, several bacon-wrapped shrimp with bleu cheese, and a crostini with bacon salsa. I added what was left of my reindeer bread cookie and dug in. I didn't have much time before I needed to be out with the guests, commemorating the party for Eliza.

My curiosity got the better of me, and I pointed to the garage hallway. "There were some men arguing over there. Did you see them?"

"Hard to miss. I thought they might've ended up with

blows," the young man said. "Didn't pay much attention, though. I gotta unload another batch of appetizers. It's been crazy, you know?"

I did know. I swallowed the bacon-wrapped shrimp, said, "It's delicious," then popped another one in my mouth.

"I didn't cook it, but thanks. I'll let Renee know."

I choked on a shrimp. "Renee?" I croaked. "As in Renee Ranson of Divine Cuisine?"

The young man looked quizzically at me. "Yeah, you know her?"

That depended on how you defined the word *know*. When I'd first moved back to Santa Sofia, one of Olaya's best friends had been killed. I'd gotten wrapped up in the case, and it had led me straight to Renee Ranson and her catering business. The woman was in a wheelchair, the victim of a hit-and-run accident.

I spun my head around, looking for her.

"She's outside. I'm holding down the fort in here till she comes back in. Even after, actually. I'm new, but the party was last-minute and there was a lot to do, so they were short-staffed. I had an in, so bam! Here I am. Luckily it's not hard to fill trays," the young man said. "Maybe I'll be a chef someday."

It was good to dream. "Well, um . . ."

"Zac," he said, filling in the dead air I'd left.

"Well, Zac, tell Renee the food is amazing."

He remained serious about filling the trays, but nodded. Two servers, dressed just like the others in black and white, strode into the kitchen and swapped their empty trays for filled ones, striding right back out without even a hitch. For hourly seasonal workers, which I figured was standard in the catering business, they operated flaw-lessly.

I went back to my small plate full of appetizers and moved on to the stuffed mushrooms. The first bite practically melted in my mouth. "Oh my God, thish ish sho good," I said, putting my fingers over my full mouth.

"Yeah. Renee told me they were pretty popular. The Parmesan crisp really elevates it. That's what she said, anyway."

Renee Ranson certainly knew what she was doing. "She's right."

I kept eating, and Zac kept talking. "My fiancée, Rita? She's working tonight, too. We're saving up. We're moving to Seattle."

"Seattle. Wow, that's exciting." I beamed at him, but inside I wondered if he was even old enough to get married. He was baby-faced and looked about eighteen. Other than this last-minute part-time gig, did he even have a job? But instead of asking him his age, I went with, "Congratulations!"

He glanced around, as if he was making sure the coast was clear—of what, I had no idea. "Rita's had a rough year. We almost split up. Actually we *did* split up after her fifteen minutes of fame. This whole acting business . . ." His expression changed a hair, taking on a frustrated edge. He hesitated and shook his head for a beat before continuing. "But it was only for about a minute. She came back around. We can get through anything together, you know?"

It's amazing what people—perfect strangers, to be specific—tell you when you leave air space for them to fill. I'd never seen Zac before in my life, but now I knew that his girlfriend had broken up with him after having some sort of acting success, and also that she'd come back to him. I hoped whatever they had was true love. I knew from experience that couples couldn't make it past every obstacle they faced. Case in point, my failed marriage to Luke. It was the main reason I'd wanted to take things slowly with Miguel, but slow or not, our future was calling. If Zac and his girlfriend had found that commitment early, I was happy for them.

Chapter 3

Walking into the great room of Eliza Fox's contemporary house, now that the party was in full swing, was like walking through a time portal whose wires had gotten crossed. I was in Dickens's London in a house with glass walls and the darkening ocean just beyond. The people dressed as Scrooge and Marley, Bob Cratchit and his wife, Mrs. Fezziwig, albeit much thinner than the original character, nameless carolers, chimney sweeps, and shopkeepers looked like they'd been transported through time into some future world where they didn't fit in . . . only they didn't realize it. They sipped their cocktails and ate from the small plates they'd filled up in the library. Some snagged appetizers from the wandering servers.

Despite the weirdness, a festive spirit wafted through the air. I threaded my way through the crowd, snapping photographs. Once or twice, quizzical eyebrows rose or someone said, "Hey!"

All I had to do to quell any concerns about my motives was smile, hold up my camera, and say "For Eliza."

Bits of conversations came at me from all sides.

A couple dressed as paupers snuggled up to each other. "We don't have to stay long," the woman said with a suggestive hint in her voice, but the man clucked with disapproval, then replied in a British accent, "Of course we do. We paid for these bloody costumes. You better believe we're going to get our money's worth. Drink as much as you want, baby. It's Eliza's dime."

I rolled my eyes. Even the friends of the rich and famous weren't above getting something for nothing. I left them to discuss the free alcohol, managing to snap a photo of them before I moved on, catching bits and pieces of conversations in progress.

I came upon two women, one of whom, despite her high-society 1800s dress and bonnet, looked a bit familiar. "You know I beat out Cordelia Knight for the part in the new Ron Howard film," she said.

The woman with her, dressed as her twin but in a different color, clapped silently. "And congrats to you. You're perfect for the part."

The first woman beamed before pulling her brows together in a show of empathy. "Yes, but what a blow to her."

"After that bombshell story, are you surprised?" the second woman asked. "The men, now, they can get away with anything—"

"Not anymore, now that we have the Me Too movement."

"I don't know. There's still a double standard."

The first woman gave a flippant wave of her hand. "Of course there is. That'll never go away. Still, I feel a little bit bad for her. A person should have some expectation of privacy, I think, even in our business. Those reporters are unconscionable."

I remembered the Cordelia Knight scandal from a few months back. The actress had allegedly been caught with two unidentified men at a private beach, all of them scantily clad—if clad at all. The rumor mill went wild. I remembered one of the headlines: *Is the girl next door* starlet *actually a* harlot?

Cordelia Knight's denials of anything sordid fell on deaf ears. The actress had taken matters into her own hands by giving an exclusive interview about the incident and how misunderstood she was. After all, she wasn't married, and didn't she have a right to have a little fun?

I tended to agree with the woman who'd claimed that men weren't judged as harshly as women when it came to sexual antics. The actions of Harvey Weinstein and the like notwithstanding, if a hot young actor had been caught cavorting with two willing and able women, the photo would have run in *People* magazine under Celebrity Sightings. The image of Cordelia Knight had run in the tabloids, and her exploits had been judged with an iron gavel rather than passed over with a roguish smile and a dismissive *boys will be boys*.

Hollywood had a short memory, though. Cordelia Knight might have lost a part thanks to her indiscretion, but I thought it was pretty likely she'd rise to the top again.

I kept walking, more snippets of party chitchat coming at me.

"Can you believe he showed up? The gall!"

"You don't believe it's true, do you?"

"Pst."

"I mean, that Yentin article wrecked her career, didn't it—"

"And that picture of—"

"Pst."

I had no idea what the people I passed were talking about, but I admit, my curiosity was piqued. Ear-hustling, as my feisty eighty-something neighbor called it, was an entertaining pastime when you didn't know anyone.

"Pst!"

Whoever was *pst*ing needed to try another method.

"Ghost of Christmas," someone hissed. "Ivy!"

Oh! I spun around, realizing the *pst*ing was for me. The person before me was dressed as a nineteenth-century beggar, but through the makeup and costume, I recognized the face. "Maggie! Wow, great costume," I said, completely mesmerized by the depth of her commitment to the role.

"Oh yeah, well, you know, I had to go all in."

That she had.

Without warning, she grabbed my arm and yanked me aside. I let out a surprised *"umph."* "Maggie—" I started, then worry sliced through me. Had something happened to Olaya? "Is everything okay—" I started, but stopped and breathed a sigh of relief when I spotted Olaya manning her bread table.

"What? Yeah, everything's fine."

"God, you scared me," I said.

"Sorry." She looked contrite for a split second before her eyes bulged. I could almost feel the electrical current flowing through her body, amping up with every passing second. "Well?"

"Well what?" I asked coyly. Watching her eyes frantically scan the crowd, I knew exactly what had her so anxious.

"Did you meet her?" she demanded. "Is she as wonderful as she seems? Please tell me she's not one of those stuck-up stars."

"Who?" I asked, making my expression blank.

"What? You know who! Eliza Fox!" Maggie practically screeched, then she looked at me, blinked, and backhanded my arm. "Oooh, Ivy. Don't do that!"

I dragged her away from the partygoers before she raised a crazy fangirl alarm and Nicole fetched Security to have her removed. "I haven't seen her come downstairs yet," I said, realizing it had been close to an hour since I'd descended those stairs. "She should be coming anytime now."

"Dammit, stop," someone snapped. "It's over."

I glanced to my left in time to see a man dressed all in black—another chimney sweep; they were a dime a dozen—storming away from a petite young woman, a black shawl around her shoulders. She stared after the retreating figure, lips trembling from the rebuke, before throwing her shoulders back in defiance. She held her head high, spun around, and marched away. *You'll be okay*, I wanted to tell her. *There are other fish in the sea.*

I looked around again, searching for the party's host. Still no Eliza, but Nicole stood off to one side of the stairs. She'd changed into a full-skirted period dress. Her hair and makeup were done so perfectly that she could have been the real deal—a woman straight out of Dickens's England. Only her frown as she stared at the guests and the clipboard she held in the crook of her arm kept her firmly rooted in the present.

I followed her line of sight straight to a server weaving through the crowd, heading to the door leading to the small backyard. Nicole tried to beckon to the girl, pointing to the stairs. Eliza's big moment must be imminent, and Nicole wanted everyone present, but the server didn't notice.

I turned back to see Nicole shake her head, clearly exasperated. Meanwhile, a slow clapping began. It grew louder and faster. A few whoops and hollers rose above the frenetic crowd as Eliza Fox appeared at the top of the stairs. I watched with everyone else for a moment before I started snapping photos. Eliza slowly descended the stairs looking like a princess, the crowd below her adoring subjects. She paused at the landing halfway down, tilting her head coquettishly and fluttering her fingers in a wave. Her Dickens costume was unexpected, yet somehow perfect. She was a female Scrooge in a cream dressing gown and nightcap, her golden hair in a single braid draping over one shoulder.

I took more pictures as she threw her head back and gave a jaunty laugh. "Thank you all for coming tonight and for indulging me in my love of Dickens." She could see everyone from her position, and she stood silently for a moment taking them all in, nodding *hellos* here and there. For the briefest moment, her gaze hitched and her smile wavered, but she summoned it back and continued acknowledging her guests. But then she froze again. This time the color drained from her face, making her look all the more like Scrooge when he encountered the Ghost of Christmas Past and faced the realities of his childhood.

Eliza Fox, though, really was a good actress. Just as quickly as her face had come undone, she put it back together. Whatever—or whoever—had spooked her had been pushed to some hidden compartment in her mind. The air in the crowded room suddenly felt stale and heavy. I shook off the feeling of claustrophobia and turned around to try to see whom Eliza had been looking at, but all I saw was a wall of nineteenth-century Londoners, along with the modern-day servers in their black and white.

I spotted Zac by the bar, clutching a tray filled with appetizers with both hands. I didn't blame him. Balancing the tray on an open palm seemed like a disaster waiting to happen in the crowded room.

Beside me, Maggie squealed. "She's so beautiful, isn't she?"

"She is," I said, but something about the expression that had passed over Eliza's face bothered me. It had looked like fear or shock, or a combination of both. Even though I'd only just met her for the first time, I felt a kinship with her. I wanted to go to her and ask if she was okay, but when I turned back around, she'd finished descending the stairs and had been absorbed by her guests.

Checking in with Nicole would be the next best thing, but the assistant had also melted into the crowd. A ribbon of cool air suddenly filtered through the room. I silently thanked whoever had just opened the door leading to the small backyard. The fresh air now circulating kept the room from feeling suffocating.

Beside me, Maggie was on her tiptoes trying to spot her idol. "There she is!" She pointed toward the glass windows. A few low lights now illuminated the outside space.

Somehow, Eliza had made it through the maze of people and stood outside with a small group of people. From where I stood, I couldn't make any of them out.

Behind me, a man spoke, a note of playfulness in his

voice. "I don't think I've ever seen you eat so many carbs."

I turned to see him raise a single eyebrow at a woman in a cinch-waisted dress. She gave a heavy sigh, and her eyes rolled up in ecstasy. "I know, but it's so freaking good." She had a plateful of Olaya's baked goods—one of everything, by the looks of it. "I think my dress zipper might actually pop open."

"Well, I like you with a little meat on your bones," he said, the suggestive tone in his voice unmistakable.

"Yeah, well, the camera doesn't, but right now I don't care." And with that, she bit Santa's hat off a bread cookie and let out a satisfied groan.

Another happy customer. I stepped out of their line of sight, snapped a photo, then dragged Maggie back to the library.

Olaya stood behind the bread table, hands on her hips, her chin lowered. "Maggie, you are here to help me, not to star gaze," she scolded.

Maggie did her best to look sheepish, but didn't quite pull it off. Her gaze strayed past the people gathering at the food tables and toward the backyard, still searching for another glimpse of Eliza. "I know but—"

"No," Olaya said in a tone that brought Maggie's head back around. Olaya snapped her fingers three times. "I am paying you, yes?"

Maggie nodded.

"*Bueno.*" And that was it. With five little words, Olaya had made it clear that she expected Maggie to tamp down the fangirl and stay put at the bread table.

Maggie looked appropriately chastised.

"Oh God, the carbs!" a woman said as she took two slices of panettone.

Olaya's lips curved into an almost imperceptible smile. I suspected that she'd worked a little of her magic, the mere aroma of her bread drawing in the perpetual dieters, making them disregard their carb-counting and caloric intake for the evening, instead giving them the mental boost of satisfying a long-suffering hunger for all things baked.

I knew better than to take too many pictures in the library with all the food being consumed, so I left Maggie and Olaya and drifted back out to the great room. Some of the partygoers had made their way upstairs to the loft. The great room felt manageable now, and I was able to catch people in candid poses just as Nicole had requested. One by one, I took shots of each and every person downstairs, which took a solid hour and a half. Some people were not as photogenic as others. Even though they were candids, I wanted each subject to be shown in their best light. Finally, I headed upstairs to capture the rest. Outside, the ocean had become an inky expanse, a few lights appearing far in the distance. Even with the low lights, the backyard was still dark. It was eerie knowing that with the blackness outside and the bright lights inside, we were all on display.

Not that it was possible for anyone to actually see in. We were on a cliff, after all. I gripped the metal railing and continued upstairs, freezing when a shrill scream cut through the party chatter.

The entire house seemed to have gone mute for a few seconds. I spun around, trying to place the location, realizing suddenly that it was coming from outside. A few of the guests had come to the same conclusion. I raced back down the stairs and through the frozen crowd, joining those who had propelled themselves into action by plowing through the side door. Down the square cement steps. Onto the patch of grass.

A serving tray lay upside down on the grass, bits of bread and smashed appetizers scattered around it. A young woman, who couldn't have been older than twenty, backed away from the huge boulders, one hand covering her mouth, the other pointing past the edge of the yard and down over the cliff.

Those of us who had rushed outside moved forward while the girl continued to back up. "Someb-b-body—" she stammered.

That's when I noticed her outstretched arm, her finger pointing . . . down.

My heart climbed to my throat as I dropped to my knees and inched forward. Carefully, I peered over the edge. Sure enough, splayed out on the rocks below, was the dark form of a body.

Chapter 4

My sister-in-law, Emmaline Davis, was also Santa Sofia's elected sheriff. She'd arrived with her deputy and the new-ish Captain Craig York. The sheriff's department, under Emmaline's command, was running as smooth as a bowl of risen dough. Once she'd taken office, Em had restructured, putting York in charge of the criminal division, allowing her to concentrate on everything else—warrants, securing courthouses in the county, dealing with the unincorporated areas in the county, and overseeing the county jail.

"This is going to be high-profile," she said when I asked her why she hadn't just let York handle the crime scene. Not that I *wanted* York in charge. He'd recently had his sights set on Miguel as the responsible party in the death of a schoolboard member. Thankfully, with my help, he'd seen the truth. I hadn't quite gotten over the affront, though.

It was going on half past nine. Some of Emmaline's

people were grouping the distressed party guests into sep-arate rooms, while another team, led by York, along with the paramedics, made their way down to the beach below.

I'd tried to take stock of the people, to see if I could discern who was missing. So far, we didn't know if it was a man or a woman who'd presumably plunged off the side of the cliff. I'd spotted Eliza and heaved a relieved sigh. I remembered seeing her standing amidst a group of people outside. Thank God it wasn't her who'd gone over the edge. She sat with one of Emmaline's deputies, her arms folded across her chest, rocking back and forth. Not even an actress of her caliber could pull it together after what had happened.

Olaya and Maggie were still at the bread table, all the giddy excitement Maggie had been feeling earlier re-placed with distress. It wasn't every day someone plum-meted to their death at a holiday party.

I spotted some of the secret carb-lovers; Zac and all the other catering employees who'd been serving; two of the chimney sweep guests; a passel of carolers; Nicole, who'd looked so perfectly put together a little while ago, now looking pale and ghostly; the variety of shopkeepers and flower girls, each more shaken than the last. There was no way to tell who was missing, and it appeared that no one had seen anything.

Emmaline sat in a corner of the library next to the server who'd screamed the alarm, her two-way radio in one hand. "Rita, how did you happen to look over the cliff?"

"I-I . . ." Her eyes were wide and scared. "I was m-making the rounds. A m-man outside called me over and asked me to get him a d-d-drink. A Tom Collins. I went in to get it, picked up a new tray of appetizers in the k-k-kitchen, and went b-b-back outside, but he was g-gone."

Poor girl could hardly get the words out, but Emmaline gently urged her on.

"I s-saw a coat on the rocks. Caught on the edge," Rita clarified. "I tried to pull it up, but it w-w-was s-s-stuck. I put my tray d-d-down and reached over and that's when I s-s-saw the—" She jammed her fist to her mouth, squeezing her eyes shut for a second as if she could block out the memory.

"You dropped your tray?" Emmaline said.

The girl's eyes had turned red and glassy. She stared straight ahead, blankly.

Emmaline laid a gentle hand on Rita's knee, and the girl snapped back from her daze. "What?"

Em repeated the question, and Rita scrunched up her face for a few seconds, thinking. "I d-d-don't know. I g-g-guess. And I f-f-fell on it." She twisted her body, arching her back to look at the seat of her pants. "I hope they're n-n-not ruined," she said, as if that was the most important thing in that moment. It was a deflection, I thought. A way for her to think about something other than the body she'd discovered.

"And you didn't see anyone hovering near the edge when you were taking drink orders?" Emmaline asked.

Rita shook her head.

"And you didn't see anyone jump?

Rita recoiled. "N-n-no!"

"You'll let me know if you think of anything else?" Emmaline asked.

Rita nodded, but her eyes had dazed again. Em thanked her, leaving her with one of her deputies.

I walked with her out to the backyard. The grassy area

had been cordoned off, so we stopped just outside the perimeter. Em shook her head, looking baffled. "All these people at the party, and no one saw anything. It doesn't make sense. Was he a jumper?"

I took the wreath from my head and let it dangle around my forearm on top of my camera strap. "But why would someone come to a party only to jump off a cliff?"

"Right. It's unlikely," she said. "And if the deceased didn't decide to leap off the edge of their own accord, that means someone pushed—"

Her handheld beeped, followed by a crackly voice. "Sheriff."

Even through the spotty reception, I recognized Captain York's voice, and I gave an involuntary grimace.

"Go ahead," Em said into the device.

"Victim is male. Mid-forties. ID in his wallet identifies him as one Edward Christopher Yentin. He's a reporter for one of those grocery store rags. *The Scout*. Looks like he was holding a small camera. Smashed to pieces on the rocks."

Instantly, I forgot about my disdain for York. Edward Christopher Yentin. Hadn't I just heard that name? I thumped my finger against my forehead. It came to me a second later. Someone had dropped Ed Yentin's name inside, I was sure of it.

I turned, looking back to the house as if the person in question might be standing right there. No such luck. It was bright inside, with every lamp and recessed light turned on. A short while ago, costumed people had filled the spaces upstairs and downstairs. Now they were huddled together like survivors of a hostage situation. Even from here, I could see the irritation on some of the faces. The party was done, and so were they, but Emmaline had given strict orders for her people to take statements from everyone.

Being back in Santa Sofia had exposed me to death. If Edward Yentin hadn't jumped off the cliff of his own accord, then someone had done it to him. Off the bat, I knew Cordelia Knight had a motive if this was the guy who'd snapped the photos of her. She quite possibly blamed the man for the article and photos that had put her career on a collision course.

But was Cordelia Knight even here? I hadn't seen her. Then again, with the costumes, it was nearly impossible to identify people.

Were there others at the party who'd been the victim of Yentin's reporting?

My mind circled around to the argument I'd overheard between the two men in the hallway off the kitchen. The first man had claimed the other had nearly ruined his career with whatever salacious story the other had written. Could Edward Yentin have been one of the two men?

"What's he wearing?" I asked Em, clarifying that I meant the dead man and not York.

"Is the deceased in costume?" she asked into her two-way.

"Affirmative," York said over the crackling airwaves. "All black. Sooty marks on the face and smudges of dirt on the clothing, although that could also be from the impact. Hard to say."

"A chimney sweep?" I asked. Em arched a perfectly shaped eyebrow at me as she repeated my question to York.

"Could be," the captain said. "Yeah, could be."

"Let's get the scene processed and get him out of there,"

she said. York gave an acknowledgment and signed off. Em spun to face me. "What do you know, Ivy?"

I threw my hands up and backed up a step. "Nothing. It's just . . ." I relayed the argument I'd overheard, followed by the retreating figure of a chimney sweep.

Emmaline was a processor. She listened to me, and then she folded one arm across her middle, rested the opposite elbow on her hand, and tapped one finger against her lips. It was one of her thinking poses. After a solid thirty seconds—which felt like five long minutes—she sighed. "Okay. If the chimney sweep you saw walking away from the argument is our victim, then based on what you overheard, we have a potential motive by one of the guests."

Exactly what I'd thought. "How do you determine if he was pushed . . . or not?" I asked. I didn't want to throw someone under the murder bus if Yentin hadn't, in fact, been murdered.

Em was one step ahead of me. "A forensics team is on their way. They'll sweep the area and put together the most probable scenario. If there's anything to find, they'll find it."

"There's something else," I said, but I hesitated. Should I wait until the cause of death was determined to find out if Cordelia Knight was even present? But I'd opened my mouth already, and now Emmaline waited expectantly. I told her about the career derailment of the actress, courtesy of Edward Yentin's investigative reporting.

"According to someone you overheard," she clarified.

"Yes."

"But we don't actually know if that's what caused

Knight's career to tank. It could have been something else."

Em loved playing devil's advocate. It was one of the things that made her so good at her job. When others developed a theory and sought to prove it, ignoring all other potential leads in the process—cough, cough, York, cough, cough—Emmaline took a different approach. She sought theories and worked to prove or disprove them, following wherever a lead might take her.

"Could be," I said.

"But it very well may have been Yentin at the wheel of that vehicle."

I had to agree.

"So," she said. "Let's find out if Cordelia Knight is at this party, and if *your* chimney sweep is *our* chimney sweep."

Emmaline operated on the side of caution. Without knowing exactly what had happened, she'd directed her people to gather statements from everyone present. Her team had made a list of party guests and gone down it one by one, finally releasing people into the temperate December night.

I checked my watch through bleary eyes. 10:43. I'd been up more than sixteen hours. No wonder I was fading. I was about to go find Olaya and Maggie when a hand clamped around my arm, the velvet of my Ghost of Christmas Present costume padding the grip. Eliza Fox yanked me into a little alcove under the stairs. Between the spaces of the steps, I saw York come in. Emmaline, with her eagle eyes, had noticed, too, and beelined for him. They disappeared back outside and out of sight.

Eliza's grip on my arm tightened. "Ivy, no one will tell me anything. What are they saying? What happened? Who *is* it?" The black coal that had lined her eyes had smudged. She opened them wide now, turning her from Scrooge into a raccoon.

Emmaline hadn't announced who the dead man was, so I certainly couldn't. "They're IDing him and—"

"So it's a man!"

I gave myself a mental head slap. I needed to get out of here and get some sleep before my drowsiness clouded my ability to filter. "I don't know if—"

"But they don't know who it is?"

I didn't want to lie, so I just didn't respond. Turns out it had been more a rhetorical question and Eliza charged ahead. "Ivy, this is bad. Someone died at my Christmas party!"

She was right. The optics, no matter how you looked at it, wouldn't be good. Then again, they were worse for the victim.

Of course, didn't they say that any publicity is good publicity? I narrowed my tired eyes, considering. It hadn't worked for Cordelia Knight. Would Eliza's It Girl status remain intact after the press deemed this a "murder house"?

A crazy thought flew into my head. Could Eliza have orchestrated a publicity stunt gone bad, just for the attention?

But I dismissed the idea. Her anxiousness seemed genuine.

Then again . . . actress.

Oh boy, I really needed to get out of here. She'd moved her grip from my arm to my hand. I gave her a squeeze, then uncurled her fingers and slipped my hand free. "It'll be okay, Eliza."

I spotted Nicole and beckoned her over. She switched places with me, mouthing, "*Thank you.*" I left them under the stairs and beelined for the library. Olaya and Maggie, as well as the servers from Divine Cuisine, had gotten permission to pack up and were nearly finished by the time I got to them. What was left of the bread would be donated to Crosby House, the women's shelter, in the morning. Olaya's leftover bread never went to waste.

I helped pack up the remains of the day and went to find Emmaline.

"Are we good to go?" I asked her.

"Sure." She gave me a hard stare, her brows pulling together. "Are you okay to drive? You look beat."

"I only have to get from the bread shop back home. I am beat, but yeah, I'm okay."

I turned to leave but stopped when Em called my name. "Ivy, I'm going to need an official statement from you tomorrow."

I threw up one hand in acknowledgment. "Okay."

I followed her gaze to the camera hanging by my side, the strap still looped over my forearm alongside my halo wreath. "Did you take a lot of pictures?"

"Hundreds."

"I'll need to see those, too."

Tomorrow was going to be a long day.

Chapter 5

After helping Olaya and Maggie unload at Yeast of Eden, I'd called Miguel. He picked up my pug Agatha from Mrs. Branford and met me at my house just as I pulled up. "So it could be murder?" he asked after we went inside and I filled him in on everything that had happened.

"Might be," I said, my eyelids drooping.

"Come on." He pulled me up and led me to my bed. "I'll let Agatha out."

"Stay here," I said drowsily, holding on to his hand.

"I'll be right back," he said, then called Agatha. I let his fingers go. "And don't worry," he added. "The last thing I want you involved in is another murder. I'm not letting you out of my sight."

I had no connection to anyone at that party, and certainly no connection to Edward Yentin, so Miguel had nothing to worry about. Still, I was glad not to be alone, and extra glad for the bonus time with Miguel.

The next thing I knew, it was Saturday morning, and the sun was streaming light through the edges of my bamboo shades. Miguel and I didn't always have weekend schedules that matched up. He usually took Sunday off, and his restaurant, Baptista's Cantina & Grill, was closed on Mondays, but my photography business had slowly been picking up, and weekends were prime for weddings and events. Often our paths didn't cross for very long on weekends and sometimes not at all.

December was not the first-choice wedding month for most brides, which meant Miguel and I both had the day off. My plan had been a lazy day at home with a good book, Agatha by my side on the couch, and Miguel puttering around in the kitchen, experimenting with new recipes.

A late-afternoon walk on the beach, wrapped in a sweater and snuggling next to Miguel, sounded like a pretty good way to end the day.

Miguel stirred beside me, turning over and settling back to sleep. I had to admit, it was awfully nice waking up next to him. Agatha gave a wheezy little sound when my cell phone buzzed, dropping her little pug head again as I answered, my voice groggy with sleep.

"You're not up?" Emmaline asked.

I groaned and pressed the heel of my hand to my forehead. "What gave it away?"

She ignored my sleepy sarcasm and said, "I need that statement from you, and the photos. I can be there now, but I'll give you an hour, okay?"

"An hour?"

"Maybe less."

The fog in my brain started to clear. Oh boy. Emmaline was on sheriff time. She was champing at the bit now, but gave me sixty minutes, which meant she'd be here in twenty-five, tops. When she had a crime to solve, she didn't let any grass grow under her feet. I pushed myself to sitting, afraid that if I stayed horizontal, I'd drift right back into my dreams. "Are you—"

"Bringing coffee? Yes," she said, answering the question I'd been about to ask.

"Mind reader."

"Best friend," she said, and I detected a little smile in her voice despite the dead body from the night before and the reason for her visit. She had to do her job as sheriff, but she'd always be my childhood friend underneath it all.

A hot shower woke me up. Once I was dressed, my hair pulled into a messy bun, spirally ginger curls fighting to escape the containment, I started out of the bedroom, leaving Miguel to sleep. Agatha, though, perked up and jumped off the bed, the *clickity clack* of her nails against the hardwood floors like a siren in the silence. "You silly goose," I whispered, scratching her head. "Guess I need to clip those claws."

She looked up at me, her tail wrapped into a curlicue. She had a bladder of iron and could have let me keep loving on her. Sweet pup. I let her into the backyard through the French doors. It had been a temperate beginning of winter so the primroses, winter jasmine, and pansies I'd planted were doing especially well. Agatha trotted off to her favorite spot behind an evergreen shrub, turned herself around three times, as if she were doing the hokey-pokey. Finally, she found the perfect spot and took care of business.

Back in the living room, I breathed in the faint scent of pine from my Christmas tree. It sat in the living room's bay window facing the street. It was small, flickered with white lights, and held only seven shiny silver balls and three original ornaments. I didn't want to buy a bunch of tree decorations that held no meaning. Instead, I'd bought three at the beginning of December from a local craft fair. A miniature rolling pin tied with a tiny strip of holiday ribbon, a camera with a Santa hat, and a coffee cup. They'd spoken to me at the time, and now they adorned my tree.

Next year, I'd find some more, as well as a few decorations to holiday up my house.

I unlocked the door for Emmaline before filling a watering can and topping off the base that held my tree. Next, I grabbed my laptop, plugged the memory card from my camera into an external reader, and uploaded the photos from the night before. There was a sound in the hallway behind me. I turned, and my heart did a little flutter. Miguel wore plaid flannel pajama pants and a white T-shirt. His dark hair was mussed from sleep, and his morning stubble was enticingly appealing. He scratched his jaw as he padded toward me.

"I figured you'd sleep in," he said, his voice tinged with morning scratchiness. He dropped down next to me and gave me a light kiss on the cheek.

"Emmaline's on her way over," I said.

"Ah," he said, drawing out the word. "Official business?"

"I have to give her my statement. You should go back to bed." Just because I was up didn't mean he had to be. It was only eight fifteen, and Miguel often worked late nights at the restaurant. Last night had been no exception. He needed the sleep as much as I did.

"Nah, I'm awake," he said, but he stood and walked back toward the bedroom, saying, "I'll get dressed."

Fifteen minutes later, uncharacteristically close to the hour timeline she'd given me, Emmaline arrived. I heard the car door slam, and a minute later she knocked once on the door, then let herself in. "Coffee, as promised," she said, holding up a cardboard coffee carrier. Four disposable cups were lodged into the openings. She looked fresh and alert, especially given the long night she'd surely had. Her braided hair was pulled back and secured with a hair tie. Her bright eyes sat in contrast to her dark skin.

She read the unspoken question on my face. "One for you, one for me, one for your honey in the bedroom."

As if on cue, Miguel appeared in the hallway. His hair was damp and towel-dried, and he looked fully awake now. He kept a few things here, just like I kept a few things at his house. He'd dressed in jeans and a mustard-yellow three-quarter zip pullover that set off his green eyes.

Emmaline smiled, handing him one of the cups. "Black, little bit of cream."

The corner of his mouth lifted in a little grin. "Nice. Thank you, Sheriff."

She nodded at him, then handed me mine. "I went with the spiced pumpkin," she said.

"Oh my God, thank you." I cradled the cup with two hands and put it to my lips, the feeling of that first sip spreading through me like rays from the sun. "Who's the fourth for?" I asked just as the front door opened. Billy strode in.

"Ah," I said, but then cocked my head. He already had a cup in his hand.

"We're here," he announced. "Now we can start."

"Who's we—?" I started to say, but stopped when Penelope Branford stepped out from behind my broad-shouldered brother.

"Saw Mrs. Branford here crossing the street and heading this way, so I waited for her."

"Lovely young man," Mrs. Branford said, patting his arm.

She looked fresh in a Christmas red velour lounge suit—she had one in every color of the rainbow—with a sparkly Christmas tree brooch. Her snowy hair floated in loose curls around her head, her eyes alive and fiery. "Let's have the full story," she said.

"What full story?" Emmaline asked, throwing me a side-eye. I shrugged and shook my head. I hadn't spoken to my octogenarian neighbor since yesterday afternoon, so if she knew anything about last night, it wasn't from me.

Mrs. Branford *pshaw*ed. "Emmaline Davis, you should know by now that I am the eyes and ears of Santa Sofia."

"Do you ever sleep, Mrs. Branford?" I asked her, halfway wondering if she had ticker tape running somewhere through her house giving her alerts to the mischief and mayhem of our town.

"Penny," she said automatically—her once-a-day attempt to get me to call her something other than Mrs. Branford—"and of course I do, but I have a sixth sense, and right now I'm sensing that something is afoot."

"Righto, Watson," Emmaline said in a terrible British accent. "Come on in."

Mrs. Branford breezed right by us and sat on one of my living room chairs as if she were ready to hold court.

Emmaline pulled the final cup from the carrier and handed it to her. "For you. Hibiscus tea."

Wow. Emmaline *was* good. She'd known my neighbor would make a beeline for my house the second she realized something was amiss, which would have happened about the exact second Emmaline had parked. Mrs. Branford was the leader of our Neighborhood Watch. She knew everything.

Every. Thing.

Right now, she nodded approvingly. "Nicely done, my dear. Now, indulge an old woman. Did someone at the party push that man to his death?"

Emmaline's smile flattened, and she didn't mince words. "The initial forensic report is inconclusive, but as of now, we have no reason to believe Mr. Yentin would have jumped on his own. We're considering all possibilities."

"But there was a house full of people," Miguel said. "It would be pretty risky for someone to push the guy, wouldn't it?"

At this, Emmaline shrugged. "It would, but that doesn't mean it didn't happen. If someone pushed him, it was most likely a crime of passion."

"A crime of *opportunity,*" Mrs. Branford said.

Emmaline pointed at Mrs. Branford, then touched the tip of her nose. "Exactly. Either way, it's unlikely it was premeditated."

"Right, because how could someone have planned that Yentin would be standing in just the right spot at just the right time so he could be pushed over a cliff? Whoever did it—assuming someone did—had to have seen him standing there, come up behind him, and shoved. Otherwise, Yentin would have fought. There would have been a struggle." I looked at Emmaline. "Right?"

"My thoughts exactly," she agreed. "So either he jumped, or he was pushed by someone who saw an opportunity."

"*Carpe diem,*" Mrs. Branford mused.

We all paused for a moment, giving Edward Yentin a moment of silence. Whatever had happened, the man was dead.

After a few seconds, Emmaline sat in the chair opposite Mrs. Branford, a pen poised over her standard narrow notepad. I sat between Billy and Miguel on the sofa.

"Right now, I need to have a clear picture of the party. All the guests have been interviewed, but nobody saw anything. Take me through the evening, Ivy," she said, and I did, starting with my arrival at the beach house with Olaya and Maggie, the tour Nicole had given me, and meeting Eliza Fox, adding that we'd had a best friend–level conversation immediately after meeting.

"Did she confide in you?" Em asked.

"No. It's like she was craving time to be normal. She wanted to talk about music and family and food. She loves cooking shows." In all the commotion, I'd forgotten to tell Olaya how much Eliza said she'd liked the *Best Bakeries in America* show Yeast of Eden had been featured on. It was what prompted her to contact the bread shop to cater the party.

"What else?" Emmaline asked. "After your girl talk, what did you do?"

"She outfitted me with a costume for the party. I went downstairs, talked to Olaya for a few minutes, then went to the kitchen to get something to eat to hold me over." I took a deep inhalation before launching into the argument I'd overheard and the chimney sweep I'd seen retreating.

Emmaline stopped writing and looked at me. "Would you recognize him?"

"Nope. I didn't see his face," I said.

"Do you think it could have been Edward Yentin?"

I'd asked myself that question over and over, but the truth was, there had been several chimney sweeps at the party—all dressed in black with sooty faces and hats. Adam Driver could have been one of them, and I wouldn't have recognized him. "Honestly, Em, I don't know."

She nodded, making a note on her pad. "What next?"

I recounted the rest of the evening to her, including the bits of gossip I'd heard, and ended with Eliza's descent on the stairway.

"Back up," Em said. "The two people talking about someone who had the gall to show up—"

I nodded.

"Who were they?"

"I don't know. The room was crowded."

"And the people talking about the Cordelia Knight scandal?"

At this, I grabbed my laptop from the coffee table and opened the collection of photos I'd uploaded. I scrolled past the two paupers who'd talked about plowing through as much alcohol as possible, stopping on the candids I'd taken of the gossipy women. "These two," I said, placing the open laptop back on the coffee table and spinning it around so she could see it.

Emmaline leaned in and peered at the photo, then she pressed the arrow key to scroll through more of my shots.

"I need copies of all of these. They still on the memory card?" she asked.

"Yes." I'd already moved them to the cloud, so I ejected it from the reader and handed it over.

She pocketed it, then asked, "Did anything else strike you, Ivy?"

She was earnest. I'd contributed to the solving of more than a few recent cases in Santa Sofia, including one while Em and Billy had been on their honeymoon. She thought I had a knack for crime-solving. My dad thought I had a knack for getting into trouble. I thought I had a knack for being either in the right place at the right time, or in the wrong place at the wrong time, depending upon how you looked at being wrapped up in murder.

I shook my head. "Not that I can think of."

She consulted her notes, then tapped the tip of her pen against one of her bullet points. "Let's backtrack to the argument you heard. You said they were two men."

"That's right. They were in the hallway off the kitchen. I know, because that's where I put my camera bag when I first arrived."

"Okay, Ivy. Think," Em said. "What exactly did you hear?"

I didn't have to think hard. The angry tones in the men's voices had seared themselves into my mind. "One of them said the other one had ruined his marriage. The other guy didn't care."

"So that could have been Yentin."

"Definitely possible," I said.

Emmaline rolled her pen in the air. "Go on."

I closed my eyes, calling up my memory of the moment. "The first one said, *Then she lied—*"

"Who's she?" Em asked.

"No idea. but the second guy just kind of laughed. Like a harsh laugh. He didn't care at *all* that the other guy was upset." My eyes opened wide as I remembered something. I pounded my fist into the palm of my other hand. "The first man, he said he should . . . no, *could* sue him for all he was worth."

Emmaline wrote that down, then looked up again. "Was it a threat?"

That I couldn't say for sure. "Mmm, maybe?"

Emmaline just nodded. "Okay, what else?"

"The reporter basically said that the article the other guy was upset about was old news. Then he said, 'Wait till you see the *next* piece I'm printing.' Emphasis on next."

I closed my eyes, replaying the conversation in my head. "The first guy said, 'You can't mess with people's lives,' then the reporter said, 'Messing with people's lives pays the bills.'"

"That could have been a veiled threat," Emmaline mused. "Anything else?"

I felt like I was missing something, but I couldn't pull it out of the weeds. Finally, I shook my head. "That's it. The guy left, but I only saw him from the back."

"So let's assume that Yentin was the reporter you over-heard. Who was he talking to?"

The conversation I'd overheard between the two women at the party careened into my mind. "Those women," I said. "The ones I overheard later? They were shocked that someone had the *gall* to show up. That was the word they used. Gall." I remembered Eliza's face as she'd scanned the room. She'd frozen when she saw someone. "Who would Eliza have *not* invited, and then be shocked to see?"

Yentin himself was a strong possibility, but someone else came to mind. My eyes met Miguel's. He turned to look at Mrs. Branford. Billy met his wife's eyes. Emmaline looked at me. We all spoke at the same time. "Brad McAvoy."

Eliza's estranged husband.

Chapter 6

The first phone call came just as I was elbow-deep in a hunk of bread dough. Miguel had gone to run a few errands, including picking up groceries for dinner. I'd stayed home to try my hand at a sourdough loaf with the starter I'd had going for weeks now. I was far from perfecting it, but I wanted, at least, to come up with a decent one—crunchy on the outside and pillowy soft on the inside.

"Okay, okay! Hang on!" I shouted, as if whoever was calling could hear me. I grabbed a hand towel and scraped enough dough from one hand to answer, but the phone stopped ringing before the pad of my finger made contact with the button.

Unknown Caller.

I waited, in case whoever it was called back, but they didn't. Instead, a few seconds later, my phone alerted me to a voice mail. I pressed it to play, but it was just a long silence. An accidental dial, followed by an accidental message.

After another quick wash, I was just about to plunge my hands back into the dough when it rang again.

This time, I was able to answer it with a quick, "Hello?"

Silence.

I listened for a few seconds. I definitely detected breathing on the other end of the line. "Hello?" I repeated.

Click. The line went dead.

I stared at the phone, frowning. What was that about? I set it down, giving it another look and waiting for a beat to see if it would ring again. It felt like watching a pot boil or grass grow. Nothing happened, so I washed my hands again. Back at my bread mat, I dug into the dough, folding and turning, folding and turning, folding and turning. I was on my fourth turn when the phone rang again.

This time I didn't bother to clean my hands. I grabbed the phone. Unknown Number. I pressed the Answer button, followed by the Speaker button. "Hello?"

"Ivy? Is that you? Ivy Culpepper?"

The voice was breathless, but recognizable. Eliza Fox.

"This is Ivy. Eliza?"

She heaved a stress-laden sigh. "Thank God. When I didn't hear anything, I thought I had the wrong number."

"Nope, you got me," I said, the mysterious caller identified. I felt a little flustered. Why was Eliza Fox calling *me*? "Can I help you with something?"

"I hope so. I heard . . . um, I think . . . mmm, I'd like to see the pictures you took last night."

"Oh, yeah, of course," I said.

I moved to the sink, setting the phone down and quickly washing my hands for the umpteenth time. Flour dusted the device, but I'd clean it later. I clicked the speaker off and held the phone to my ear. She was a celebrity, so it felt right to contain her exposure, even in the privacy of my own home.

She let loose another sigh, this time one of relief. "Great. Can you email them?"

"Oh, no, sorry. I haven't had a chance to do any editing on them, and they're, you know, proprietary. You pay for the ones you buy."

Agatha strolled into the kitchen, her nails giving away her approach before she actually materialized. She looked at me before sniffing the ground for bits of food. When all she found was flour dust, she plopped down, front legs extended forward like a sphinx, watching me.

Eliza made a clucking noise with her tongue. "Of course! Stupid of me. Of course I'll pay you for them."

This time, I exhaled. Edward Yentin's death notwithstanding, this was still a business. I'd collected my fee up front for the shoot itself, but I hadn't been holding out much hope of Eliza buying any of the photos I'd taken, what with the pall that now hung over her party. "All of them?" I asked, trying to hide my surprise.

Her voice had a lightness to it now. "Uh-huh. All of them."

This was highly unusual, and my curiosity piqued. "Mmm, usually I go through them, pick out the best ones, do some editing—"

"I don't care about any of that," she interrupted, and I imagined her hand flying up, palm out.

I was flabbergasted and didn't know what to make of her request, so I moved on. "Are you wanting prints or digital—"

"Digital is fine. Today is great. How can I get them?"

Today. Now my mild curiosity shifted to something more acute. What was her hurry? "I can put them on a thumb drive—"

"Perfect. When can you come?"

Whoa. We'd gone from me putting the photos on a portable disk drive to me delivering said drive. I wasn't super excited about revisiting the cliff house. Frankly, I was a little surprised *she* was still there in the direct aftermath of the death. "Um, I'm in the middle of baking some bread—"

"Oh my God, fresh bread? Never mind. *I'll* come to *you.*"

Eliza Fox, I was discovering, had a bad habit of interrupting. And like every starlet worth her box-office numbers, she also seemed to get exactly what she wanted.

Still, the fact that she was licking her lips at the idea of my freshly baked bread made me like her a little bit more. Carbs be damned.

I glanced around my untidy kitchen and cringed. Eliza Fox was coming here. Eliza Fox was coming here! Maggie was going to flip when I told her.

"How does four o'clock sound?" I asked. That would give me time to let the bread rise and bake, as well as straighten up the house, take a shower, and look presentable for the visit of a movie star.

*　*　*

Before I knew it, I'd cleaned the kitchen, and Miguel and I had put away the groceries he'd come home with. While I'd showered, he'd prepared a pot of winter vegetable soup, which was now simmering on the stove. The aroma of garlic and onion filled the house, on top of the scent of a fresh-from-the-oven sourdough round.

"Thank you for making the soup early," I said to him, stretching up to give him a kiss on the cheek.

He laughed. "Well, we can't just feed her bread." On the table, he laid out three bowls, spoons, and small plates. He knew where everything was in my kitchen, just as I'd learned the placement of everything in his.

Based on her reaction over the phone, I thought Eliza would probably have been just fine with bread, but serving her a meal was the hospitable thing to do. The fact that it would give us more time with her had its appeal. Why was she so gung ho about getting her hands on the photos I'd taken? I suspected she wouldn't cough up the answer to that question right away, but I was a curious cat.

An hour later, she arrived, looking very incognito in jeans and an oversized lightweight navy jacket. The brim of a white bucket hat covered part of her face. I stepped onto the porch to see if an entourage or her personal assistant had joined her as much as to see if Mrs. Branford was lurking across the street.

If she was, she was staying behind closed doors.

The coast was clear on all fronts.

When I came back inside, Miguel had already introduced himself and taken Eliza's coat. Agatha stood at Eliza's sneakered feet, her bulbous eyes peering up. She usually barked when strangers came into the house, throwing her little head up, dragging in a ragged breath, and yapping for all she was worth. But with Eliza Fox, she just looked smitten.

Eliza cooed over her, bending to pet her. "She . . . he . . ."

"She," I said. "Agatha."

"She's precious!" After a solid minute of loving on the pug, Eliza stood straight again and gushed. "I love your house! It's a gem. A complete gem."

I smiled and thanked her. I couldn't agree more. The quaint Tudor had been a lucky find at just the right time, even if the down payment had zapped almost all of my savings and the monthly mortgage often made things pretty tight. It was worth it. I loved the house.

"Give me a tour?" she asked hopefully.

"Sure." I led her through the living room on the right, and pointed down the hallway that led to the master bedroom, with access to the garage on the right side of the hall. We stopped at the French doors leading to the backyard, then turned left and went through to the kitchen and eating nook. "And there are two small bedrooms that way," I said, indicating the hallway off the kitchen.

"It's adorable," she said, her palms crossed against her chest.

She looked sincere, but that niggling thought that she was an actress had come back. Was she putting on a show for us? But if she was, why? Did it have something to do with the photographs I'd taken the night before? What was she hoping to find . . . or not find?

Eliza's nose crinkled as she sniffed. She'd been facing the bay window overlooking the backyard, but spun around, eyeing the crusty loaf of sourdough resting on a breadboard. She bit her lower lip, and I could practically see her salivary glands working overtime.

"Have a seat," Miguel said, gesturing to the table.

Her crystalline-blue eyes went wide, and she whipped off the bucket hat. "Seriously? Are you having me for dinner?"

I stared at her, trying to figure her out. On the one hand, she was a movie star, but on the other, she was like an innocent girl craving normal interactions. "If you'd like to stay," I said. "Miguel's an amazing chef. He owns Baptista's Cantina and Grill on the pier—"

"He does!" She whirled her gaze to him. "You do? I've heard it's so good. I've wanted to go, but I don't eat out much. Paparazzi."

Enough said. Having photographers constantly following me, angling for the perfect shot that would net them a pretty penny, would keep me indoors, too. "You're in for a treat, then," I said.

I poured a glass of wine for each of us, set a bottle of olive oil and dipping dishes at each place setting, and sliced the sourdough loaf. I piled it into a basket and set it in the center of the table while Miguel ladled soup into shallow white bowls. Eliza didn't know where to start. She held her spoon with one hand and a piece of bread with the other. Finally, she dug in, spooning soup, dunking bread in oil, and offering satisfied groans along the way. "So. Good," she said. "This soup should be bottled and sold everywhere."

I had to agree. He'd outdone himself.

"And the bread. Oh. My. God." Eliza eyed me. "How do you not look like Gweneth Paltrow in *Shallow Hall*? God, I love that movie."

"I'm sure when I hit forty, it'll catch up to me," I said with a wry laugh. That was only a few years away. I knew I'd better start upping the exercise.

We started the meal with idle chitchat, but before long, Eliza's animated stories of her life in Hollywood turned somber. "It's hard to know who your friends are," she said. "Who you can trust. I grew up looking over my shoulder. *Always* with the creepy guys around. *Always* with the creepy bosses. I thought if I just got away." She sighed, deep and heavy. "It worked, and before long I had an agent and a manager and a starring role in *The Beach*. And I fell in love."

She stopped, her eyes turning glassy. "I should have known better than to trust a man," she said, then shot an apologetic glance at Miguel. "I mean, I'm sure you're fine. Totally trustworthy, so no offense."

"None taken," he said with a reassuring smile.

"You fell in love," I prompted.

She threw up her hands dramatically. "I mean, what was I thinking? True love doesn't exist. My parents split up before I was even born. My father, he had some creepy friends. The more I"—she gestured to herself—"developed, the creepier they became."

"That's when you left home?"

"Not quite. I was sixteen and got a job at this dumpy diner. The Pit. And it was, one hundred percent, a pit." She stopped long enough to take a sip of wine and another bite of sourdough. "I can't even tell you how many times Mr. Tucker came on to me. Too many." And then her voice faltered. "Too many."

I wondered if it was the wine that had loosened her up,

or just her desperate need for real connection. Either way, she'd started, and she wasn't done yet. "Are you okay?" I asked.

Tears pooled in her eyes. One broke free, sliding down her cheek. She swiped it away and closed her eyes, taking a full breath in and out before opening them again. She sniffed and blinked hard. "I'm fine. I shouldn't be unloading on you."

Miguel took that as his cue to leave Eliza and me alone. He made a hasty retreat to the bedroom. "What happened?" I asked Eliza once we were alone.

She pushed her bowl and plate toward the center of the table, leaving room for her to interlace her fingers. Her crystalline eyes had turned steely, her emotions neatly tucked away again. "I'll tell you what *didn't* happen. I didn't stick around long enough for Mr. Tucker to get tired of me saying no. Your parents are supposed to take care of you, right? Well, mine didn't. My mom disappeared, and my dad couldn't see what was happening right in front of him."

"You mean with your boss?"

"With every single man I met. They never saw me. All they saw was this." She gestured to her body again. "When I met Brad, I thought, now here's a guy I can trust. He'll take care of me. Of course, *that* didn't happen."

I wondered again if her estranged husband was the person she wanted to look for in the mess of photos I'd taken. "I can show you the photos now, if you'd like."

"Yes, please." She stood abruptly, stacked her bowl on top of her plate. She picked them up with one hand, grabbing her wineglass with the other "Refill?"

I topped her off. She took a sip before depositing her

dishes at the sink. I cleared mine and Miguel's, setting them on the counter next to Eliza's, then led her into the living room. It had grown dark, the short December days growing shorter, the darkness staying longer and longer.

I knew I could just hand over a thumb drive with the photos, but I was hoping Eliza would agree to go through them with me. We could at least eliminate the bad ones and the duplicates. There was no reason for her to pay for those.

I explained all of this. "That's fine," she said. She sounded casual. Nonchalant, even, although I knew from what she'd said and from the way she clutched her wine-glass that she was anything but calm. She was putting her acting chops to good use, but inside, I knew her emotions were roiling.

Agatha's nails clicked against the hardwood floor behind us as she followed us from the kitchen. Once Eliza and I settled side by side on the couch, Agatha climbed into the plush circular dog bed I'd moved to the base of the Christmas tree. She was asleep one second later.

"Oh, to be as carefree as a dog," Eliza said.

I smiled. "She lives the good life."

I set a pillow on my lap and placed my computer on it, positioning it so we could both see the screen. I entered my password and waited for the operating system to boot up. "I'll just scroll through them, and you can tell me the ones I should delete," I said.

She nodded, her hands twisting around her wineglass. "Okay."

I double-clicked on the folder I'd dropped all of the party photos into, clicking to open the first shot. From there, I'd use the arrow keys to move through them. They were in chronological order, starting with the few I'd taken of the outside of the house when I'd arrived, moving to the inside and the bits of the interior I'd captured as Nicole had led me upstairs to meet Eliza for the first time.

The next set were from Eliza's dressing room. I'd managed a few candids of Eliza and Nicole, individually and heads together as they whispered about some party detail. It was clear from the photos that Nicole was a mother figure to Eliza in the same way Olaya and Mrs. Branford were for me.

I moved through them, noticing how Eliza scooted closer to me. She'd put her glass on the coffee table and placed a pillow on her own lap, propping her elbows there, her fisted hands against her mouth. She drew in an audible breath as we finally got to the shots of the party guests.

"Slow down a little," she said, leaning closer.

One by one, I scrolled through the pictures. "Stop," she said, putting a hand on my arm.

The photo was of a chimney sweep, but not Edward Yentin, I knew. The daily newspaper had printed a photo of him alongside the brief notice of his death. The man I'd photographed was not the dead man. I peered at the face, but it was no one I recognized.

"No," she said to herself, lifting her hand. "Go on."

I did, moving through five or six more before her fingers came down on my forearm again. The photo I'd stopped at showed the pauper couple. "Those two," she grumbled. "Freeloaders."

I raised my eyebrows. So she knew. "Why'd you invite them?"

She scoffed. "Hollywood is all about image. I can't snub someone like Mickey Trampton."

I did a double take. I *knew* the guy had looked familiar, but I hadn't been able to place him. Now that she said it, though, I recognized the comedian right away. He hadn't seemed too funny from my brief encounter with him.

"Go on," Eliza said, rolling her finger in the air.

I paused for a second. "Are you looking for someone in particular?"

She hedged, holding her breath for a beat before exhaling. "Brad."

I knew it! It was exactly the conclusion Emmaline, Miguel, Billy, Mrs. Branford, and I had come to earlier. Brad McAvoy. "Your husband?"

She nodded slowly. "Estranged husband. And I didn't invite him, but . . ."

Her lower lip trembled, just barely, as her real emotions fought to surface. "Are you okay?" I asked.

Her hands started trembling, and her face grew pale. "I don't know. What if . . ."

She trailed off, as if she couldn't bear to finish the thought. I waited, knowing she'd continue if I gave her enough silence to fill.

"What if that man didn't jump? What if he was pushed?"

I hadn't told her that the sheriff had already fast-forwarded to that theory, but she'd gotten there on her own. "What does that have to do with your husband?" I asked.

Her voice became scarcely more than a whisper. "Brad hated that reporter—"

This time I interrupted her. "Enough to kill him?"

Eliza buried her head in her hands. "I really don't know." She peered up at me through her eyelashes. "Maybe."

After Eliza left, I called Emmaline to fill her in, and now I could hear the tip of her pen tapping against her desk. "Brad McAvoy wasn't among the people we got statements from. Were there any photos of him?"

"No. And we went through every picture I took. Of course, I didn't get shots of every guest. The commotion—" I stopped. The server's scream had stopped the party before I'd gotten to even half the guests. "There is one thing, though," I said.

"I'm listening." Emmaline had the ability to compartmentalize. When she was on duty or working a case, she was single-minded. Our long friendship was put on the back burner. In those moments, she wasn't my friend or my sister-in-law. She was the sheriff, seeking information, so I didn't take offense at the brusqueness of her tone.

"There was one photo toward the end . . ."

"What about it?"

"When she saw it, she sort of gasped and became . . . upset."

I replayed the moment in my mind. With Eliza by my side, I'd come to the last few shots I'd taken. The first in the final set showed Eliza standing on the landing of the stairs, descending in her Ebenezer Scrooge outfit, the partygoers enraptured by their hostess. I'd turned to capture a few shots of her adoring guests. One of those shots had caused Eliza to start. "Wait. Go back," she'd said.

I had, stopping on a photo of the crowd, not focused on any one person. "This one?" I'd asked.

She'd nodded slightly, and leaned forward, hugging herself, her mouth gaping. "Oh no," she'd whispered.

"What?" I'd stared at the photo. Who had she seen? "Is it Brad?"

Slowly, she had shaken her head. Her lips pressed in against themselves, and her nostrils flared. Finally, she had let out a shaky breath and uttered, "It's my father."

Emmaline's tapping brought me back to the moment. "Interesting," she said.

"And sad." Estranged from her father and her husband. I felt sorry for her.

I knew Emmaline the woman did, too, but Sheriff Davis kept her emotions in check. She moved on from the bombshell that Eliza's father had been at the party, but I knew she'd only filed it away temporarily. For now, she said, "We're matching the photos you took with the people on the guest list. It's tedious. Here's the problem. So far, Brad McAvoy is the only person connected to Eliza Fox and the party who had a motive to murder Edward Yentin. But Mr. McAvoy wasn't in attendance, as far as we know."

"What about the Cordelia Knight scandal?" I asked.

"Cordelia *was* on the guest list, but as far as we can tell, she was a no-show."

"Was Yentin on the guest list?"

"Nope."

So, how had he known about the party, and why was he there? Curiouser and curiouser.

I'd spent some time Googling Edward Yentin. What I'd discovered was that he seemed like the type of reporter who'd acquired a mountain of enemies. He did tell-alls, outed people who didn't want to be outed, revealed hidden secrets, and basically reported all the things that any other reputable reporter would steer clear of. I wondered if he had legitimate sources for even half of what he printed.

"We're scouring his computer as we speak," Emmaline said. "I'm sure we'll turn over some dirt."

Of that, I had no doubt.

Chapter 7

I sat up in bed, a flashing light bulb hovering overhead. It had finally come to me. I'd fallen asleep to the nagging feeling that I was forgetting something. Now I'd awakened with the answer.

I jumped out of bed with the force of a gymnast. Agatha bounced awake and gave a disturbed little screech. "Sorry, Ags," I said, slowing just enough to pat her head. I'd plugged in my computer to charge before going to bed the night before. Now, clad in my red-plaid flannel pj's, I raced down the hall, past the living room, through the kitchen, and down the opposite hall to my little office to grab it. I plopped onto the floor, sitting cross-legged, pulling an old, pilled afghan that my mother had knitted around my shoulders.

A second later, I opened the file with the photos from Eliza's party. I pulled up the first picture, then used the arrow key on my computer to quickly scroll through the images until I found the one I was looking for. I'd taken a shot of Olaya's bread table, as well as the appetizer table. Beyond was the dining room and the opening to the kitchen.

Zac, the server I'd spoken with just after I'd overheard the argument between those men off the kitchen, stood with his back against the island. He had one arm draped around a young woman. Presumably this was Rita, his fiancée.

I zoomed in on her face, but I already knew I was right. This was the same woman with the bright eyes who'd been rejected by the chimney sweep. In this photo, she wore her black and white caterer's uniform, but when I'd seen her with the chimney sweep, she'd had a shawl around her shoulders. For a few minutes, she'd been able to blend in with the guests.

My first thought was: *Poor Zac*. The woman he'd fallen for and whom he planned to whisk away to Seattle, didn't look like she was quite so committed to her betrothed.

After that thought, three questions immediately surfaced. Was the chimney sweep who'd rejected her Edward Yentin? If it was, could she have pushed him over the cliff? After all, this was also the same young woman who'd discovered the body.

The third question that came to mind, which I didn't want to believe, but which I also had to consider, was: Had something gone on between the chimney sweep, again, assuming it was Yentin, and the woman I now suspected was Rita, and if so, did young Zac know about it?

Because if he did, that was clearly motive for murder.

It was barely light outside, but Emmaline was an early bird, so I didn't hesitate to phone her immediately.

She answered with a bright, "Morning, sunshine. You're up early for a Monday."

How right she was. Yeast of Eden was closed on Mondays, which meant I usually slept in—at least until seven or seven thirty. I glanced at my computer's clock in the upper right corner: 6:07. I yawned in response to the early hour. "I remembered something. It woke me up."

"Let's hear it," Em said, immediately shifting to sheriff mode.

I told her about the new server, Zac. If Rita already worked for Divine Cuisine, it suddenly made sense how he'd gotten the job at the last minute. He'd had an in. "He's engaged to one of the other employees. But here's the thing. I saw Rita being rejected by a guy at the party." I paused for dramatic affect. "A chimney sweep."

"*Our* chimney sweep?" Em asked.

"I'm not sure." From the photos I took, there were at least four, maybe five men dressed like some version of Bert from *Mary Poppins*. They were so similar that it was difficult to tell them apart. That number didn't include whatever costumed guests I hadn't managed to photograph.

"Thanks, Ivy. I'll let York know."

I wished I could pursue the clue, but I wasn't law enforcement, so leaving my discovery in the hands of Captain York was the best I could do.

Still, I felt a certain amount of ownership over my revelation, and that ownership led me to Divine Cuisine, a catering outfit in Santa Sofia that jangled up my nerves. The last time I'd been there, Renee Ranson had had an ax to grind. The hit-and-run she'd been the victim of had put her permanently in a wheelchair.

If I wanted answers, I had to suck it up and face her.

Divine Cuisine was located in the warehouse district of Santa Sofia, well off the beaten path. It was flanked by an embroidery and uniform business on one side, a cheerleading and tumbling studio on the other. Two white vans, similar to the one Olaya used for deliveries, sat in front. I'd bided my time, waiting until I thought the business would be in full swing. Now, at nine thirty, they were backed into the parking spots, the back doors of each open. Just as I'd anticipated, Divine Cuisine had more holiday parties on the catering docket.

The roll-up garage door, which was the loading area, was open. The back doors of one of the vans was being filled with bins and trays. I walked in through the front door to the hustle and bustle of what could have been Mrs. Claus's kitchen. A woman—definitely *not* Mrs. Claus—barked orders as several people flew around the kitchen and holding areas, moving trays, piling food into giant rectangular stainless-steel chafing dishes, covering them with heavy-duty tinfoil. I jumped out of the way as one of the employees lumbered by me, weighted down with an armload of folded white linens.

"Can I help you?" a voice said from behind me.

I turned back and found myself face-to-face with Renee Ranson. She took one look at me and jerked her wheelchair back with a lurch. "I know you."

"Ivy Culpepper. We met—"

"I remember. Your mother was Anna Culpepper."

Only recently had I started to get used to the casualness with which people referred to my mother. She'd died far too young. And tragically. It had taken me a long time to accept her death, let alone talk about it. But I managed to nod my head. "That's right."

"You work for Olaya Solis," she said.

I nodded again. I knew Olaya was occasionally contracted by Divine Cuisine when specialty breads were needed. It didn't happen often, and Olaya rarely delivered the bread herself. Usually one of Divine Cuisine's employees picked up an order. Olaya kept me out of those interactions. She was always trying to protect me, and I knew she didn't want me to suffer reminders about the particulars surrounding my mother's death.

"Well, what can I help you with? Our holiday schedule is completely full."

I waved away the idea that I was here to book a party. "I was at Eliza Fox's party Saturday night," I said. It wasn't an answer to her question, but it got her attention. She pointed to a stool, and I had a déjà vu moment of sitting at this stainless-steel counter the first time I'd been here, not long after I'd returned to Santa Sofia.

I pushed the thought away as she wheeled herself up to the counter next to me. "One of my servers mentioned that someone I knew was at the party," she said. "With what happened and the police and everything, he couldn't remember the name. It was you?"

"Zac. Yeah," I said, surprised he'd remembered to tell Renee about me asking after her. "We met in the kitchen there. He and his fiancée."

She scoffed. "If those two actually get married, then I'll walk again." She pulled a face that clearly said neither of those things was going to happen.

"He seemed pretty smitten," I said.

"He's only done a few gigs, so I don't know him well, but I'd say *he's* more smitten than *she* is."

That made sense given Rita's come-on to the chimney sweep. "Zac told me he's new—that party was his first gig—but Rita's been with you awhile."

Dark circles mooned under her eyes, and she looked haggard. I imagined she needed a break from her work, so a little respite during our conversation with me might be just what she needed. I hoped it would keep her talking.

"Rita's been with me for about six months. Turnover in this business is high, so that's a lifetime. Especially when you factor in the Hollywood wannabes." She let loose a heavy sigh and shook her head. "Too many of those around here."

I remembered what Zac had said about Rita's fifteen minutes of fame. "So Rita's an actress, too?"

She let out a harsh laugh. "Bah! She *wants* to be, but so does half of Southern California. And they all keep creeping up the coast into our little slice of paradise like they'll get their big break up here. They need to get themselves back to Los Angeles."

I supposed being discovered up here wasn't outside the realm of possibility given the growing number of actors who'd moved to Santa Sofia and the surrounding areas. Maybe agents knew this was a hot spot for the young and eager, and Hollywood hopefuls probably thought they had decent odds of meeting one of them, buddying up, and getting access to an otherwise-out-of-reach network.

Like I had at Eliza's party. I'd been wondering why Rita would make a move on Edward Yentin at the party with her fiancé right there. The guy wasn't an agent, so what was the draw?

Renee Ranson spoke again. "I told Rita she needed to lie

low after that scandal. Of course, why would a twenty-year-old who knows everything listen to someone like me?"

My head almost jerked back from the power of her cynicism. Before I could question her about it, though, one of her employees sidled over, clutching a clipboard. He flipped to the second page before handing it to her. As they spoke in hushed voices about a catering crisis, my mind wandered. The word *scandal* had triggered two snippets of conversation I'd heard the other night. The first was about Cordelia Knight, an invited guest, but as of now, a no-show at Eliza's party. The second was the argument between the two men off the kitchen. I was going with the premise that one of the men had been Yentin and the other was Brad McAvoy. With that scenario, Brad had been accusing Yentin of nearly ruining his marriage and his career with photos of him and a younger woman. *I could sue you for everything you're worth.*

Could Rita be the home wrecker that had been referred to?

Fifteen minutes of fame.

My mind fast-forwarded to Rita being rejected by the chimney sweep. A different scenario surfaced. I'd thought it might have been Yentin, but if I stuck to the theory that it was Yentin and Brad McAvoy arguing in the back hallway, it could have been McAvoy who'd rebuffed Rita.

I rewound. Yentin had told Brad, "You both won." I'd thought he'd been referring to the old adage that even bad publicity is good publicity. If that was to be believed, then both Brad's and Eliza's careers would have gotten a boost from the scandal of Brad's alleged affair.

But what if Yentin hadn't been referring to that? What if he'd been referring to Rita? She wanted a foot in Hollywood's door. Would she have created a scandal in order to get herself linked with one of Hollywood's hottest leading men? So both Brad McAvoy and lovely Rita had "won."

Renee muttered something under her breath, still flipping through the pages on the clipboard. My mind drifted back to Rita's fifteen minutes of fame. Zac had said they'd figured out how to get past it. Rita's face flashed in my mind. Whoever the chimney sweep was, she'd been disappointed at his lack of interest. Zac had said Rita had finally come around. Around to leaving her dreams of stardom behind? I suddenly knew what Zac had left unsaid. Seattle hadn't been enough for her. *Zac* hadn't been enough for her. Rita wanted what Eliza Fox had. She wanted stardom, but Zac said she'd come back around to him, and to Seattle.

But had she? Had she really? That interaction between her and the chimney sweep niggled in my mind. Something wasn't jibing. Had it been Edward Yentin, or Brad McAvoy?

Another idea hit me suddenly. What if Rita wasn't as ready to leave her dreams behind as Zac thought? What if she and Yentin had concocted a scheme for Yentin to get a photograph of Rita and Brad McAvoy so she could try to *trap* Brad and get herself in the news again? Extend her fifteen minutes to twenty . . . or thirty?

Maybe she thought she could steal Brad away from Eliza. After all, they were already estranged. She could step in and fill the void in Brad's heart.

Renee cleared her throat, dragging my attention back. "I have to cut this short. Is there something else you need?"

I jumped up. "No, I'm good. But thanks."

She stared at me for a long second, her eyes wary.

"What's your interest—" she started, but a young woman hurried over, cutting her off by saying, "Renee, there's a problem with the cheese order."

"Of course there is," Renee muttered.

I scurried out with a wave, my mind skittering back to the conversation I'd overheard in the hallway at Eliza Fox's house. Brad had said that his marriage and his career were ruined. But the reporter had scoffed at that and said, "You're here." I'd thought he meant, *You're here at this party hobnobbing with the rich and famous.* But what if he'd meant, *You're here at this party, thrown by your wife. How ruined could your marriage be?*

I remembered Eliza sitting on my couch, looking through the pictures I'd taken . . . looking for Brad, I thought. If Yentin was the reporter in that back hallway argument, and Brad was the other man—both present at the party despite not having invitations—that gave Brad a very clear motive. Get rid of the guy who'd wrecked his marriage.

If the chimney sweep Rita had been talking to had been Yentin, and if he'd given up on trying to capture Rita and Brad together, that gave Rita a motive.

By the time I was back at my car, my head was swimming. Those Dickens costumes. They were making things very difficult.

I pulled my cell phone from my back pocket and quickly texted Emmaline. *I'm 95% sure that Brad McAvoy was at the party.*

Three flashing dots appeared. Her response came a few seconds later. *Your gut was on target. Two guests confirmed they saw McAvoy there. Dressed as a chimney sweep.*

My heartbeat surged with satisfaction. I'd been right! My fingers flew across the screen. *I'm 50% sure that Rita, the server from Divine Cuisine, was working with Yentin so she could get "caught" with Brad.*

Fifty percent wasn't a strong sell, but I threw it out there anyway.

Emmaline tap backed the text with a thumbs-up. It was as much as I'd hoped for. The ball was now in the sheriff's court.

Chapter 8

My mind whirled as I left Divine Cuisine. Had I
jumped to a bunch of unfounded conclusions, or
had my deductive reasoning skills discovered a truth? I
couldn't answer that question on my own. What I needed
were reinforcements.

Mrs. Branford was always ready at a moment's notice.
She was a grandmother figure who was the furthest thing
from an old-fashioned Grandma Ethel or Mildred. She was
Betty White at her spunkiest. If I had half of Mrs. Branford's energy when I hit eighty, I'd be a happy camper. I
swung home to give Agatha some attention, alerting my
neighbor with a text that I'd be picking her up in thirty
minutes.

She replied with a red car emoji, followed by a black-
and-white-checkered starting flag. I took that to mean she
was ready and waiting.

I took the time to do a quick internet search, typing
Brad McAvoy scandal in the search bar. The results were

plentiful, although what Google considered a scandal wasn't entirely accurate. There were photos of Brad with a variety of starlets, but most of them were pre-marriage to Eliza Fox. I searched the top posts, including the ones about Brad's estrangement from his wife, and found what I was looking for. Two photos were part of an article about the demise of Hollywood's hottest marriage thanks to the wandering ways of heartthrob Brad McAvoy. The article was sympathetic to Eliza Fox, lamenting the fact that her girl-next-door heart had been broken, this time by her husband and a woman named Margarita Lewellyn.

Rita.

I enlarged the first photo on my computer screen. It *was* salacious. A shirtless Brad had his arms around a dark-haired naked woman whose back was to the camera. Clearly *not* Eliza Fox. One of Brad's hands splayed across the woman's backside. His eyes were trained on the camera. His expression was twisted into a scowl, and he held up his other arm, giving the photographer, in no uncertain terms, his middle finger.

I closed that photo, then enlarged the second one. I studied it for a minute, turning my head this way and that as I looked at the composition and the figures. Something about it was off. Brad walked down the street, a disposable coffee cup in his left hand. His right hand held his cell phone, his head dipped and thumb poised over the screen like he might be sliding it over the keyboard. Just to his left, a full step behind him was a young woman with the same color hair and general build as the woman in the first photo. In this one, her face was in full view. It was definitely Rita. She grinned, looking coyly at the camera as if she knew the photo was being taken.

Brad McAvoy, on the other hand, looked like he had

no idea he was being photographed—or if he did, he was choosing to ignore the paparazzi this time. No flashing the bird. No acknowledgment whatsoever.

He was not tuned in to Rita's presence at all. She *looked* like she was with him, but I was left wondering if it was simply a trick of the eye and she was merely a stranger walking up from behind him.

The whole thing felt wrong.

Awkward.

Staged.

The argument between the two men at Eliza's party came back to me again. Brad had said there had been no affair. Yentin had just scoffed. Because he didn't actually care about the truth?

I went back to the first photo, enlarging it again and looking more closely. The girl *could* have been photographed using a green screen, then Photoshopped into the picture, replacing whomever Brad had actually been embracing. If it was, it was done expertly. Still, it was possible.

And if it was true, then Rita had definitely worked with Yentin to set up Brad.

I'd parked my car on my driveway when I'd gotten home. Now, with my purse slung over my shoulder, I headed out the front door, ready to pick up Mrs. Branford. Agatha tried to follow me, making her little whimpering sound—the one she knew would pierce my heart.

"I can't take you to the bread shop, Ags," I said, giving her my pouty lips.

She wasn't placated. She sat down on her haunches and looked up at me with her giant eyes. That was all it took. "Okay, you win," I said. "Come on. Doggie day-care!"

I harnessed her up and led her to the car, depositing her on the blanket stretched across the backseat. Her tail curled, and she almost seemed to have a smile on her face. Impossible, I knew, but still . . .

Agatha was a little diabolical.

From my driveway, I could see Mrs. Branford standing at the curb in front of her cute, old Craftsman-style house. The warm taupe siding, combined with the creamy white window trim, made it one of the most welcoming houses on a street filled with lovely, welcoming homes.

A person's home, I'd come to realize, was as telling as his or her wardrobe. Mrs. Branford's spruced home reflected her spruced countenance. She had her tidy collection of velour lounge suits. She had notebooks chock-full of neat scribblings about each of the local crimes we'd had a hand in solving. Her furniture was old, but it was all highly functional, and not a trace of dust could be found in the house, or in her mind.

Her porch tilted slightly—as if some part of the house wanted to show its external age just like Mrs. Branford's snowy hair and slightly hunched shoulders showed hers, but overall, Mrs. Branford and her house were tidy reflections of each other.

In the same way, Miguel's bungalow was as laid-back as he was, and my Tudor reflected my traditional side. People whose houses had perfectly kept yards tended to be more fastidious than their neighbors who had a ladder carelessly lying in the front yard, or who had a flower bed crowded with weeds. It was an interesting way to study people.

I backed out of my driveway and drove the short distance to Mrs. Branford's house. She stood there with her cane resting on her shoulder in the same way a happy fisherman might have carried his pole. Her cane was more for show than it was for physical support, although I had seen her manipulate its use a few times when it suited her need.

Mrs. Branford jumped spritely into the car's passenger seat, spinning around to greet Agatha with, "Why, hello there, sweet girl."

I smiled. Mrs. Branford was Agatha's second mama. When I had a long day at Yeast of Eden, or a photography shoot that would keep me away from home for more than a few hours, it was usually Mrs. Branford to the rescue. She loved the company, and Agatha loved the attention. "It's a doggie daycare day," I said, turning the car around again and heading to the Waggin' Tail to drop her off.

A short while later, Mrs. Branford perched on a stool in the Yeast of Eden kitchen. The bread shop was closed, but the ovens were fired up, and the scent of baking bread filled the kitchen. Olaya was working on several Christmas Star Twisted Breads. The dough had already risen. She'd divided each mound into four sections, patted each one into a twelve-inch circle, and slathered three of them with raspberry jam.

This particular holiday bread had several steps to it. She layered the jam-covered rounds, one on top of the next, four-high, like stacks of thin crepes, the final layers without jam. She placed a round cutter smack in the center of each stack, pressing just enough to make a faint circle in the dough. Next, she took a knife and created a starburst design by cutting from the embossed circle out to the edge, slicing through all the layers. Finally, two by two, she twisted the strips together, which revealed the layers of jam. "It is messy, but as it rises and bakes, all that messiness disappears."

"Quite beautiful, Olaya," Mrs. Branford said.

Olaya dipped her head. A small thank-you. Their relationship hadn't always been smooth—or even existent—but they'd found common ground and had become friends, though they didn't like to admit it. They were more alike than not, and they each knew it deep down.

When she was done twisting all the dough and had set them all aside to rest, Olaya took four baked star breads from the oven. They were golden brown, the layers of raspberry jam giving them a festive look. She set them next to another four, which had been cooling. "Ivy, if you would, brush these four with the melted butter and dust with the sugar," she told me, indicating what had to have been the first four she'd baked that day.

I used a pastry brush to coat each star loaf with butter, then sprinkled confectioner's sugar over it with a small sieve. It looked like a light layer of snow had fallen. Olaya was right. There was not a bit of messiness to the twists.

"Now, try one," she said as she continued to work, measuring the ingredients for another set of four.

"What are they for?" I asked.

"Some for a book club holiday party this evening, others for another office party, and the last four for a dinner group," she said.

I cut three pieces, placing each on a white napkin. I set one next to Olaya's workstation, handed one to Mrs. Branford, and kept the third for myself.

"Mmm." Mrs. Branford dabbed her lips with her napkin after tearing off a hefty piece and plopping it into her mouth. "It tastes better than it looks. And it looks spectacular, so that's saying something."

I took a bite, practically smacking my lips at the lightly sweetened bread mixed with the jam. "So good," I agreed.

Olaya's eyes sparkled as she worked, keeping an eye on us as she mixed the new batch of dough. One of her greatest joys was seeing people savor what she baked— and Mrs. Branford and I were savoring on a very high level.

I waited until I'd finished eating the buttery bread, groaning with delight after each bite, before bringing up the murder. "I have a theory to run by you both before I take it to Emmaline," I said, brushing away the remnants of powdered sugar from my shirt.

Olaya simply nodded, while Mrs. Branford said, "It's about time. Let's hear it."

I filled them in on my visit with Renee Ranson, as well as the photos I'd found of Rita and Brad from my internet search and my doubts about their authenticity.

"What is this green screen?" Olaya asked after I suggested my theory.

I explained the process of using a solid green background to photograph something. "You can then replace that solid color with a different background."

"Interesting," Olaya said. "And this can be done?"

"It would take someone who knows what they're doing, but I bet Yentin would have had that skill." I paused long enough for them to consider what I'd said. "It makes sense, right?"

"Perfectly," Mrs. Branford said. "I believe it is quite a good deduction."

Despite the fact that we were talking about murder, warm fuzzies bloomed inside me. I felt like Mrs. Branford had just given me genuine praise on a particularly well-written essay.

Olaya looked reflective, finally nodding. "I agree with you, Penelope. This young woman, the Rita—sadly, she seems lost."

I couldn't have agreed more. To entrap someone in an effort to be discovered was underhanded; to compromise yourself with a naked Photoshopped photo was just sad.

"Call Emmaline, *mija*," Olaya said.

I'd felt anxious about making yet another call to Em. I was pretty sure I was right about the photos, but what if I was wrong? I didn't want to throw somebody under the bus if there was a chance I was offtrack, but Olaya and Mrs. Branford had agreed with my line of thinking. That was the reassurance I needed. Plus, I'd never held out on Em before. I couldn't start now.

I stepped outside to the back parking lot. The flower beds, which were usually blossoming with an array of flowers, had been pruned back for the winter. It was fifty-seven degrees, a bit cooler than the average December afternoon. I'd left home without a sweater or jacket, and now I shivered. Instead of suffering in the coastal California cold, I unlocked my car and sat in the driver's seat, the door closed against the chilly breeze.

Emmaline answered before the second ring. "Hey, Ivy."

"Hey." I bypassed the small talk, knowing Em would want to hear what I had to say. I relayed my story once again, falling silent at the end and waiting for her response.

"That's a great lead," she said. "Much clearer motive for Brad McAvoy. So far, still no solid evidence he was at the party, though."

My anxiousness had abated after getting Olaya and Mrs. Branford's reassurance, but after I hung up with Em, it came back with a gale force wind. I'd hoped to alleviate the strife in Eliza's marriage by discounting the affair, but Em was right. Now Brad had an incredibly solid reason for pushing Yentin off the cliff.

Chapter 9

For a bakery, the holiday season is beyond busy. Yeast of Eden was no exception. On top of the regular seasonal parties, customers came in droves. The front of the store was rarely empty. Felix, his small morning crew, and I had trays of croissants in the oven and had moved on to the sourdough rolls and rye loaves. The scent of baking bread spiraled in the air like vapory lengths of ribbon. For a moment, I closed my eyes and just breathed it in. As it always did, the yeasty scent softened the hard lines in my mind and took the edge off my anxiety—which at the moment was centered around Eliza Fox, the death of Edward Yentin, and Brad McAvoy's motive for killing him.

I let it go as I picked up a mound of dough, dropped it again, and dug the heel of one hand into it. Baking bread Olaya's way, which was to say with the traditional long-rise method, was physical and could be cathartic, if you let it.

I was letting it, one hundred percent.

Olaya breezed in, her caftan billowing behind her. "I have hired someone to help in front," she announced. "Amanda quit last night."

I glanced up. Amanda had only worked here for a little over a month, and I'd only seen her a handful of times. She was a junior at Santa Sofia High School who, apparently, cared more about hanging out with her friends than being committed to her job. "She quit? Just like that?"

Olaya snapped her fingers. "Just like that."

"And you already hired someone?" I asked. Olaya wasn't the type of person to sit on her hands, but a new hire in the matter of a few nighttime hours was fast, even for her.

From her smile, I knew she was more than pleased with herself. "What is the American expression—a door closes fast before a different door, it opens?"

"That's it exactly," I said. More or less.

"To Amanda, *vaya con dios*, because the door opening brought me"—she paused, the silence filling the air with an imaginary drumroll—"Zula."

I dropped my hunk of dough. It fell with a *thud* on the stainless-steel counter. "Zula?! Zula Senai? Really? She's going to work here?" I asked, resisting the urge to jump up and down with excitement.

Olaya had a passion for helping and empowering women. One of the ways she did that was by running a program called Bread for Life. Bread was a staple in every culture and country. Olaya's program was designed to bring women together and to share their stories through baking. Zula Senai had been one of the women in the first cohort. "Senai was my father's first name," she'd explained when she'd filled out the initial application. "It is different than a surname here."

We'd all loved her name . . . and her. If I had to choose three words to describe Zula, they'd be: boisterous, stunning, and enthusiastic. She was an Eastern African version of Sofia Vergara in *Modern Family*. She had a tween daughter named Ella and worked as a hospice-care nurse. "What about her current job?" I asked.

"Zula told me she wants to spread her wings. Those were her words."

She had loved baking bread and teaching the other women in the Bread for Life program about hembesha and other traditional Eritrean foods, and she was full of energy and life to the point that she made the rest of us seem downright dull. "So she'll do both?"

"She will work mornings here, and schedule her hospice shifts in the afternoons," Olaya said.

"It sounds perfect." Honestly, I couldn't wait to have Zula around all the time. I might never want to leave the bread shop.

As if on cue, a woman's voice boomed from the front of the house. "I am here!"

Zula swept through the swinging doors separating Olaya's commercial kitchen from the shop. She was tall—five feet, eleven inches—and she had pronounced high cheekbones, and deep, rich skin that had the beautiful shine of polished mahogany. Her long braids were banded together at her shoulder blades. But it was her smile, which spanned the width of her face, that captured the attention of anyone she encountered. She wore a deep shade of red on her lips and her white teeth practically glistened. The woman was supermodel-gorgeous, down-to-earth, and humble. It was a killer combination.

She came over to Olaya, towering over her. "You just tell me what to do, boss, and I will do it."

"You are where you are meant to be," Olaya said, perfectly sanguine, as she always was.

Zula's grin grew wider, if that was possible. "Of course I am!"

"Come with me," Olaya said, and she led Zula back through the swinging doors to start her training.

The phone call from Eliza came at exactly 11:03. "They arrested Brad!"

I clamped the phone between my shoulder and ear as I washed my hands at the commercial sink. My heart sank. Captain Craig York must have had enough suspicion to bring Brad in for questioning, which I feared I'd had a hand in.

"Ivy, you have to help me!" Eliza's voice shrilled in my ear.

"Help you how?"

"Brad *couldn't* have killed that man!" she wailed.

I perked up. "Does he have an alibi?"

"Yes! I mean, no. I don't know. What I mean is that he doesn't have it in him. He's not a . . . a *killer*!"

That might be true, but I'd seen Brad McAvoy in plenty of movie roles where he'd adeptly used a gun or simply his fighting skills to take down the bad guys. Brad had killed in the movies, and any prosecutor would surely use that preconceived perception to sway a jury into thinking he could do the same in real life.

"I saw you talking to the sheriff. Aren't you friends? Can you find out what's happening with Brad? Please, Ivy."

This was not the pleading voice of a woman who wanted to divorce her husband. This sounded like a woman desperate to *save* her husband. Despite the estrangement, she still loved Brad.

"I don't know if I can find out anything, Eliza, but I'll try," I said, knowing Em would tell me only what she felt she could, and not a single, solitary bit more.

I was about done with my bread shop shift, so I dialed Em's cell right away. Sounds from the front of the shop drifted back to the kitchen, the holiday spirit heightened with Zula's effervescent presence.

"Hey," Em said by way of greeting. "You have me on speed-dial lately."

That was true. She was in my Favorites list, anyway, but lately I'd called her more than anyone else. "I just got a frantic call from Eliza Fox."

That was all I had to say. "York brought Brad McAvoy in for questioning," she said. "He's a person of interest."

Nerves coiled in my stomach. "Based on what I told you?"

"Partially, but also, we found some things on Yentin's computer and in his home office."

I knew Yentin's computer would reveal something sordid, but I hadn't considered that that something might include Brad McAvoy. It took the responsibility off of me—he'd have been looked at by law enforcement without the motive I'd handed Em—but that didn't make me feel less guilty. Before I could ask what they'd found, Em said, "You're becoming friends with Eliza?"

Was I? That might be a stretch, because even if she did seem like a lost puppy, whatever connection we'd forged was based on the transactional relationship of me being her party photographer. Still, we had broken bread together. Literally. "Um, maybe? A little bit."

A rustling. Footsteps. It sounded like Em had moved the phone from one ear to the other and was moving from one place to another. "Look, I can't give you details," she said, her voice lower than it had been, "but Yentin was working on an article about . . ."

She trailed off, as if she wasn't sure if she should say anymore. She probably shouldn't, but I pressed her anyway. "About Brad McAvoy?"

"No. About Eliza Fox herself."

Forty minutes later, with Emmaline's blessing—and encouragement, truth be told—I stood at the island in Eliza Fox's kitchen sipping a cup of hot tea.

Eliza and Nicole stood shoulder to shoulder. "What did he want?" Eliza muttered into her teacup, referring to Yentin.

"He was a hack," Nicole said. She set down the set of car keys in her hand. "It doesn't matter."

Eliza didn't look convinced, but she nodded.

Nicole looked at me. "Let me get this straight. The authorities think Brad pushed the guy off a cliff in the middle of a party, in plain view of half the party guests, because a) he was getting revenge for the article about him having an affair—"

"He didn't have an affair!" Eliza interrupted. "It looks that way, but he didn't!"

"Okay, okay. I know he didn't, but the article and the pictures are still out there," Nicole said, then continued. "Or b) because the guy was writing an article about you and, what, Brad wanted to stop it? What was the article even about, and how would Brad know about it, and why would it matter? It's not like you have skeletons in your closet, Eliza. And I'm with you, I don't think Brad is capable of killing someone."

Those were excellent points, and I said so. "Maybe Yentin baited him," I suggested. The second the words left my mouth, I knew it was true. Yentin *had* baited Brad McAvoy, and I'd overheard it. Brad had threatened to sue Yentin about the so-called affair, but Yentin had no fear. I could hear his response in my head. *I've moved on. You're upset about that hot little thing? Wait till you see the next piece I'm printing.* Could he have been talking about whatever tell-all he was planning about Eliza? And more importantly, did Brad *know* what Yentin was referring to? *Did* Eliza have skeletons that Nicole didn't know about, but that Brad did?

"But what if Yentin told Brad—"

Eliza broke off, her face ashen and her voice shaky. Nicole pushed her glasses up the bridge of her nose. "It doesn't matter. He couldn't possibly have anything interesting to write because he didn't know you."

Eliza didn't look so sure of that. "But what if—"

"There is no 'what if'," Nicole said, putting her foot down. "It's a nice idea to think Brad would protect you, but he had nothing to avenge. He would have gotten a lawyer. A restraining order. Something. He wouldn't kill the guy. He had no reason to even want to."

Eliza's expression clouded with doubt. The best way

to combat that was with facts. "I heard two men talking. If we assume Brad came to the party—"

"Uninvited," Nicole inserted.

"—and it was him with Yentin—"

"Also uninvited," Nicole said.

"—in the back hallway, and that Yentin was the chimney sweep I saw walk away, then where did Brad go?"

"Into the garage?" Eliza suggested.

"Exactly," I said. "It's the only thing that makes senses. He must have snuck in and out through the garage."

"He'd have to have the remote for that," Nicole said, stopping when she saw the color drain from Eliza's face. "Oh no. Eliza, no, no, no. You didn't give him a remote, did you?"

"He's been here before, then?" I asked, realizing that maybe they weren't as estranged as I'd thought.

"I still love him," Eliza practically whispered. "He's been over a few times. I told him he had to tell me the truth. *Did you have an affair?* I asked him. He said no. *He. Said. No.* I want to believe him. I gave him the remote because I wanted him to come back—"

"Without me knowing—" Nicole snapped.

Eliza managed to look both sheepish and defiant. "He's my husband. I don't want to believe he cheated—"

Nicole's irritation drained from her face. "He didn't."

Eliza carried on. "I told him not to come to the party. It was too soon, and I didn't want to be explaining all night about whether or not we're together when I didn't even know the answer to that question myself."

Nicole just shook her head, keeping whatever chastisement she'd been about to say to herself.

"Did anyone actually *see* Brad at the party?" Eliza asked. "Because he's not in any of the pictures you took, Ivy."

That was true. Emmaline, Eliza, and I had all scoured every detail of every one of those photos. Em had two guests confirming his attendance, but if Brad had been at the party, I hadn't gotten a candid of him. "Have you spoken to him since the murder?" I asked Eliza.

Her eyes went wide, and I thought this was probably the first time she'd heard it put so bluntly. Edward Yentin had been murdered during Eliza's holiday party. Slowly, she nodded. "He called me late Saturday night. After he found out what happened."

I managed not to raise my eyebrows at that. Emmaline had managed to keep the details of the paparazzi reporter's death out of the news. No media blitz had gone out so unless McAvoy had been at the party, how would he have known what had happened?

Nicole put a comforting arm around Eliza. "What did he say, sweetie?"

Eliza's eyes had welled with tears, but so far, she'd kept them from spilling. They just pooled there perfectly. "He said he l-loved me, and that at least Yentin wouldn't bother me anymore."

That phrase ricocheted in my mind. *At least Yentin wouldn't bother Eliza anymore . . .* why? Because Brad McAvoy had taken care of the guy?

"*Had* he been bothering you?" I asked, because she hadn't even admitted to knowing the guy.

Now a single tear spilled, falling in a streak down her cheek. It was a small blessing to be able to cry pretty instead of ugly. I didn't have that gift. When I cried, it was a full-on red-faced, drippy-nose, tortured-mouth kind of experience. No solitary, poignant tear for me, but it didn't surprise me that Eliza cried with understated drama and poise. She was gorgeous, so why not have a beautiful cry, too? The pause was pregnant, but finally she nodded. "The thing is, he called me last week to see if I wanted to comment on a story he was going to run."

Nicole's face drained, and her side hug tightened. "He didn't," she said, but Eliza nodded, another tear slipping down her cheek, and said, "He did."

Those coils in my gut tightened again, and I bit my lip. "What was the story about?" I asked.

"He was, um, researching my, mmm, childhood."

"What about it?" I asked, remembering what she'd told me about being the object of too much male attention.

Eliza shook her head. "I'd rather not . . . I don't like to . . . mmm, talk about it."

I got that, but I wanted to make sure she understood what was happening here. I didn't know if Yentin had already sold the story he was writing about Eliza. Maybe he didn't really care about a comment from her at all. Maybe him reaching out to her was all for show, or maybe it had been a move to rattle her cage.

"You mean it might be out there, ready to be published?" she asked when I pressed. Her eyes grew wide and . . . worried.

"I don't know, Eliza," I said, wondering about the way she'd reacted to seeing photographic proof that her father had been at the holiday party. Did he have something to do with her leaving home at such a young age? "It's a possibility, that's all."

Nicole moved her arm from Eliza's shoulders and took her by the hand instead, squeezing lightly. Reassuring her. From the way Eliza had responded when she realized her father had been at her party, there was definitely something between them. I didn't know what would happen if Yentin's story came to light, but I was glad Eliza had steady support now.

The thing was, though, she now also had a motive for murder.

Chapter 10

The doorbell rang, startling the three of us. Nicole and Eliza didn't budge.

"Are you expecting someone?" I asked.

"No," Nicole said. She raised her eyebrows at me and nodded toward the living room. "Would you mind?"

"Oh. Sure." I headed toward the front door as the bell rang again, its sonorous tone matching the somber mood in the house.

I opened the door to two men standing on the slate front porch, looking down on me from their six-feet-plus heights. One had dark hair and wore an old ball cap, while the other was dirty blond and had slight waves that dusted his shoulders.

The long-haired man gave a strained smile. "I'm looking for Joh—" The second man backhanded the first, cutting him off. He started again. "I'm, uh, John. I'm looking for Eliza? Fox?"

I raised a skeptical eyebrow. "Do you know her—" I

stopped when recognition hit. "Wait, you're . . ." I decided it was better not to say any more, instead acting like Eliza's personal secretary. "You're here to see Ms. Fox? Do you have an appointment?"

"I think she'll see me. Tell her her . . . mmm, tell her John is here."

That speech pattern—the hesitation and the *mmm*. John Fox. Eliza's father. "Wait here, please," I said. I shut the door on them, turning the deadbolt before hurrying back to the kitchen.

Eliza still stood against the kitchen counter, but Nicole had gone. "She went to pick up a prescription for me," she said when I asked. "Bladder infection. I can't take it anymore."

Sure enough, the car keys Nicole had set down when I'd shown up were gone. I empathized with Eliza and hoped Nicole would get back with the meds quickly. UTIs were the worst.

I looked over my shoulder, as if checking to make sure the two men hadn't followed me inside. Impossible, I knew, but Eliza's reaction to the photo of her father told me was that she had not been thrilled to know that he'd been in attendance at her party. It followed that him showing up here unannounced would not be a celebratory reunion. An unwelcome thought sped into my head. Eliza had left home so young. What if her father . . . ? I let the question drift away, too horrible to even think of.

Eliza didn't ask who rang the bell. Was it her stardom that made it irrelevant to her? Or was it that she didn't have anyone who'd come to visit? Or did she assume it was some service person who'd come to the front rather than the side door like Nicole directed people to do?

"Eliza," I said, drawing her attention. "There are two men at the door."

She looked at me with her giant crystal-blue eyes, tucking a strand of her blond hair behind her ear, but she waited for me to continue. In that moment, I realized that it wasn't her ego that made her aloof or disconnected. It was her naiveté. She knew how to use her star power, as she'd done when she'd descended the staircase at the party, but that was an act. Inside, I was pretty sure that she was an innocent girl who felt like she was playing dress-up in a grown-up world.

"Um, I think one of them is your father?" I said, lilting the last word. I didn't know what I'd expected, but the reality wasn't even in the realm of possibilities I would have considered. She flew into frenzied action, fluttering her hands in the air like she was fanning her face, and scurrying around in tight circles. Like a chicken with its head cut off.

I didn't know whether to leave her be or put my hands on her shoulders to try to calm her down. She was outside of herself. Why, oh why, had Nicole chosen this moment to leave? We needed her calming presence.

"Eliza?" I said, then more loudly and with authority. "Eliza!"

She stopped spinning around just as suddenly as she'd started. She came to a full stop, hands on either side of her head, like she was in the movie *Frozen*, touched by Elsa's hand.

I surged forward, crouching my body enough to move my face into her line of sight. I looked into her face. "Eliza, are you okay?"

She blinked, coming back to life. Slowly, she lowered her hands. "M-m-my father? Are you s-sure?"

Well, no. I wasn't a hundred percent sure. I'd never met the guy, after all. "It's the same man you saw in the photo Sunday."

She started to grow frantic again. Her lower lip trembled. "He's here?"

"Yes. With another man. Short hair. Baseball cap."

"Russ," she said, her voice scarcely more than a whisper.

Was that a first name, or a last name? I didn't bother asking. "Should I let them in?"

"No! I don't want to see him."

"Okay. So, I'll tell them to go?"

"Why is he here?" she asked.

I had no idea. "I don't know. Um, should I tell them to go?" I asked again.

Her eyes bugged, and she started nodding frantically. "Y-yes! I c-can't . . . I d-don't want them here. He cannot come in here. I can't face him. But . . . no, maybe I should . . ." She spun around as if she was searching for something. "Where's Nicole?"

I tried to steady her with my hand on her forearm. She was losing it. "Nicole went for your prescription, remember?"

The words sank in. Just as I thought she might pull herself together, the doorbell rang again, followed by a fist pounding on the front door. One of the men yelled, "Eliza! Please. I just want to talk!"

Eliza screeched. "Oh!"

I could feel her trembling through the light sweater she wore. "What do you want me to tell them?"

The pounding stopped suddenly, and we fell silent. She grabbed my hand. We both held our breath, waiting to see if they'd start up again.

A long minute passed. Then another. Finally, we both exhaled, and our hands loosened.

"Oh, thank Go—"

And then someone pounded on one of the front-facing kitchen windows and a face appeared, rising up from the shrubs like a defectively slow jack-in-the-box.

Eliza screamed.

My heart shot to my throat.

"I just want to talk!" he yelled through the glass.

Eliza's nostrils flared. Her entire body trembled, but she spun around to face the window. Her hands fisted. "I can't!"

"Please. Baby, it's been so long," the man said.

Her hair flew around her face as she shook her head. "I can't."

"I miss you, baby. I love you," he said through the glass.

Her face collapsed, and this time it *was* an ugly cry. I was secretly mollified. She was mortal after all. "Dad. I. Could. Not. Stay. There."

He pressed his palms against the glass. "But why, baby?"

Eliza's lower lip quivered with emotion. Conflicted emotion, I thought. Part of her, I suspected, wanted to talk to him, but the other part had built a story up around her reasons for running away, and now that story was too big to let go of.

The story Edward Yentin had been writing . . . what had he discovered about Eliza's childhood?

And just like that, the suspicion pendulum swung firmly in her direction again. If Yentin had been writing a story about what Eliza had been hiding all these years, that could be motive to stop him.

"You c-came to my party," Eliza said, her voice elevated enough for her father to hear.

"To see you."

"I d-don't want t-to see you." She flung her arm out, pointing beyond the window. "Leave or I'm going to c-call the police. You're t-t—" She hit her clenched fist against her thigh. "Trespassing."

John's forehead made a dull *thump* as it fell against the window. For a second, I thought he might smash his forehead right against the glass to shatter it, but instead he backed away without another word.

Eliza sank against the counter as I raced to the window. John Fox had already disappeared around the corner. I hurried through the living room to the entry, peering through the clear square windows of the front door. There was no sign of the men.

Back in the kitchen, I led Eliza to a stool at the island. "We should call the police," I said, my phone already out.

"He's gone? You're sure?"

"I'm sure."

"Then I'm fine. Please don't say anything."

She was far from fine, but it was her father, and he hadn't broken into the house. Showing up at a party uninvited wasn't a crime. If it was, half the students in Santa Sofia Unified School District would be holed up in jail.

Still, the incident had been unsettling. Whatever friendship—if you could call it that—I was forging with Eliza Fox was brand-new. My friendship with Emmaline practically spanned our entire lives. Did I owe it to Eliza not to tell Emmaline about the surprise visit from Eliza's father, or did I owe it to Emmaline to tell her what I knew? I knew what it meant to be between a rock and a hard place, but this was not one of these times. The fact was,

John Fox's sudden appearance was alarming. I didn't know how—or if—it was connected to Edward Yentin's death, but Emmaline needed to know about it.

I filled a glass of water and handed it to Eliza as I sat down on the stool next to her. "I don't know what your relationship is with your dad, but, Eliza, he showed up to your party, he showed up here with his friend, and he clearly scares you. We *have* to tell the sheriff about this."

She didn't move. Didn't react. For a second, I wasn't sure she'd heard me, but then she raised her teary blue eyes to mine. "I c-can't hold on to anything."

"What do you mean? You have a wonderful career. People love you!"

"My f-family. M-My m-marriage . . . I m-miss Brad."

I took her hand, feeling the bones underneath her cold skin. "You can call Brad. That scandal . . . it was made up, Eliza. It was fake."

"I thought so," she said, but her eyes clouded. "Sometimes you can't take things back after you say them."

"Okay," I agreed. "But sometimes you can." The nearly twenty years of silence between Miguel and me was proof enough of that. We'd both reacted to stories that we'd believed, but that weren't actually true. The result had been his enlistment and exodus from Santa Sofia, and my long stint in Texas, plus a failed marriage. "You have to talk it out."

"I'm back," a voice called. The door leading to the garage slammed shut.

My head snapped up. Nicole appeared in the hallway, a white paper sack in one hand. That garage door opener had to be the quietest in existence.

Quiet enough for someone to escape through, unnoticed.

Nicole registered the tension in the room and the anxiety emanating from Eliza. She dropped her purse and the paper sack on the hallway bench and surged forward, crouching down next to Eliza. "What's wrong?"

I'd come to recognize the slight flaring of Eliza's nostrils when she took deep inhalations, or when she was bolstering herself. This was one of those moments, on both counts. "My father was here."

Nicole didn't react, but a splotchy red crept from her neck to her cheeks. Unspoken panic for Eliza. "At the door? I thought it was a delivery. Oh my—Eliza, are you okay?"

Her response told me that Nicole had insight into Eliza's situation with her father. It didn't surprise me. The starlet had to trust someone.

Eliza's head waggled in an unconvincing nod. "Ivy thinks I need to call the police," she said.

"You can't," Nicole said immediately. She swiveled her head to me. "She can't. A police incident on the heels of that man's death is the last thing she needs."

"I think the last thing she needs is to go through this again if he comes back." I tried to communicate with Nicole just using my eyes. *You should have seen her. She barely held it together.*

If Nicole got any of my unspoken messages, she didn't let on. "Eliza. Sweetheart. We can handle this without the authorities."

I wasn't so sure. "But the mur—"

Nicole shut me down with one terse look. "She cannot be wrapped up in a scandal."

"Her father showing up is not a scandal," I said. "So what if she doesn't have a relationship with him? Her not wanting him here is not newsworthy. But him showing up

at her party, then at the front door, could constitute ha-
rassment."

Nicole gave me an indulgent smile. "I agree, but a
celebrity's star shines only as bright as her next marquee.
Did you not hear about Cordelia Knight?"

That was not the same thing at all, and I said so.

"You don't know Hollywood," Nicole said.

"But I do know women who have needed to escape
bad situations. It sounds to me like that's what happened
to Eliza." The moment I spoke the words, I knew they
were true. Eliza hadn't left home over some creepy boss.
No, something had happened. Something to do with her
father. Why she opted to live her life in the public eye if
she was escaping something in her past was a mystery,
but there was no accounting for people's decisions.

"Stop talking about me like I'm not here." The chill in
Eliza's voice cut through me. She'd transformed from
scared and withdrawn to a steel magnolia.

Later, as I drove off, the thought that Eliza's emotions
weren't a hundred percent authentic stuck with me like a
splinter just far enough under the skin that it was un-
reachable. Once again, I reminded myself that Eliza Fox
was an actor.

Chapter 11

Instead of another phone call to Emmaline, I headed straight to the sheriff's department. The squat beige building was a quintessential government structure, which is to say it didn't have much personality. Then again, it didn't need to have personality as long as the people inside kept the county safe.

"I'm here to see the sheriff," I told the uniformed woman at the front desk. Her dark hair was shorn close to the scalp on both sides just above the ears, with a row of curls running over the top of her head like a Mohawk. In her private life, I suspected the deputy lived a little on the wild side.

"She's not in."

Coming in without calling had been a risk, but I went with plan B. I knew I needed to let my residual dislike of Captain York fade away. No time like the present.

"Sure. What's your name?" the officer asked after I requested to see York.

"Ivy Culpepper," I said, wondering if my name would make York sneak out the back door.

"Hang on." She picked up the phone and dialed an extension, saying, "Someone to see you, Captain. An Ivy Culpepper." She listened while the captain said something to her, replying with an obedient, "Sure thing, Captain." Then to me, she said, "He'll be with you in a few minutes."

After a solid *twenty* minutes, more than a mere few, the captain sauntered out to greet me. "Ms. Culpepper," he said, and just like that, his smugness reignited my distaste for him.

"Captain York," I said. His wispy blond hair and saunter reminded me of a washed-up TV show detective. All he needed was an open shirt collar and a brown leather 1970s jacket.

He led me into the back of the building. I'd been here before to see Emmaline, but it never ceased to surprise me how different the Santa Sofia Sheriff's Department was from the huge departments shown on television with their grungy interiors and partners' desks positioned so the detectives faced one another.

Here there was a common room with workspaces running along the perimeter wall, each space divided by a cubicle partition, but the room was clean and bright and would never have been a set for a gritty city police drama. Instead, it could have been the model for an ensemble comedy. It looked like each deputy had their own space, some decorated with family photos and other personal items, each with a computer and a chair on casters.

"This way," York said. We passed the sheriff's office, the door closed, the lights out. I wanted to ask where Emmaline was, but I knew he wouldn't tell me. He led me into an office at the end of one side of the room, going in and leaving the door open for me to follow. Chivalrous he was not. I felt like any TV detective worth his salt would have held the door for me, not that it actually mattered.

Still . . .

He circled around his desk and sat, extending his arm toward one of the chairs facing it. I sat, noticing how neat and tidy the man was. I hadn't had any expectations about that, but I liked that the things in his office were in order. No file folders lay scattered about. No old coffee cups sat abandoned on his desk. No layer of dust coated his shelves. Either the man liked things orderly or he didn't actually do any work.

My bet was the former.

He leaned back in his chair, folding his arms like a barrier against whatever I might have to say. "What can I help you with, Ms. Culpepper?"

Right. No pleasantries. I cut to the chase. "I have some information about the murder at Eliza Fox's house."

He jolted forward, dropping his forearms to his desk. "What now?"

"The murder at Eliza Fox's? I have some information. I don't know if it means anything, but I wanted to share it with . . . well, actually, with Emmaline, but she's not here, so . . ."

I was rambling. The guy made me nervous, like he might randomly decide *I* was the mastermind behind Edward Yentin's death. I had been present, after all.

The way his eyes narrowed, I suddenly couldn't tell if he was curious or skeptical. "What kind of information?" he asked.

I counted to four as I inhaled to slow my racing heartbeat. "First I want to say that I really like Eliza—"

"*Pfft*," he scoffed.

I raised my eyebrows at him. "What?"

"She's a celebrity," he said, as if that explained his response.

Apparently in his book, celebrities couldn't be liked for themselves. Their fame drove everything. I couldn't completely disagree. Still, I ignored his remark and proceeded. "As I was saying, I like Eliza Fox—"

"But?"

I held in the grumble rising in me. "*But* I learned a few things that I thought were worth sharing."

This time I paused on purpose. "Go on," he said.

And so I did, telling him about the two reasons Eliza Fox might have wanted Edward Yentin out of her life.

"So she avenged her husband for the licentious photos Yentin sold, which were at the core of their estrangement, or she has a secret from her past she wants to keep a secret, but you don't know precisely what that secret is," he summarized when I was done.

The way he repeated the word *secret* three times made it seem like my concern was comical, but I held my head high and said,"Correct. And then there's Brad McAvoy, and John Fox," I said.

He cocked a brow. "John who, now?"

"Eliza's father, John Fox. He was at the party uninvited, and he showed up at Eliza's house earlier today. He's really upset her. The thing is, the timing is off."

He used my own tactic on me, sitting silent until I filled the space by continuing.

Which I did. "Is it coincidence that he showed up the same night Edward Yentin died?"

York nodded slowly. "I see what you're getting at. What if Yentin rooted around in this secret Eliza wants to keep on the down low and John Fox emerged from the woodwork."

"Exactly." I didn't know if it was warranted, but I was relieved that, at least for the moment, York's attention was off of Eliza and onto her father.

He plucked a file folder from the metal organizer on his desk, flipped it open, and ran his finger down a list. "There's no John Fox on our list of guests, and we didn't interview anyone with that name."

So he'd slipped out before the police had arrived. Did he know about the door to the garage and the silent opener? Then again, how could he? And even though he did show up at the party, did he even know who Edward Yentin was?

"How, exactly, did you come by this knowledge that John Fox has come out of the woodwork?" York asked.

"I was just at Eliza's—"

"For what reason were you at Ms. Fox's residence?"

I bristled, suddenly feeling as if I was the subject of an interrogation rather than a concerned citizen trying to help get a murderer off the streets of Santa Sofia. "She called me this morning, upset," I said, leaving out the fact that Emmaline had encouraged me to go.

"Upset, why?"

I threw my shoulders back. "Because *you* brought her husband in for questioning."

It felt like I'd thrown down a gauntlet, and he responded with a silent growl. "And what did Ms. Fox have to say about *that*?"

"Like I said, Captain York, she was upset. She said her husband wasn't capable of pushing a man to his death."

The complicated-looking phone on his desk beeped. He picked up the receiver with a gruff, "York."

He stood as he replaced the handset. "Ms. Culpepper, thanks for coming in."

"But—"

"You let the Santa Sofia Sheriff's Department handle it from here."

Meeting over.

He strode to the door and opened it. I followed, breezing past him as if his abrupt behavior didn't bother me in the least.

Just as I stepped into the common room of the station, the deputy with the edgy haircut from the front desk appeared, ushering an unhappy Eliza Fox and a placating Nicole Leonard into an interview room opposite from where we stood.

I'd left Eliza's house only a short while ago. I must have just missed the authorities barging in on her. My eyes locked with Eliza's, and I saw the fire rise in her. "You?"

It was an accusation, as if *I* was the one responsible for her being here. I shrugged helplessly, glancing at York, who stood beside me. The smirk on his face said it all. The phone call he'd just answered had alerted him to Eliza's arrival. He'd suddenly ended our interview and led me out of his office so Eliza would see me . . . and think that *I'd* ratted her out.

"I didn't—" I started, but of course I actually *had* given her up as a potential suspect to York. He'd simply played out his hand early, arranging to bring Eliza in for questioning before I'd given him my suspicions. That didn't make me feel any better.

"This way, Ms. Culpepper," York said, interrupting my

thoughts, and he ushered me back the way we'd come. He spoke loud enough for the entire room to hear. "Thank you for your cooperation."

I started to say that I hadn't cooperated, but I couldn't get the words out because I had.

Maybe I was a rat after all.

"Drink this," Miguel said as he placed a steaming mug of green tea in front of me. We sat in his office off the restaurant's kitchen, away from the hustle and bustle as the back of house prepared for the dinner rush.

I cupped my chilled hands around the hot ceramic, letting the warmth infuse my skin before taking a sip.

He sat in the chair opposite me, clasping his hands together, forearms resting on the table. "Start from the beginning," he said, and so I did.

By the time I finished, his brows were pinched together, two vertical lines carved into the space in between. "He orchestrated it to make you look like you'd turned her in."

I nodded slowly. "Exactly. And it was diabolical, because it's not like he knew I was going to show up with information."

"You said you had to wait a while for him. Sounds to me like he saw an opportunity, and he ran with it. He used you to bait Eliza." Miguel gave a nonchalant shrug. "Doesn't surprise me at all."

I guess it didn't really surprise me, either, but it irked me nonetheless. "But Eliza likes—or maybe *liked*—me. If York really thinks she had something to do with Yentin's death, why would he deliberately drive a wedge between us? I might have been able to get him more information."

Not that I wanted to be an informant for York, but the question remained.

"What are you going to do?" he asked.

I hadn't known what I planned to do, but I answered without thinking. "I have to go talk to her."

"I think she'll listen to you," he said matter-of-factly.

One of the things I loved about Miguel was his unquestioning support of me. He rallied behind my efforts at building my photography business back up after leaving Austin. He never questioned the time I spent working at Yeast of Eden. He was always willing and able to try out my practice loaves of bread. He walked Agatha with me. He indulged Mrs. Branford whenever she showed up—usually unannounced. And especially in a situation like this, when someone else might have discouraged me from getting more involved, he reassured me with his words.

Was *I* as supporting of *him*? I thought I was. I helped him concoct new recipes for the restaurant. I cheered him on during his bike races. I picked the dead leaves off the potted plants in his house. I listened when he talked about his goal of opening a second location of Baptista's Cantina & Grill, scouting locations with him and giving my ten cents.

We were there for each other, I decided.

"You think so?" I asked. I knew *he'd* listen to me, always and forever. I was skeptical Eliza Fox would give me that same attention, given she thought I'd betrayed her trust.

"Tell her the truth," he said.

Tell her the truth. He made it sound easy. Like if I did, Eliza would instantly believe me, and all would be forgiven. I hoped he was right.

A knot of nerves had twined inside me, and I wanted nothing more than to unwind them, pronto. The only way to do that was to, as the saying goes, get back on the horse. I finished my tea, gave Miguel a kiss, and headed right back to the beachfront cliffs of Santa Sofia.

Chapter 12

I pulled through the open gate and drove through the trees to what was becoming my spot on the driveway. An unfamiliar truck sat off to one side, and I hesitated. I didn't want to interrupt Eliza if she had company.

But I was here now, and I had to mend this broken fence before it completely rotted away. As I walked to the front door, I thought about what I could say. That I hadn't turned her in? It was technically true—I hadn't been the source of information that had caused York to bring Eliza in—but I *had* told him my suspicions.

I stopped, ready to turn around. What had I been thinking? Whatever trust I'd established with Eliza was surely gone. And what if she was behind Yentin's death somehow? She'd been on the staircase in front of all her guests, so her alibi was foolproof.

A new thought struck me. She could have had someone do her bidding.

Nicole?

She *was* a devoted employee, after all.

I spun around again. Maybe if we talked, I'd come up with another idea about what had actually happened to Edward Yentin and I could steer York *away* from Eliza. I started toward the door again, jerking to a stop when the door suddenly flung open and Eliza emerged, cheeks stained red, that same fire I'd seen earlier in her eyes.

"What do you want?"

I held my hands up, palms out, like she had a pistol pointed at me and I was a hapless victim. "I just want to talk. Eliza, I—"

"There is nothing to say."

"I didn't—"

"Oh, you didn't?" She folded her arms over her chest and cocked a hip. "Then why were you at the sheriff's station talking to that horrible man?"

"I—the sheriff, she's my best friend. Emmaline, remember? You'd asked me about Brad," I said, rationalizing that if I'd been able to actually talk to Em, I might have been able to get some information about Eliza's estranged husband.

As if on cue, Brad McAvoy appeared beside Eliza. I couldn't help my inaudible intake of breath. Miguel had my heart, but this guy, he was gorgeous, there was no denying it.

And he was free. Clearly there wasn't enough evidence to hold either of them for Yentin's murder.

In all his golden boy splendor, Brad moved closer to Eliza. I thought he was going to drape his arm casually over her shoulder in a nonchalant devil-may-care manner, but instead he took her hand in his, lacing their fingers together. It struck me as authentic and in complete opposition to the photo of him hugging the naked Rita and flipping off the camera.

The gentle manner with which he took Eliza's hand made me think that Brad McAvoy really cared about his wife.

I strode to the front porch, determined, ignoring the stream of cold that ran through me. "I don't know why the sheriff's department brought you in. It wasn't because of anything I said."

Her defiant expression wavered enough to know that her determination to hold me responsible for her being dragged into the station was faltering. "They questioned me for a long time."

"Because a murder happened on *your* property, during a party *you* held," I said. There was no point in mincing words. "They *have* to question you. They wouldn't be doing their job otherwise."

She frowned. Brad leaned in and whispered in her ear. She gave a slow blink and nodded, sidestepping in unison with him. "Come inside. It's too cold out here."

It was only about fifty-five degrees—not bone-chilling by any stretch, but I shivered, as if her words had carried the cold air straight from her mouth to my insides.

We went through the living room to the smaller library with the evergreen tree and the book-shaped Christmas tree in the corner. The room looked more spacious with the food tables gone, but it was still cozier than the wide-open modern space of the huge great room.

We all sat, no words spoken. A glass of red liquid and a bottle of cranberry juice sat on the coffee table. I let the awkward silence percolate until, finally, Brad McAvoy cleared his throat. He held Eliza's hand against his thigh, giving it a reassuring squeeze. "This is taking a toll on Liza," he said to me.

Eliza's eyelids closed slowly, fluttered for a second as her nostrils flared, then reopened. Being hauled into the sheriff's station would rattle anyone's cage, even the most adept actor in Hollywood. She was clearly gathering strength for this conversation and reacting to her husband's support. Were they still estranged? I thought maybe not.

"I'm sorry this has been so hard," I said to Eliza, trying to emanate sympathy. "It wasn't your fault there was a murder during your party." I hoped. "I'm sure you understand that the authorities are just doing their job."

She pressed her lips together, pulling them in over her teeth as she looked up, those long, dark eyelashes batting again. She fanned her face with her free hand, as if stopping tears from coming. "I want this to be over. Look!" She pointed to her forehead. "I'm getting a pimple!"

My chin quivered. The fact that she was worried about a pimple nearly sent me into a fit of laughter, but I managed to contain it. "Ohhh."

She collapsed against Brad. "This is too stressful!" she wailed.

It was worse for Edward Yentin, who was dead, I wanted to say, but I settled for, "Eliza. The police know you couldn't have pushed Mr. Yentin. You were on the staircase." I shifted my gaze to Brad. "But they might think *you* had something to do with it, acting on Eliza's behalf." Or Nicole, I thought.

Eliza balked, sitting up, staring at me, swiveling her head to look at Brad, then back to me. "Brad. Did not.

Have anything. To do. With. What. Happened. To that man," she said slowly. Her voice was calmer than it had been a few seconds ago. Measured, almost. Firm.

"But you *were* at the party," I said, speaking directly to Brad.

Eliza sputtered. "He was *not* invited."

I shrugged. "Maybe not, but that doesn't mean he wasn't here, does it?" It was the theory I'd led the sheriff to, and that two guests corroborated. I looked at Brad again. "I heard you arguing with Mr. Yentin."

Crickets.

"You're on Captain York's *person of interest* list," I said. "That's why he brought you in for questioning."

Brad grimaced, and Eliza exhaled a shaky breath. "What are you talking about, Ivy?" she asked, then spun to face her husband. "What is she talking about, Brad?"

His broad shoulders folded in, and his chin dipped. He looked up at Eliza through his lashes. Contrite or just caught and forced to fess up?

"She's right. I was here."

Eliza's breathing instantly grew shallow. She scooted away from him. "Wha—?"

I could see in her eyes that she'd feared it was true— that he'd used the garage door opener she'd given him— but she hadn't wanted to believe it. I had been wondering if I could identify Eliza's real emotions, compared to her fabricated acting emotions. In this moment, she was doing a good job of convincing me of her innocence.

Brad turned to face her. "I miss you, Liza. I've tried to tell you. That man . . . what he wrote simply is not true. You know I did *not* have an affair with that woman, or with anyone. I needed to see you."

"I want to believe you," Eliza said, and I thought deep down she did, "but the naked woman."

"It was doctored, baby. Don't you remember that day in Santa Monica? We were on the boardwalk together. You and me. I told you I saw a paparazzi taking our picture."

Eliza's brows pinched with uncertainty. He prompted her again, talking about how they'd walked on the shoreline and how she'd collected shells. Her eyes popped open with realization. "I do remember that!"

Brad's expression lightened. "Right? He Photoshopped you out and put that other woman in your place. He had to, because I have not been with anyone else since the second I met you."

I tried to become invisible, to let them have their moment, but it was impossible, of course. Invisibility was not my superpower.

Eliza swiped at a tear. "I do."

Brad reached for her hands, nodding his head so emphatically that the gentle curls of his hair lightly bounced. "I love you."

She fell into him, and he pulled her close. It looked like she believed him.

If I could have escaped from the room unnoticed, I would have, but any movement from me would have reminded them of my presence, and I didn't want to interrupt their reconciliation. I stayed statue-still, hardly breathing and looking down at my hands, my fingers twisting in my lap. I turned the wide silver band I wore on my right ring finger, then absently slipped it off and, one by one, slid it onto each finger of my left hand. It didn't go past my knuckles on my thumb, forefinger, and middle finger, and it swam on my pinkie, but it fit my ring finger perfectly. I stared down at it. It had been a long time since I'd worn a ring there. I kind of liked the way it looked.

Brad cleared his throat again. I quickly put my ring back on my right hand and looked up.

"Ivy," Eliza started. "You can't . . . you won't . . ."

I knew what she was getting at. I zipped my lips and turned an invisible key. "Your relationship is between you two. I won't say a word."

"Thanks," Brad said. He looked as pulled together and leading-man handsome as ever, but the slight crack in his voice betrayed his emotion. If I had to guess, I'd say he really did love Eliza, and my heart warmed for them both.

I just hoped he wasn't a murderer.

That thought led me to circle back to Brad and Yentin. How good of an actor was he? Could he lie on the spot? And even if he fooled me, could he fool Eliza? "You argued with Edward Yentin at the party."

The impact of that fact suddenly dawned on Eliza. "Oh my God, Brad, you didn't...mmm, you didn't kill him, did you?" Her voice dropped to a whisper. "For me?"

He was affronted. "Eliza, no. Of course not. I didn't even know he'd be there!"

Not that that fact had anything at all do with him possibly killing the reporter, but his declaration seem to satisfy Eliza.

"Where were you when it happened?" I asked.

One side of his lip rose in a little smirk. "Nicole spotted me as Liza was coming down the stairs," he said. "I saw her coming toward me—probably to kick me out—but I managed to duck into the kitchen, then out to the garage. I waited in there for a few minutes. I came back in when I heard the scream."

"There's no 'probably' about it," a voice said from the archway between the library and the dining room. Nicole was there, one hand on her hip. "I *would* have kicked you out."

She looked at Eliza. "I'm so sorry. He'll be leaving now." She pointed toward the door. "Exit's that way," she said to Brad, but Eliza waved her hand to stop Nicole.

"It okay," she said. "I want him to stay."

Brad's eyebrows stretched up, crinkling his forehead, and his eyes widened. "Really? You mean it?"

He looked like he'd just won the Oscar but had expected to lose to a more seasoned actor. True elation tinged with disbelief.

Nicole clamped her mouth shut. From how close she was with her employer, I thought she probably didn't hold back what she thought when she and Eliza were together in private, but in front of Brad and me, she held her tongue. It was clear, though, that she wasn't buying Brad's Academy Award–winning performance.

Not that it was remotely in the cards, but I decided then and there that I could never spend my life with an actor. It was exhausting.

Chapter 13

Santa Sofia did the holidays right, even on a Wednesday night. First there was the tree lighting, followed by the annual Here We Come A-Wassailing event. The town's businesses had a friendly competition, each offering nonalcoholic wassail to passersby. The townspeople spent the evening sampling wassail, then would vote for the winner.

I parked my car at one of the beach lots, harnessed up Agatha, and started walking. Our quaint downtown was decorated with festive flags hanging from each of the old-fashioned lampposts that lined every street. Some had wreaths and *Happy Holidays* written in bold red letters. Others had a *kinara*, a candleholder with a single black candle in the center, flanked by three red candles on the left and three green candles on the right, and *Happy Kwanza* written in green letters. And still others featured the image of a lighted menorah and *Happy Hanukkah* spelled out in yellow lettering.

Each lamppost was wrapped with red and white ribbon, candy cane style, and storefronts on all the town's main streets were decorated with faux greenery garlands, with giant shiny ball ornaments. In Santa Sofia's historic town gazebo, we had our own version of the Rockefeller Center Christmas tree. Agatha and I stopped in front of it, gazing up at the twinkling white lights. It was about a thousand times bigger than the tree I'd put up, and I had to tilt my head back to look up to the golden star topper.

For a few minutes, it made me forget about the murder that had enraptured the town.

I felt a presence behind me before I felt arms slip around my waist and Miguel's face move next to mine. "Hey, *chula*," he said, an endearment he'd been calling me lately. I'd looked it up once to find it could mean "hottie," "beautiful," "cute," or even "girlfriend." I wasn't sure which meaning he applied when he called me *chula*, but I'd take any of them.

"Hey, yourself," I said, twisting around to face him, draping my arms around his neck, and arching on my tiptoes to kiss him hello. "Right on time."

Miguel was always punctual. He valued other people's time and would never make them wait if he could help it. Just one more thing to love about him.

As the sun set over the Pacific, the streetlamps lit up. Santa Sofia was a beach town, but even without snow and icy weather, the spirit of the holidays was in the air.

Miguel took my free hand in his as we strolled around the park, Agatha trotting alongside me. After a while, the murder came back to the forefront of my mind. I'd had a quick lunch with Emmaline earlier, and she'd dropped a bombshell. John Fox was now an official person of interest. Apparently they'd found information on Yentin's computer that led them to believe Yentin had visited Fox just a week prior to him showing up at Eliza's party.

I'd spent the day mulling it all over and had concocted a plausible scenario between Fox and Yentin. It had played like a movie in my head.

> *Edward Yentin arrives in a small Central Valley town. Knocks on the door of a modest house.*
> *John Fox, looking rumpled, answers the door.*
> *Yentin: You're Eliza Fox's father.*
> *Fox scratches his stubbled chin.*
> *Fox: So what?*
> *Yentin: I'll pay you for the exclusive story about your daughter.*
> *Fox thinks.*
> *Fox: How much?*
> *Yentin sneers.*
> *Yentin: More than enough to make it worth your while.*
> *Fox steps aside so Yentin can enter.*
> *Fox: You got a deal.*

From everything I'd learned about him so far, Edward Yentin had a line of people with potential motives to murder him. If whoever actually *did* kill him hadn't done the deed, someone else probably would have eventually. He'd made enemies left and right, and now John Fox was on the list.

Miguel pulled me to a bench facing the Christmas tree. Agatha lay at my feet. "Wait. So Eliza's father knew Yentin?"

"Apparently Yentin went to Eliza's hometown and met her dad."

I knew the scenario I'd crafted in my head wasn't the way Yentin and Fox's meeting had actually gone down. I hoped Yentin had had to do some serious persuading before John Fox turned his daughter's life upside down with whatever tell-all information he'd shared about her.

"This Yentin guy was a piece of work," Miguel said. "He worked every angle."

That he did. "Seems he probably double-crossed Rita Lewellyn, promising her more 'publicity', but not providing it. Maybe he did the same thing to Cordelia Knight that he'd done to Brad."

How did that old saying go? One time was chance. Twice was coincidence. Three times was a pattern. I didn't know who else the guy had schemed with, then turned on, but my guess was Rita was not the only one, which made Yentin's hoodwinking people who thought he was being straight with them his modus operandi.

I went back to my Yentin/Fox scenario. "If Yentin made an agreement with John Fox, then double-crossed him, that gives Fox a motive for murder," I said. "And Fox was at Eliza's party."

"What would that double-cross look like?" Miguel asked as we stood again. "If he made a deal with Fox to do some sort of exposé on the guy's daughter, who would have come in with a better offer?"

I didn't have an answer to that. I filed the question away as we walked toward Yeast of Eden, stopping at every storefront we passed, sampling their wassail and chatting along the way.

"Ivy!"

I turned to see my dad crossing the street, waving to us. He looked sprightly, and dare I say it, downright happy. I knew the reason behind Owen Culpepper's new-found joy, and her name was Olaya Solis. I'd followed the clues like a trail of breadcrumbs to a gingerbread house. The baked goods that appeared at my dad's house. The times I'd wanted to go by for a visit only to be put off. The easy banter between them at the Spring Festival. My dad's increased visits to Yeast of Eden. The tint of red on Olaya's cheeks when Owen's name was mentioned.

It all amounted to a clandestine romance.

"Miguel," my dad said, offering his hand to him.

"Dad, I didn't know you were coming out tonight," I said after a hug.

He shrugged, a sheepish grin playing on his lips. "I hadn't planned on it, but why not, right?"

Why not, indeed. We all still mourned the loss of my mother, but my dad was doing exactly what Anna Culpepper would have wanted. He was figuring out a new normal and how to move forward with his life.

"Want to come with us?" I asked. "We're tasting all the wassail."

Owen seemed to consider the option, but I got the feeling it was more for show than anything else. "Just for a few minutes," he said, but he didn't elaborate on what other plans he had. He had a destination in mind, though, and my guess was that it had to do with bread.

We stopped in front of the mini antique mall diagonally across from the bread shop. The place had a new owner and was going through an identity crisis. Ancient knickknacks filled the shelves. The store had everything from cracked teapots to vinyl record albums to camouflage clothing to samurai swords to Madame Alexander dolls. If you were looking for something specific, the mini mall was *not* the place to go, but if you were open to being drawn to something completely unexpected, you were likely to find a treasure you didn't even know you wanted.

Nina, the new proprietor, channeled Mrs. Claus with her red skirt, red sweater, and blond hair under her Santa hat. "Olaya's outdone herself," she said as she handed each of us a small paper cup of wassail.

I glanced across the street, but a crowd of people blocked my view of Yeast of Eden. "How so?" I asked her, turning back to face her.

Nina pointed to a green napkin stacked with Santa skull cookies. "These things are to die for," she said. She leaned toward us, placing her hand to the side of her mouth like she was telling us a secret. "Don't tell her, but I sent my niece over for seconds." She chuckled and patted her side. "They're going straight to my hips, but I don't care."

With that, she broke off a piece of one of the cookies, put it in her mouth, and emitted a satisfied groan. "So. Good."

The mention of Olaya made my dad grin. He sipped his wassail, but a moment later he ditched us. As he left us behind, walking purposefully up the street, Mrs. Branford appeared out of thin air, her cane hooked over one arm. Her red velour lounge suit, sparkling white orthotic sneakers, and snowy hair made me smile. Now *this* was Mrs. Claus on vacation.

"I'm so glad I caught up with you," she said. "I have some scuttlebutt."

Any scuttlebutt Mrs. Branford had was sure to be fire. I looked for a private place to hear it. Santa Sofia was a town made for walkers and bicyclers, complete with well-lit common areas connecting the main streets. We turned into the nearest, stopping under the balcony of one of the loft apartments. "What is it?" I asked.

"Well, I was picking up a prescription—arthritis, you know—when I overheard two women talking about your Eliza Fox."

I perked up. Fire scuttlebutt, indeed. "What did they say?"

"It's a small-world thing. One of them said she was from Eliza's hometown . . . only she wasn't Eliza back then."

I tilted my head. "What do you mean?"

"She changed her name?" Miguel asked.

"That's what I gathered."

This wasn't earth-shattering news. A lot of stars had done that. Marilyn Monroe had grown up Norma Jeane Mortenson. Caryn Elaine Johnson had become Whoopi Goldberg. Ilyena Lydia Vasilievna Mironov spent her adult life as Helen Mirren. Mark Sinclair's alter ego was Vin Diesel.

"There's more," Mrs. Branford said. She looked this way and that, as if she was afraid of someone overhearing us.

Miguel and I waited. Mrs. Branford had the sharpest mind around. If she thought Eliza Fox's name change was important, it probably was.

"The young woman is running from something. It's not common knowledge that she's not who she says she is."

"She is who she says she is," Miguel said. "She's Eliza Fox. She just may be someone else, too."

Mrs. Branford waved an annoyed hand at him. "Yes, yes, quite right. She lives her life as Eliza Fox, but her past is something she wants to keep secret."

Also not a huge revelation, since I already knew Eliza had something she was hiding. "Did the woman say what her real name is?" I asked, still wanting whatever information I could get.

"Sadly, no," Mrs. Branford said. "One of their blasted cell phones rang, effectively stopping the conversation."

Eliza having a different name growing up didn't jibe with Eliza's father being John Fox, though. I filed this information away to think about later, then Mrs. Branford, Miguel, Agatha, and I ambled to the next store. Holiday spirit emanated from it. Where the mini mall's setup had been utilitarian, the Kitchen Shop's was pure magic. Music played from inside the store. A miniature Christmas tree decorated with tiny rolling pins, teacups, miniature mixers, and other kitchen goodies sat beside the table, which was draped with a white tablecloth embroidered with colorful nutcrackers, bells, and holly. Even the Kitchen Shop's slow cooker, which kept the mulled cider warm, was red.

"Merry Christmas!" Beth Spalding sang out, followed by a zippy "Happy Kwanza, and Happy Hanukkah!"

Her smile stretched from ear to ear. If Nina from the mini mall was a walking Mrs. Claus, Beth was the epitome of a joyful elf. She wore red and green horizontally striped tights, cute-as-a-button red elf shoes, bells adorning the curled-up ends, and a ruffled red dress topped with a white apron that said *'Tis the Season for Cocktails* in festive writing.

Another apron hung on a coatrack next to the open shop door. This one said *It's the Most Wonderful Wine of the Year*.

"Can I interest you in some of our world-class wassail?

Nonalcoholic, of course." Everything Beth said sounded singsongy.

We each took one of the proffered cups. I had to admit, Beth's mulled cider was excellent. I didn't know what made wassail world-class, but in my opinion, this one qualified.

Beth ladled more cider into our cups and held out a plate of shortbread. It was a perfect combination. I was surprised Nina hadn't stocked up on Beth's shortbread right alongside Olaya's sugar cookies.

"I heard you're friends with Eliza Fox," Beth said, her eyes bright with the excitement of knowing a celebrity through association.

Eliza was the topic du jour, that was for sure. "A little bit," I said.

"I heard she was at your house for dinner! At least that's what people are saying."

This news took me aback. "Who's saying that?" I asked. Eliza had been incognito the afternoon she'd come over, and I'd seen no evidence that she'd been followed by paparazzi.

"It's in *The Scout*," she said, and like magic, she pulled out a copy of the grocery store rag. Right there on the front page was a photo of Eliza Fox. Her cap was pulled low on her forehead, but there was no mistaking the identity. And there in the background was *my* Tudor house.

There was no such thing as privacy, I realized.

At the Yeast of Eden table, Olaya was conspicuously absent. In her place were her sisters. Consuelo was a few years younger than Olaya, so somewhere in her early sixties. Unlike Olaya, who'd settled into her gray hair and kept it short and a little spiky on top, Consuelo's deep brown hair was shoulder-length and currently pulled into a bun at the nape of her neck. She was boisterous and a chatterbox, especially compared to Olaya's sanguine demeanor. They definitely looked like sisters, both with almond-shaped eyes, noses that curved down slightly at the end, hollowed cheekbones that gave their faces definition, and warm olive skin.

The youngest sister, Martina, had a darker complexion, and her hair was as black as Santa's belt and gloves. Olaya and Consuelo had stronger European genes, while Martina had more Aztec blood running through her. Even Martina's facial features—her straight nose; her big, round dark eyes; and her fuller lips—were night and day from her sisters. She was the quietest of the three, and definitely the most youthful. She dressed in skinny jeans and fitted tops, and she currently had on low-heeled booties. Instead of jeans, Olaya tipped toward palazzo pants, culottes, and maxiskirts and Consuelo went for middle-aged neutral. Martina, by comparison, was the height of style.

"Where's Olaya?" I asked.

Consuelo and Martina looked at each other, both of them wearing a similarly sly smile. "For the first time ever, Olaya is drinking other shops' wassail instead of staying here serving her own," Martina said.

"With Owen," Consuelo sang, sounding like a middle-school student ribbing a friend.

I smiled, my suspicions confirmed.

Miguel and I chatted for a few minutes before continuing down the street. As we sipped the next offering of wassail, something occurred to me. *I'd* been calling Eliza's father John Fox, assigning him the same surname as his daughter, but obviously Fox *wasn't* his last name. If I found out what it actually was, would it help get to the truth?

Emmaline had said that Yentin had been doing a piece on Eliza's childhood, and the women Mrs. Branford had overheard talking said Eliza was not who she said she was. She had taken a different name, divorcing herself from her childhood. What if Edward Yentin had unearthed the truth and confronted John about his daughter leaving home as a teenager? Eliza was trying to hide from her past. It was just as possible that her father was trying to hide, too.

Which made him another person with a motive for murder.

Chapter 14

By the next day, not a single remnant of the Here We Come A-Wassailing extravaganza was evident on the streets of Santa Sofia. It was as if Dumbledore had waved his elder wood wand and magically put everything back in its rightful place.

I stood under the awning in front of Yeast of Eden, soaking in the festive air. Cloud cover had floated in, and a light drizzle was expected later in the afternoon, but for now it just felt like a lovely December day, and a little bit of magic was in the air.

The bell dinged as I pushed through the bread shop's door. A chorus of voices chimed.

"Ivy!"

"Come sit with us!"

"My dear!"

"So good to see you!"

I laughed at the last comment. "I see you nearly every day, Mabel."

It was true. It was a rare occasion when the Blackbird Ladies didn't show up at the bread shop for a cup of coffee and a baked treat.

Mabel Peabody, the flamboyant one of the group, with her bright red hair, equally bright lipstick, and colorful clothing, guffawed. "Didn't mean it literally."

I'd dubbed them the Blackbird Ladies when I'd first met them as a group, and the name had stuck. While it was true they each wore a hat for their daily meetups at Yeast of Eden, and each hat had a little blackbird tucked into the daisies, roses, or whatever flower adorned them, the name fit them just as much for their blackbird behavior. Even when they talked over each other, their voices blended together in melodic song. At least one of them always had a bit of red, just like female blackbirds had a tuft of red feathers on their chests. And blackbirds, just like the ladies before me, had eclectic diets. Case in point, while Mabel Peabody always gravitated to Olaya's chocolate croissants, she would happily eat almond croissants, rye bread, a piece of cranberry walnut loaf, or whatever goodies were laid before her.

Maybe most importantly, though, was a blackbird's ability to adapt. My Blackbird Ladies had lost one of their members in an unbelievable situation, but they'd all dealt with the loss and had moved on.

These women were originals, through and through.

Alice Ryder was the exact opposite of Mabel. She was put together and had the demeanor of a Southern socialite with her refined features, floral dresses, and pointy-toed heels—even in December. Needless to say, the hat she wore was demure and tame. Her short mahogany curls flipped up at the bottom. Her hat sat atop her head at a jaunty angle and could have been worn by a stylish woman in the 1940s, and while the other Blackbird Ladies looked a little Red Hat Society vivacious, Alice was restrained. She was an ice queen, even when you got to know her, but this group had been friends for so long, they accepted each other, warts and all.

Lastly, there was Mrs. Branford, who fell somewhere in between the two women on the personality bell curve. She was smart, funny, a killer poker player, and an unabashed lover of the English language. Incorrect grammar was her pet peeve. There was so much to love about the woman who'd become an honorary grandmother to me, but the thing that topped the list was her propensity for direct honesty. She said it like it was, no holds barred.

Mrs. Branford patted the seat of the chair between her and Mabel. "Have a seat, Ivy, and unburden yourself."

I scooted behind the counter to grab a cup of coffee and one of Olaya's to-die-for bran muffins, then sat.

Olaya's Saturday morning helper was a young man who was a high school sophomore. He wore no hat, and the other customers coming and going, of which there were many, also had no hats. Still, amongst the Blackbird Ladies, I felt a little naked without my own. "I have nothing to unburden," I said.

Alice *tsk*ed. I couldn't say she was exactly friendly, but she'd warmed to me in the time I'd known her. She simply wasn't a warm and fuzzy person. "That isn't what we've heard," she said, her slight Southern drawl the softest thing about her.

I raised my brows at Mrs. Branford, knowing she was the source of whatever information they had.

Mabel caught the look and *pshaw*ed. "Ivy, you know we have no secrets between us. Isn't that right, Penny?"

Mrs. Branford dipped her chin. "That is correct."

I went all in, telling them about the murder, the suspects, and my affinity for Eliza, right along with my hope that she wasn't somehow behind it all.

The ladies, for their part, *tsk*ed and *pshaw*ed and *ooh*ed and *aah*ed in all the appropriate moments, listening raptly to my story.

"I think the husband did it," Mabel announced.

Alice threw her a scornful look. "You always think it's the husband."

"Not true," Mabel said, but we all knew it was a hundred percent true. She'd even thought Alice's husband had murderous secrets once upon a time.

"Well, I think it's Eliza Fox," Alice said. "You heard what Ivy said. That's not even her real name."

Mabel brushed a spattering of croissant crumbs from her lap. "Could be any of them. The caterer. The assistant. The father."

Olaya appeared from the back, sweeping up to us, her solid black caftan billowing behind her. "Do you ladies need anything?" she asked, a twinkle in her eyes. I smiled to myself, pretty sure the lightness in her step was due to her budding romance with my father.

"We're fine, aren't we, ladies?" Mabel said.

Alice pushed her plate away. "I couldn't muster another bite."

Olaya nodded, pleased. She loved satisfied customers. "Join us," Mrs. Branford said, pulling out the chair next to her.

Olaya moved to it, but stood behind it rather than sitting down. "What is the topic of the day?" she asked.

"Ivy's mystery," Mabel said. "She's at it again, mixed up in murder."

"I have something to say about that," Mrs. Branford

remarked. She rested her forearms on the table, taking a moment to meet each of our gazes. After this dramatic pause, she said, "*Pygmalion*."

We all raised our brows at her. "What is that, *Pygmalion*?" Olaya asked.

I didn't know either. Was it a story? A play, maybe?

Mrs. Branford gave an exasperated sigh. "None of you know it?"

"I do."

The voice came from the high school student behind the counter. He was ringing up a customer, but had apparently been listening to our conversation at the same time. Of course, why not? The dining area of Yeast of Eden was quaint with its bistro chairs and tables, but it was also small, so it didn't afford much privacy.

"Do you, Nick?" Olaya asked, clearly pleased that her employee was so worldly. "Please tell us."

He finished with the customer and came closer to our table, still behind the counter. "It's about a professor, Henry Higgins, and this woman he trains to be a lady."

Mrs. Branford made a low, grumbling sound in her throat, but she gave credit to the boy. "A bit simplified, but that is the gist of it, young man. Thank you."

It was a clear dismissal. Olaya tried not to smile too broadly, but nodded at him with approval before he scurried over to help a customer who'd just come in.

"Henry Higgins, as in *My Fair Lady*?" I asked.

"One and the same," Mrs. Branford said. "He makes a wager that he can take a lowly cockney flower girl, teach her to speak properly—he is a phonetician, you see—so that she will pass as a lady in society."

"And they fall in love!" Mabel sang with a little waggle of her head.

"They do, indeed," Mrs. Branford agreed.

Alice's tight lips pinched tighter, her sign of bafflement. "What does *Pygmalion*, or *My Fair Lady*, or Henry Higgins have to do with anything?"

At this, Mrs. Branford leaned forward and lowered her voice. "We know Eliza Fox is not the name our young actress was born with. She left her childhood home and came to Southern California. Why, if not because of some dream of stardom? I suspect that she watched old movies as a child, and *My Fair Lady* was one of them. Eliza Doolittle goes through a comprehensive change under the professor's tutelage. I believe Eliza chose the name Eliza because she saw herself as Miss Doolittle—a girl who could reinvent herself entirely."

"Mrs. Branford!" I pressed my palms together, putting my fingers in front of my lips. "That's brilliant!"

She gave a satisfied smile. She knew perfectly well how brilliant she was.

"Who's her Henry Higgins, then?" Mabel asked.

That was a good question. We all sat silent, thinking, and then it hit me. She'd told me the story about when she'd been discovered, and her feeling of being in the right place at the right time. What was his name? I closed my eyes, replaying that conversation. It started with a *G*. I was sure of it. *G* . . . *G* . . . *G* . . . "Gunther!" I blurted. "Gunther Hoffman."

Olaya asked the question I'd been thinking. "Would this man, this Gunther Hoffman, have had a reason to kill the journalist?"

"To protect his Miss Doolittle?" Alice suggested.

Mabel took a bite of a ham-and-cheese croissant. "Seems possible."

Alice took a sip of her coffee. "People have killed for less."

Wasn't that the truth? We all knew about a particular murderous situation firsthand. It had been connected to a local boardinghouse and a horrible secret we'd uncovered.

Eliza hadn't mentioned Gunther, her agent, being at the party, but that didn't mean he hadn't been there. I excused myself and went to call Emmaline, excited at the new theory.

I stood outside under the awning again, pulling my lightweight red coat tighter around me, wishing I'd gone for the warmer, but less festive wool jacket I had. Sometimes fashion won over common sense. I asked for Emmaline, but my call was routed to Captain York. Again. It was as if my phone number was flagged.

"Ms. Culpepper." A warning was already in his voice, which irritated me because I was only trying to help.

"Hello, Captain," I said, trying hard to sound upbeat and neighborly rather than irate.

He waited silently.

I cut to the chase. "Gunther Hoffman is Eliza's agent. He discovered her—"

"It wasn't him," York said, cutting me off. "He's out of the country. Has been since mid-November."

And bam, just like that, the theory that Gunther was protecting his asset was shot down. Easy come, easy go.

In a way, it was good, though. It kept the potential suspect pool smaller. But on the other hand, so far most of the suspects were people I kind of liked and didn't want to be guilty.

"Anything else?" York asked gruffly.

I was just about to ask him if he knew Eliza Fox's given name, but changed my mind at the last second. He'd only tell me to butt out, which I just couldn't do. I'd rather find out that information for myself. Ask forgiveness rather than permission, as the saying went.

"Nope. All good," I said, and hung up before he could give me his warning.

Back inside, I relayed the information to the Blackbird Ladies.

"Stick with it, Ivy," Mrs. Branford said.

Mabel pumped one arm in the air, crumbs flying from the croissant she held. "You can do it, Ivy!"

Alice simply looked at me. No smile. No words. Just a single nod. I was touched by what amounted to encouragement from her.

I looked to Olaya last. She gave me her best sanguine expression. "You will discover the truth. You always do."

I left Yeast of Eden with my head held high. The Blackbird Ladies believed in me.

I spent the rest of the afternoon working at Crosby House. Earlier in the year, I'd learned about the women's shelter and had volunteered, helping to create keyhole gardens. I'd come to love my weekly volunteer time, sometimes teaching baking classes, often reading to the children staying there with their mothers, and, like today, yanking out dead weeds and clearing out the old growth from the garden boxes to get them ready for spring.

The women at Crosby House came and went. Some used their time there to contemplate their next steps. Others quickly transitioned, leaving to stay with family members somewhere else. Still others were there for longer periods of time. There was one commonality. They'd all ended up at the shelter because they were trying to escape from something—or someone—untenable.

I wrapped my gloved hand around a thick-stemmed weed and yanked it out, tossing it onto the growing pile of brittle debris. The idea of escaping from something—or someone—lingered in my mind right alongside the fact that Eliza had changed her name. She'd left home when she was just a kid. She'd needed to escape from something. She couldn't stand to talk with her father.

I'd been trying to avoid this line of thinking, but the more I thought about it, the more sense it made. Eliza Fox had been abused. And now her past had caught up with her.

Chapter 15

Walking the path that ran alongside the coast usually cleared my mind. Today, however, it wasn't working.

I'd left Yeast of Eden feeling empowered, and my time working at Crosby House had given me clarity. The problem was that I liked Eliza Fox, and helping to prove that she had nothing to do with the death of the scumbag journalist was the right thing to do—as long as I thought she was innocent. But was she?

First there was the scandal involving Brad. Although they seemed to be mending their broken marriage, Yentin had been behind their estrangement.

And now there was the probability that Yentin had been digging into Eliza's past, unearthing something the actress didn't want exposed. If I was right about him uncovering her abusive childhood, that was a pretty strong motive for silencing him.

Two solid motives for murdering the guy.

The more I thought about it, the more I wondered if maybe York was right, and I should back away and just let him do his job.

I'd left Crosby House needing to clear my head. I'd grabbed Agatha and headed to the beach. Now I looked down at her, trotting by my side, and said, "It's decided. I should butt out." Her big mouth was open, her tongue flopping out of it. "What? You don't believe me?" I asked when she didn't bother to look up at me.

She stopped suddenly, standing stone-still, her head tilted, and now her bulbous eyes stared me down.

"I know," I said. "You're right. I like her, and I don't think she arranged to have the guy killed, even with her motives, and who else is on her side? She has Brad and Nicole, but everyone else at that party, well, I don't think she calls any of them friends."

Agatha threw her head back, gave a single bark, then plunked down on her backside.

"I get it. You think I *should* dig a little more?" I asked. A rhetorical question, because obviously she couldn't answer me, but I kept on. "The thing is, I can't keep showing up at her house uninvited."

This posed a definite problem, but only if I kept my focus on Eliza. Trying to prove her innocence was tougher than I'd thought. The better angle was to try to find out who was, in fact, guilty. Which I'd been doing, but everything kept bringing me back to Eliza.

I groaned, frustrated. What to do, what to do. I started walking again, tugging on the leash. Agatha popped up to all fours and caught up to me. We were almost to the small public beach lot where I'd left my car when I spotted two familiar faces at the back of one of the parked vehicles. They were partially hidden by the tan minivan parked next to them, and their angles meant I could only see their profiles, but there was no mistaking Nicole Leonard and the man I'd been calling John Fox.

What in the world did *they* have to talk about? Was Nicole reading him the riot act for harassing her employer, or had he ambushed her, trying to convince her to help him reach his daughter? Either scenario was possible. What struck me most, though, was that they were out here by the beach. This particular public access point was south of town, so well off the beaten path. Plus it was cold out. Not too many people spent their December days at the beach. The odds of them meeting here accidentally were slim. Slim to none. Actually, just none. There was no way it was happenstance.

My curiosity got the better of me. I had to know what they were talking about. I quickly turned my back so they wouldn't see me, then bent down and grabbed up Agatha, moving her hefty, little body until she was comfortable in my arms. I tried to act casually as I sidestepped in front of the parked cars, getting closer to them without bringing any attention to myself. Their voices became clear as I reached the front of the minivan. I edged as close as I could and crouched down, still clutching Agatha. *Please don't bark. Please don't bark.*

I stroked her head to keep her distracted as I pressed my back against the bumper of the mom-mobile. I stretched my neck to peek around the corner, catching their profiles, and listened.

"What do you want?" Nicole demanded, sounding like she was speaking through clenched teeth.

"I want to see my daughter. You can make it happen."

"No way," Nicole snapped. "*Not* going to happen."

The man ripped off his ball cap and scraped his fingers over his scalp. "Why the hell not?"

"Because it's her decision." Nicole's voice dropped to a low growl. "She ran away from you, remember?"

"You have no right—"

"I have *every* right," she snapped.

His jaw pulsed. "I am her father, and I have a lot more right to be in her life than you do. I have *always* loved her."

Nicole scoffed. "Right. And remind me, exactly when did you act like a father to her?"

"How do *you* have the right to ask *me* that, *Nicole*?" There was something about the way he said her name, as if he was driving home some point.

It hit its mark, because she threw one hand up in exasperation. "You had your chance to protect her, but you didn't. She does *not* want to see you. Stay away."

In my opinion, Nicole was going above and beyond the call of duty as Eliza's assistant, confronting the star's father like she was. She deserved a hefty holiday bonus. Part of me wanted to jump up, puff up my chest, and join her. I chickened out, though, when she started to turn. I jerked my head back. My pulse raced. Had she seen me? I looked around. Could I get to my car without being identified?

"I will not," John Fox ground out.

"Oh yes," she said slowly, "you will."

I started to inch my way along the bumper, praying the car's alarm wouldn't be triggered. I had just got to the end of the bumper when John's next words stopped me cold. "Or what? I know the truth about you. One word to Johnette and you're done."

Something slammed. Nicole's hand on the hood of the car? "And I know the truth about you, John Calvin," she said, her voice turning ugly. "I'll go straight to the press. I'm sure they'd love to know how you forced away the mother of your newborn baby and proceeded to let your daughter be ogled—and God knows what else—by your own friends—"

"That is so far from the truth, you lying—"

Suddenly a car door slammed, cutting him off. Tires squealed against the gravel. A second later, a vehicle tore out of the little beach parking lot.

I jumped as another car door opened because the minivan jostled and rocked with the weight of someone getting into it. My heart shot up to my throat as I scurried away from the bumper, scooting in front of the next car in the lot.

Johnette. Eliza. My skin turned cold. Pygmalion.

I hoped and prayed I hadn't been seen, but as I snuck a look at the minivan backing out of the space, I saw Eliza's father staring at me.

Chapter 16

I drove from the beach parking lot straight to Yeast of Eden, my heart practically pounding out of my chest. I had Agatha, so instead of going through the back kitchen entrance, I circled around the building and sat in one of the bistro chairs in front of the bread shop. Not a minute later, Olaya stepped out, the door's bell tinkling behind her. She had a sixth sense.

"Ivy? What is wrong?"

I looked up at her and managed a smile, but I was still shaking. The death stare John Calvin had given me as he'd driven away had sent chills down my spine.

Olaya popped her head back through the door, saying something to someone. Then she sat down next to me. "Something has happened," she said. "Are you all right? Ivy?"

"I'm okay," I said, though it wasn't entirely true.

"I do not believe that. *Mija*, tell me. You look like you have eaten a rotten egg."

Her statement brought my awareness to the sneer I wore. I relaxed my facial muscles and tried to smile. "I *saw* a rotten egg is more like it," I said, and proceeded to tell her what I'd seen transpire between John Not-Fox-but-Calvin and Nicole Leonard.

"She was on fire," I said, describing the red that had crept from Nicole's neck to her cheeks. "She read him the riot act—"

Olaya raised her eyebrows in a question. It was an expression she hadn't heard.

"She was dressing him down—"

Again, the eyebrows.

American idioms. "She was the one yelling at him, not the other way around."

She nodded her understanding. "Until the end."

"Exactly. Until he said that he knew truth about her." They'd been in each other's faces.

You've never been a father to her.

I know the truth about you.

This hadn't been the first time they'd met, I suddenly realized. My thoughts slowed, replaying the scene. It was like they were divorced parents arguing over their shared child.

Divorced parents.

Parents.

Could Eliza be . . . ?

No, surely not.

But maybe . . . Johnette . . .

Could Eliza be . . . *their* child? As in together?

The moment I thought it was the moment I knew it might really be true. *Eliza* could be their child. Eliza could be *their* child. Holy moly. Nicole Leonard could be Eliza's mother.

Nicole had said, "People change." If I was right, she'd left her daughter when she was a baby—or maybe John Calvin had forced her away—but she'd come back.

"You!"

I turned to see Nicole Leonard marching right up to me. Speak of the devil.

"Nicole," I said, meeting her fiery eyes.

"Eliza trusts you." Her voice rose. "*I* trusted you—"

Olaya held up her hand, stopping Nicole. "You will not yell in front of my shop," she said calmly.

Nicole practically stomped her foot. "I can do whatever I—"

Olaya made a clicking sound with her tongue. "You will *not* yell in front of my shop," she repeated.

The force of her words seemed to encircle Nicole. Her nostrils flared and her jaw clenched, but she sucked in a breath and let it go before speaking again. "Ivy, I trusted you," she said, her voice more controlled. "Eliza likes you. She welcomed you into her home. And you . . . and you . . ."

She grew agitated again, and Olaya clucked. "*Cal-mate*," she said in Spanish.

"How dare you follow me—"

So she'd seen me after all. If Nicole had been a bull in a cartoon, steam would have been billowing from her nostrils. She opened her mouth to start again, but I beat her to the punch. "You're Eliza's mother, aren't you?"

She sputtered. "W-What? N-n-n—"

"I didn't follow you to the beach," I said, stopping her attempt at denial. The truth was clear on her pallid face. "I was walking my dog." We all looked down at Agatha. "I happened to be there. Coincidence. But you and John Calvin? Not so much."

"How do you—"

"I put two and two together. He's her father, and he knows the truth about you? What else could it be?" I spoke with confidence, as if I knew without a shadow of a doubt that what I'd surmised was the truth. I tapped my finger against my lips. "It makes sense. You're so close to Eliza. More than a personal assistant. And the way you argued about her with John Calvin . . . the way antagonistic parents might if they were fighting over the welfare of their child."

Emotion bubbled just under Nicole's skin—fear? anger? I pressed on. "I do wonder, though, how you got the job?" I spoke with exaggerated innocence. "I mean, it's kind of coincidental, isn't it? Or did you set out to hoodwink your own daughter?"

"You don't know what you're talking about," Nicole said, but she'd gone from fiery to smoldering.

"Don't I? So, you're telling me you're *not* Eliza's mother?"

She sputtered again, and I could see the wheels turning as she tried to figure out what to say. How to convince me that I was wrong.

At that moment, the door to the bread shop opened. Zula, dressed in a red skirt and black and white chevron blouse, backed out, a tray laden with two Yeast of Eden mugs and a plate filled with several baked goods, balanced in her hands. With her black flats, her limbs looked coltish and never-ending.

She turned toward us at the same moment Nicole said, "You don't understand!" and flung her arm up in the air in utter frustration. The back of her hand caught the underside of the tray. Zula stumbled backward. Nicole grabbed for her hand, her eyes wide, her mouth open. It happened so fast, but it felt like slow motion as Zula tried to stabilize the tray. One mug toppled to the ground, the impact smashing it into bulky chunks of ceramic.

Nicole screeched as the hot liquid splashed her legs.

Agatha and I both jumped up. Nicole let go of Zula, lurched, and plowed into me. I fell against the bistro table. From somewhere, someone screamed. Agatha yelped and tried to bolt, the leash I held pulling taut. The table tipped. Olaya leaped clear as it fell with a clatter. I landed on the ground next to it, my legs splayed out in front of me.

In front of my eyes, Nicole teetered. She tried to regain her balance. She reached for the table to steady herself, only to realize the table wasn't there anymore. And then I watched in slow motion as she fell smack on top of me.

Her knee pressed into my gut. I let out an agonizing grunt, gasping for breath.

"Sorry! Sorry! Oh my God, Ivy, are you okay?" Nicole's words came fast and frantic, everything else momentarily forgotten. She scrambled backward. Olaya was behind me. She bent down to curl her fingers under my armpits, hauling me up, first to a crouching position, then to standing. Carrying around sacks of grains and sugars, bagging up the flour she ground herself, and carrying heavy trays had given her the strength of Hercules.

A crowd had gathered around, at least three people standing there, phones up, recording. The rest just watched the show, breaking into a round of applause when I was once again steady on my feet.

Olaya straightened the fallen table, gesturing to Zula to put down the tray she'd righted. The rolls and croissants had toppled from the plate and onto the tray itself, sitting in the liquid spilled from the second mug.

"Oh my gosh, oh my gosh—" Zula began, then stopped, shook her head, and started again. "Ivy! Do you need a doctor?"

"No, I'm okay," I said, taking inventory. I'd be bruised—no doubt about that—but nothing was broken. "Are you?" I asked her.

She checked her palms and her shins, but all appeared to be cut- and burn-free. "Me, I am fine. Olaya?"

Olaya waved away Zula's concern. "Bah. I am fine."

We all turned our attention to Nicole. Clumps of her hair had fallen from her chignon, and her glasses were cockeyed, but she looked relatively unscathed. "I'm fine," she said abruptly. She straightened her clothing. Patted her hair. "It's my business, Ivy," she said to me, and with her head held high and without a backward glance, she pushed through the crowd of lookie-loos, marching away from us.

"Who was that?" Zula asked, wide-eyed, watching Nicole's retreating figure, the small crowd that had gathered dispersing.

"That," I said, "is a woman who just had her cover blown."

Zula shifted her gaze to me. "Her cover blown?"

"She is not who she says she is," I said, cursing American idioms again.

Olaya crouched and picked up the chunky shards of the broken mug, placing them on the tray. "There is a lot of that going on," she said.

That was the truth. Eliza. Nicole. John Calvin. Was there anyone else who wasn't who they appeared to be?

"Is she a bad woman?" Zula asked, retrieving the tray from the table and looking in the general direction of Nicole's retreating figure.

That was a good question. Why would Nicole hide her identity from her daughter? How did Eliza end up living with her father rather than her mother, and why had Nicole had no contact with her daughter over the years?

The bigger question—or at least the one most related to the death of Edward Yentin—was whether the journalist had discovered who Nicole was, and if so, could she have killed him to prevent that truth from coming out?

The plot thickened.

Chapter 17

I'd been shaken after the run-in with Nicole in front of Yeast of Eden, but a little bread, coffee, and cuddle time with Agatha—plus a warm sourdough roll slathered with melted butter—brought back my equilibrium. After a while, I loaded her into the back seat of my car, and we headed from the bread shop to Miguel's bungalow. I turned onto Beach Road, which would take me to Bungalow Oasis in the Upper Laguna District of Santa Sofia. From the back seat, Agatha whimpered. I knew just what that sound meant.

I adjusted the rearview mirror so I could see her. "Can you wait?" I asked.

Her bulging eyes were latched onto my back, and her whimpering grew louder. Apparently not.

A minute later, I pulled into the parking lot of a car wash, harnessed her up, and walked over to a small embankment. Agatha sniffed and circled, sniffed and circled, sniffed and circled, finally finding the perfect spot. Bless her heart, she really had to go.

When she was done, she scratched the ground with her paws, spreading her scent and kicking up the earth in the process. I picked up the poop using one of the doggie bags I kept in the driver's door cubby in my car. I returned her to the back seat and was just getting back in myself when a tan minivan drove past on Beach Road.

I did a double take. Minivans used to be a dime a dozen, but Santa Sofians had long ago upgraded to SUVs. My nerves pricked. I was absolutely sure it was the same one John Fox Calvin had driven away in earlier.

"Hang on, Agatha!" I buckled in before tearing out of the parking lot in hot pursuit, not a single iota of a plan in my head. My instinct was simply to follow him. I didn't know what his game was, but I was determined to find out. Nicole's chastisement of him not protecting his daughter rattled around in my head.

I couldn't shake the idea that Edward Yentin had discovered Eliza's true identity and had hunted down John Calvin for an exclusive story. I took it a step further. What if Yentin and Calvin had conspired to get a candid of Eliza seeing her father for the first time in more than a decade at her own holiday party? It would have been a horrible moment for the starlet, but a great exclusive that could have minted both Calvin and Yentin a bundle.

I took the chain of events a little further. What if Nicole had gotten wind of the ambush? That gave *her* motive for stopping Yentin in order to protect her daughter. The only problem with that scenario was *how* Nicole could have gotten that inside information. Unless John Calvin or Edward Yentin had told her, it was unlikely she had prior knowledge of their potential plan to waylay Eliza. Unless . . .

Maybe she'd overheard them talking at the party?

It was a lot of supposition, but it was all I had at the moment.

Three minutes later, I'd caught up with the minivan. I lifted my foot from the gas pedal, letting my car fall back to a safe distance while keeping a watchful eye on the taillights. Once or twice, I let myself speed up enough to try to catch a glimpse of the driver in the side mirror. Dusk was settling in, but after the stare down from the beach parking lot, I'd recognize that face anywhere. It was definitely John Calvin. And after ten minutes on his tail, I knew exactly where he was heading.

The driveway entrance leading to Eliza's cliffside house came into view. Once again, the gate was open. As spooked as she'd been when her father had shown up the first time—not to mention after a murder happened on the premises—I would have thought she'd keep it closed. Sometimes there was no accounting for people's actions.

I fell back again, hoping Calvin hadn't realized the headlights behind him had been following him all this time. I watched his taillights disappear down the drive. I jerked my car off the road and quickly dialed Eliza. She answered on the third ring.

"It's Ivy," I said, dispensing with any pleasantries. "Your father just pulled into your driveway."

"Whaaat?" she asked, her instant anxiety stretching out the word.

"I saw your father—"

I broke off at the faint sound of the doorbell ringing.

My instinct was to blurt out, "Don't answer it!" but I held it in. Was John Calvin a murderer? An abusive father? Or was Eliza a puppet master, pulling everyone's strings? My mind felt stuffed with a convoluted tangle of yarn, utterly impossible to unwind.

"How do you know?" she asked in a whisper.

"I—I happened to see him drive by . . ." I said, leaving the circumstances and the fact that I'd followed him unspoken.

"Are you here, too?"

The doorbell rang again. I suspected Eliza was peering out the kitchen window John Calvin had pounded on the other evening when I'd been here, allowing her a glimpse of the driveway and his van. "I'm at the end of the driveway—"

"Come down!"

"But your father—"

"Please come," she begged. "I can't face him alone."

That was all the encouragement I needed. Three seconds later, I pulled in next to the minivan. John Calvin still stood in front of the closed front door. He turned at the sound of my car's engine, his expression instantly turning from impatient to disbelief.

I jumped out and opened the back door. I had to help Agatha out, but once she was on the ground, she broke into vicious yelping. Calvin stared at me. "You again? This place is like the freaking Twilight Zone. You're everywhere I turn."

I pressed my palm innocently to my chest and looked over my shoulder as if he might be talking to someone else. "Me?"

"Are you following me? Did that *woman* put you up to it?"

By that, I presumed he meant Nicole.

The passenger side of the minivan flung open suddenly, and the man, Russ, who'd been with Calvin the last time they'd been here, stepped out. He looked from his friend to me and back again. "Let's go, man."

Agatha's frenzied barking continued. At the sound of Russ's voice, she took off, stopping short at his feet. She darted forward like she was ready to nip at his ankles. The guy hopped from one foot to the other. "Back off!" he yelled, as if Agatha was going to listen to him.

Calvin ignored the commotion. He pressed his finger on the doorbell, leaving it there so it rang and rang and rang. "I'm not going anywhere 'til I see Johnette—"

The front door was suddenly flung open. Eliza stood there in a pair of leggings, fuzzy socks, and an oversized T-shirt, a defiant hand on her hip. Even dressed down, she had an ethereal beauty. Frankly, she seemed to glow from the inside out. "What do you want?" she demanded.

The second Eliza opened the door, Calvin released his finger from the doorbell and swung to face her. "I just want to talk. I need to tell you—"

"I have nothing to say to you."

"You are my daughter—"

The sound of the passenger door to the minivan slamming shut cut him off. Eliza's eyes darted over John Calvin's shoulder, landing on Agatha and the minivan. Her gaze faltered for a moment, but she dragged her attention back to her father. "You lost the right to call me that a long time ago," she ground out. I could imagine it being a line from *The Beach* as her character confronted the parent who'd wronged her somehow.

"Johne—"

"Get off my property." Eliza spoke through clenched teeth. "Now."

Calvin threw his hands up in surrender. "Sure. Fine. But before I go, there's something you need to know about your assista—"

"No!" Eliza yelled, her eyes glassy and wild.

I took that as my cue to intervene. I charged past the minivan toward the front door. Behind me, Agatha gave a few tepid yelps before she let loose into another frenzied fit of barking, throwing her head back with each hearty "Ruff!"

"Agatha!" I yelled as I barreled past Calvin, positioning myself between him and Eliza. To him, I said, "She said leave."

A red tint had spread from Eliza's neck to her cheeks. Her entire body was trembling.

Calvin's nostrils flared, and for a second, I thought I might see steam coming from them. "I'm your father. You owe me—"

Eliza sputtered. "I-I don't owe you anything!"

"I know you've always blamed me for your mom leaving, but I am *not* the bad guy here," he said. "I've only ever tried to protect you. And now—"

Eliza held up one hand, palm out. "Just stop, okay? I can add one plus one, you know. You show up at my party. That reporter shows up at my party. Now he's dead, and you're trying to get in my head—"

"You have it all wrong," Calvin said. "That reporter did come to see me, and that is why I'm here, but it's *not* what you think."

She scoffed. "And what do I think?"

He frowned. "I'm not here for money," he said quietly.

Her chin quivered with emotion.

"Go inside, Eliza," I told her, then I whistled. Agatha gave one more mighty bark before turning and running to me. Eliza hesitated for a second, but then stepped out of sight. I crossed the threshold, and just after Agatha scurried past my feet, I turned to face John Calvin. "Timing is everything," I said before closing the door with a low *click*, then turning the lock.

I leaned my back against the door to let my racing heart calm down, but Eliza's voice in my ear kept it going double-time. "Maybe h-he's right. I left a l-long time ago. What if I'm remembering wro—" She exhaled a heavy breath and suddenly registered the fact that she was still a little bit peeved with me, yet I was in her house. "Why are you here?"

I pushed away from the door, wrapped my hand around her wrist, and pulled her to the living room sofa—a sleek, modern piece of furniture that didn't look particularly comfortable. She perched on the edge of it, looking at me with her stormy blue eyes. I sat in the chair opposite her, which turned out to be just as uncomfortable as it looked. I scooted to the edge, mirroring Eliza.

"Look—" I hesitated, wondering if I was about to do the completely wrong thing.

"Whatever it is, just tell me."

Agatha found a spot on the floor by my feet. She lay down, her front legs extended in front of her. I scratched her head for moral support, sucked in a bolstering breath, then forged ahead before I could change my mind. "Nicole and your father—they, uh, know each other."

Eliza scoffed. "No they don't."

I dipped my chin and nodded. "Yes. They do."

She looked at me for a beat, as if she was giving serious thought to what I'd said. "They can't. Nicole would have told me."

I stayed silent, waiting for her to get to a point of receptiveness. After a few seconds, she made it there. "Why do you think they know each other?"

"I saw them together, Eliza. Today, at the beach. They were in one of the public parking lots, and they were arguing."

She drew her perfectly arched brows together and frowned. She seemed to shrink inside her oversized shirt. "Arguing about what?"

"About you."

I'd expected her to be surprised by this bit of news. Instead, she just shrugged. "Nicole is very protective. She knows I don't want to see my father."

"It was more than that."

A car door slammed outside. Eliza flinched, shooting a nervous glance at the front door. Her nostrils flared as she inhaled, her breath shaky with her exhalation. She was trying to control her emotions, but they bubbled just under the surface.

We both sat perfectly still, waiting. Had the car door been John Calvin finally getting in the minivan and leaving?

The click of the lock turning in the front door was followed by Nicole saying, "Eliza, I'm back."

Eliza and I both jumped. Eliza's hand flew to her chest. "Oh, thank God," she breathed out.

Nicole saw us sitting in the living room and stopped abruptly.

"My father showed up," Eliza said. "Ivy helped get him to leave." She peered around Nicole, as if she could see through the front of the house to the driveway. Her voice turned low and raspy. "He is gone, isn't he?"

"No one is out there," Nicole said. She dropped her purse onto the corner of the couch and glared at me. "And what are you doing here?" she asked. Her voice had a cold edge, but it was shaken. Beneath the stony exterior, I could see her start to unravel. She was asking the very question she didn't want me to answer, but she couldn't stop herself.

Eliza stared at Nicole. "I just said my father was here. What's wrong with you?"

Nicole's head jerked, and she blinked, as if coming out of a trance. "He was *here*?"

"Again," Eliza said. "And Ivy helped get him to leave."

Nicole's face softened, but only slightly, and only for a brief second. She jerked again, suddenly moving forward. She beelined for Eliza and bent to whisper in her ear.

Eliza jerked back. "What are you talking about?" she snapped, but her eyes darted from Nicole to me and back again.

Once again, Nicole leaned in, her lips close to Eliza's ear, but Eliza bent out of the way. "No. Nicole, stop."

Nicole stood up again, her body rigid. She took her glasses off and let them hang around her neck. "Eliza . . ."

But Eliza shook her head. "If that's what you think, just ask her." Nicole swung to look at me, but Eliza kept her focus on her assistant. "Go ahead. Ask her."

"Ask me what?" I said, then waited with bated breath.

Nicole kept her gaze steady on me as she spoke. "Were you working with Edward Yentin? Is that why you're always hanging around, trying to dig up information on Eliza? On her father? On me?"

I was completely floored by the accusation. "What are you talking about?"

"Exactly what I said. Were you working with Yentin? Did you take photographs you haven't shared? Or, no, you must not have. That's why you're still digging around, isn't it? You need something juicy, still. Well, you're not going to get it—"

I jumped up, waving my hands in front of me. Agatha went on full alert. "Whoa, whoa, whoa. I am not—was not—never have worked with Edward Yentin. I'd never even heard of him till he ended up dead at the party."

Nicole shot daggers at me with her eyes, daring me to challenge her. "None of this is your business."

She was right, I thought. "You're right," I said, speaking to them both. "It's not my business, except I was hired to photograph the holiday party, then Eliza, you came to my house to look at the photos, and"—I redirected my attention to Nicole—"when I saw you and John Calvin arguing, then when you practically accosted me in front of Yeast of Eden, well, all that means it became my business."

Eliza sputtered, swiveling to face Nicole. "Wait, what? You accosted Ivy?"

Nicole closed her eyes for a beat. There wasn't a strong resemblance between the two, but her nostrils flared—just as Eliza's had a few minutes ago. "She followed me," Nicole ground out, barely controlling the shaking in her voice.

"I didn't follow you. I was walking Agatha at the beach—"

"She said you and my dad were arguing," Eliza interrupted. Her eyes narrowed as she confronted Nicole. She couldn't care less that I'd been there to witness it. She just wanted to know what was going on between her assistant and her father.

Nicole flashed the briefest of death stares at me.

"Tell her," I said softly, because it needed to come from her.

"Tell me what?" Eliza's gaze swung back and forth between us. Her voice rose an octave. "Tell me *what*?"

And just like that, Nicole's face collapsed, the iron façade melting into distress. She sat on the couch next to Eliza, turning to face her. Tears traced lines down her cheeks, and her nose ran. The composed woman I'd first met with her glasses and clipboard and tidy updo had turned into an anguished woman on the verge of losing it altogether.

The color had drained from Eliza's face. She stared, openmouthed, at Nicole, panic rising. "Tell me. What is it, Nicole? Are y-you s-sick?"

Nicole looked stricken. "No! God, no, Eliza. It's nothing like that."

For a second, I wanted to melt into the background. To be anywhere but there. This was a private moment, but then again, it was only happening *because* of me.

"Then, what is it?" Eliza's lower lip started to tremble, and her eyes grew glassy. She cared for Nicole, and the worried anticipation was like a knife to her heart.

Instead of answering her, Nicole grabbed her abandoned purse and dug inside. Her hand emerged clutching a trim black wallet. She opened it and retrieved a photograph, handing it to Eliza without a word.

Eliza looked at the photo, her brows drawing together. "I don't understand. This is me when I was a baby." Then her words slowed. "How did you get this?"

Nicole swiped away her tears. "Johnette . . ." she whispered.

Eliza stared at Nicole. "What did you call me?" Eliza asked, her voice tentative. Scared.

Nicole drew in a bolstering inhalation before exhaling the name again. "Johnette."

It was as if time froze. Eliza stopped breathing. Nicole bit her lower lip, her eyes wide. I stared, waiting to see what would happen next.

Finally, Eliza spoke, her voice scarcely more than a whisper. "How do you know that name?"

There was no way forward, except for the truth. Nicole was flustered, but she seemed to realize she couldn't stop now. "Y-you have to understand. W-we didn't plan to get pregnant. I was just eighteen. I was just a kid."

Eliza's face drained of all color. "What are you saying?"

Nicole looked at her beseechingly. "You felt it," she said. "The connection between us." She reached for Eliza's hands. "Sweetheart, I'm your mother."

Eliza yanked her hands free and pressed them over her ears, as if she could block out what Nicole was saying.

"I couldn't take care of myself, let alone you," Nicole continued. "I tried. I really tried, but John was—"

Eliza's head suddenly snapped up, her confusion turning to rage. "He was what?"

Nicole heaved a shaky sigh. "A mistake. He was a mistake."

At this, Eliza dropped her hands and faced Nicole head on. "Yeah? Well, at least *he* stuck around."

My head spun. I hadn't expected her to defend the very man she didn't want to speak with. Eliza was a complex young woman battling emotions. Angry tears streamed from her eyes. "You left me. How could you leave me?"

She hadn't said, *How could you leave me with him?* but simply *How could you leave me?* Maybe the omission didn't mean anything. But maybe it did. Maybe I'd been off base about John Calvin.

Nicole reached a hand out to Eliza's knee. "He acts like he doesn't know me. Like I don't exist."

Eliza scooted away, knocking Nicole's hand off. "Am I supposed to feel sorry for you while you've been pretending to be someone else?" She shook her head in frantic little movements. "Why not just tell me?"

That was a very good question. I could almost see the wheels turning behind Nicole's eyes as she figured out how to answer that question in a way that would placate Eliza. Personally, I didn't think there was a good response. After a very long, very fraught thirty seconds, Nicole reached for Eliza's hands, clasping them in hers. "I don't know," she said simply. "Suddenly you were just there, starring in a brand-new TV show. I followed your career on *The Beach*, trying to figure out how I could be part of your life. I—" Nicole broke down, her mouth contorting with her anguish. "I was afraid you would never forgive me if I told you the truth." She looked up at Eliza through her tear-soaked eyelashes. "Can you? Can you forgive me?"

Eliza stared out the back windows toward the Pacific. I imagined the churning water of the ocean pretty well matched her roiling emotions. A moment later, she turned to Nicole and almost managed a small smile through her tears. I stared, flummoxed, as she dragged the back of her hand under her nose. "For letting him n-name me Johnette?" She forced out an indignant laugh. "N-never."

Chapter 18

The Blackbird Ladies convened in Mrs. Branford's kitchen at precisely 5 p.m. on Thursday nights, come rain or come shine. It was their book club night.

"You get together every week?" I'd asked when I'd found out about their meetings.

Mrs. Branford had given a good-natured laugh. "A book a week is quite reasonable, Ivy. Why, there are times when I read two or three in a single *day*. And if I can't sleep, well, I don't just lie there. I read. You should join us. Book club is the very best kind of social engagement."

"But I'm not a Blackbird Lady." I was in the wrong generation, for starters, and I didn't know if I had time to read an entire book every single week.

She'd waved her hand, as if she were clasping a magic wand, and said, "Bibbidi-bobbidi-boo. You are now a Blackbird Lady."

"As simple as that?"

She smiled and patted her tight, snowy curls. "As simple as that. Now perhaps you will call me Penny, or at the very least, Penelope."

"No can do, Mrs. Branford. And I can't commit to a book a week."

I'd found out that along with a new weekly book, they also had a new weekly cocktail. Lemon drops. Long Island iced teas. Whiskey sours. Raspberry kamikazes. Screwdrivers. If there was a way to tie a drink to the book selection, they found it.

I hadn't told Mrs. Branford that I was coming on this particular Thursday evening. I walked into the kitchen where the three Blackbird Ladies convened, chattering nonstop. Mrs. Branford's parents had built the house in 1899 and had left it to her. She'd lived in it nearly her whole life. Parts of it were remodeled, while other parts were original to the old house. The black-and-white checkerboard tiles on the floor channeled the whimsical side of Mrs. Branford. The backsplash was bead board. Green was the accent color, from the tiles behind the stove to the speckles in the granite countertop to the avocado refrigerator from another era.

"Ivy!" Mabel Peabody's boisterous voice sang out as Agatha and I entered the kitchen. "Penny said you'd be joining us tonight!"

She had? "You did?" I asked Mrs. Branford, wondering how in the world she'd known that when I'd only decided to pop by a few minutes ago.

Mrs. Branford stood at the counter amidst bottles of sparkling wine, vanilla vodka, clear crème de menthe, and grenadine, a satisfied grin on her face. Her cane was no-where in sight. She held a stainless-steel shaker clasped in her hands, and she gently jiggled and joggled it back and forth. On the counter in front of her were four martini glasses rimmed with crushed candy cane pieces. One for Mabel, one for Alice, one for Mrs. Branford, and one, I presumed, for me. "Of course you're here. It was inevitable."

It was? "Why was it inevitable?"

"Miguel is surely at the restaurant, and I know Olaya is out with Owen." She waggled her penciled eyebrows, clearly still enamored with the fact that my father and Olaya were courting. "That leaves us." Mrs. Branford's knowing smile remained in place. "I knew you'd come here."

It was all true, but the way she'd said it made it sound as if being here was my third choice, when, in fact, this was exactly where I wanted to be, even if I hadn't read whatever book they'd chosen and even if Miguel, my father, or Olaya had been available.

Penelope Branford had a sixth sense.

She poured the mixture from the shaker into the glasses, catching the ice with the strainer. She added sparkling wine to the festive red drink, then placed a small candy cane in each glass. "Voilà! Sparkling Peppermint Swirls." She passed out the glasses, then held up her own in a toast. "Chin-chin!"

"Chin-chin!" Mabel cheered.

Alice's "Chin-chin" was calm and imbued with her Southern drawl.

I held up my glass, tapping it against each of theirs in turn. "Chin-chin."

We sat at the table sipping our drinks. Three copies of *A Christmas Carol* sat in the center of the table. "Our book choice this week," Mrs. Branford said. "Can you believe that neither Mabel or Alice had ever read it?"

I felt my neck flex as I pulled a face. I was with the majority because I also had never read the classic Dickens tale.

"Ivy Culpepper," Mrs. Branford chided. "Not you, too."

Mabel slapped her palm on the table. "Yes! I told you we weren't the only ones," she declared victoriously. "Who needs to read it when there are a thousand and one film adaptations?"

Exactly! I'd seen plenty of film versions, from *The Muppet Christmas Carol* to Patrick Stewart as Scrooge, all the way to *A Diva's Christmas Carol* with Vanessa Williams.

"Because," Mrs. Branford said, her gentle, chiding tone shifting to a pure scolding, "a film cannot capture the nuances of Dickens's writing. You are all philistines."

"Penelope Branford!" Alice's voice came across with uncharacteristic force. "Judge not, lest ye be judged."

Mrs. Branford's terse expression cracked as her face split into a smile. "Touché, Alice."

"I'll get to it, eventually," I said. After the stack of mystery novels on my to-be-read pile.

"I will hold you to that, my dear," Mrs. Branford said. "Now. No more suspense. What is happening with the lovely Eliza Fox and the case of the dead reporter?"

She made our real-life murder investigation sound like the title to a Nancy Drew book. I filled them in on Nicole Leonard's emotional confession that she was Eliza's mother. The scene flashed in my mind. Nicole's apologies. Eliza's shock turning from fury to forgiveness.

I finished the story and took a sip of my minty cocktail. "So they'll be okay," Mrs. Branford said.

I had no idea how hard it would be for Eliza to truly forgive her mother for leaving her behind, even for the best of reasons, and then, on top of that, for hiding her identity while she pretended to be someone else. Would I be able to forgive such a thing?

Under the right circumstances, I thought I would. I couldn't fault Nicole for what she'd felt and the decisions she'd made when she was an eighteen-year-old unwed mother. She'd done what she'd thought was best for herself and her daughter. She didn't have a crystal ball to tell her how she'd feel about her decisions two decades later.

And as for Eliza, she needed both the Nicole she already had a relationship with, and the Nicole whom she now knew was her mother.

"I think so," I said, responding to Mrs. Branford.

The three women sipped from their festive martini glasses simultaneously, their six eyes staring at me expectantly.

"There's nothing else to tell," I said when I realized they wanted me to go on.

"Of course there is," Mrs. Branford said. "Did you ask her about *My Fair Lady*?"

"Is Eliza Fox still a suspect?" Alice asked. "And what about this woman, Nicole? Seems to me she had reason to kill the reporter if he was going to reveal the truth. She's lucky Eliza forgave her so easily. It might not have gone that way, you know."

Mabel waggled her eyebrows. "And what about Brad McAvoy?"

I answered each one in turn. "I did not have a chance to ask about *My Fair Lady*. I think until the killer is found, *everyone's* still a suspect. Probably including me, Olaya, and Maggie, since we'd all been present. And what about Brad?"

Mabel grinned. "Have you seen him again? Is he as gorgeous in real life as he is on the silver screen? Are they going to split up?"

Alice rolled her eyes. "Why? If they split up, are you going to make a move on him?"

"He might like a cougar," Mabel said with a growl, either completely missing Alice's sarcasm, or choosing to completely ignore it.

"He might at that," Mrs. Branford said.

Alice shook her head and sighed. "Why do you encourage her?"

Mrs. Branford laughed. "Alice, my dear, let's be realistic. What are the odds that Brad McAvoy would even come into contact with Mabel? I'll tell you. Zero. The odds are zero. Therefore, it's clearly a joke. Mabel has no expectation of hooking up with the young actor. When you react to her, *that* is what encourages her to say outrageous things."

I suspected that Mabel Peabody needed no encouragement in the *I'm going to be outrageous* department.

"There is something," I said, going back to the murder of Edward Yentin. "John Calvin. Why wouldn't he have let Nicole back into Eliza's life when she'd tried?"

"Anger at her abandoning them in the first place," Mabel said without blinking an eye.

I supposed she was right. There would have been— and from the scene I'd witnessed at the beach, there still was—a lot of resentment.

"People who are abusive isolate their victims. If that's why Eliza left her childhood behind, it explains a lot, including her father keeping the girl's mother away," Mrs. Branford said.

I thought about this. It was possible John Calvin had been abusive, but Eliza hadn't been scared of him. Angry, yes; fearful, no. That fact bothered me. She'd alluded to creepy men, and a creepy boss, but she'd never mentioned her father. I felt that something was missing from the story.

And none of it answered who killed Yentin.

I tuned back into the conversation. "Did he really name his daughter Johnette?" Alice was asking.

"I taught a girl called Johnna," Mrs. Branford said. "There are no strange names anymore."

"How true. I adore my name, but people have always thought it old-fashioned," Mabel said. "But when Paul and Jamie named their little girl Mabel—"

"Who?" Alice asked.

Mabel answered without losing a beat. "Helen Hunt and Paul Reiser. *Mad About You*, that show from the nineties? You know the one."

"Oh, right. I remember," Alice said. "Mabel was an acronym for something, wasn't it?"

"Mothers always bring extra love," Mrs. Branford said.

Alice scoffed. "Silly, when you think of it, naming your child after a television character."

"Well, obviously I was born before that television show aired, so *my* name didn't come from there," Mabel said. "I was simply pointing out that the name went through a short-lived resurgence of popularity after that TV baby bore the name."

"Jimmy and I named our daughter after a character

from literature. No less silly than that, I'd venture to say," Mrs. Brandford said.

Alice held her hands out, palms up, as if they were the scales of justice. "Mabel from an old sitcom versus a character from *The Taming of the Shrew*? Two completely different things."

Mrs. Branford shook her head. "I disagree. I have a love of Shakespeare, I spent the majority of my life teaching literature, and I've always loved books. To someone else, pop culture and old sitcoms, as you say, may hold a huge significance. As you said, judge not, lest ye be judged."

Mrs. Branford's countenance turned melancholy, something it always did when her daughter, Kate, was mentioned. She'd named her after Katherina in Shakespeare's play *The Taming of the Shrew*. Mrs. Branford's oldest son lived in San Fransisco. Jeremy was a banker who'd done very well for himself. Peter was a programmer who led a nomadic life, traveling from place to place and living life to the fullest. Kate, however, had lost her early battle with cancer. I didn't think losing a child was something anyone ever got over. From Mrs. Branford's reaction whenever she thought of Kate, it was clear she hadn't.

She'd told me on multiple occasions that I reminded her of Katherina. Bold and headstrong, quick-witted and intuitive. It was the greatest compliment she could have ever bestowed upon me. Now she patted my hand. "You be there for that young woman. I suspect she's going to need a friend."

Chapter 19

The weekend rolled around again, and before I knew it, I was side by side with Olaya preparing for yet another holiday party. "I didn't think we had one scheduled for tonight," I said when I'd showed up for my shift.

"It was last-minute. The Hollywood starlet's party, it has brought up a bit of competition."

I stood in front of one of the commercial ovens, a tray of steaming bran muffins in my mitted hands. "What do you mean?"

"That is what the woman said. *My party will be better than Eliza Fox's*," Olaya said.

I couldn't imagine what movie star would be in such overt rivalry with Eliza. Then again, it was a cutthroat industry. "Who's giving it?"

"Cordelia Knight," Olaya answered.

A series of bells went off inside my head. The no-show at Eliza's party was now hosting one of her own. Here in Santa Sofia? How interesting. "Really?"

Olaya gave one of her sage nods. "She wants every-thing exactly the same, from the food to the servers."

"Meaning me and Maggie?"

"Yes, *pero* this time with no costumes."

Extremely interesting. And thank God.

We had our work cut out for us to finish Yeast of Eden's daily baking, plus the baking for an unplanned fiesta, but Felix stayed to lend a hand. Olaya had talked Cordelia Knight down from an identical array of what had been at Eliza's party to a somewhat lighter and easier order. We made miniature candy cane loaves out of sweetened cres-cent dough, dusting them with stripes of turbinado sugar tinted red before baking. We baked mounds of cinnamon tea rings, loaf after loaf of sweet cinnamon dough filled with a buttery-sugary-cinnamony filling, all rolled up like a jelly roll, topped with a light glaze, and sliced to reveal lovely rings. Finally, Olaya made *Rosca de Reyes*, or Three Kings Bread. "It is a traditional Mexican fruit bread," she explained.

When it was finished, I saw the resemblance to a crown. The bread was braided, then dotted with dried fruit. "In Mexico," Olaya said, "we place a miniature baby Jesus figurine into the dough. It is a lucky person who finds the baby in their piece of bread."

She left that special tradition out of the miniature wreath-shaped loaves. "Not for a party like this," she said. "No one will be there to explain."

"We're not staying this time?" I asked.

She looked at me, understanding in her eyes. She knew me so well. "You and Maggie will set it all up. You can stay for a little while, but the woman, she did not say to stay for the entire party. We can pick up in the morning." She wagged her finger at me. "But watch the girl. She is too starstruck."

Wasn't that the truth. Maggie was still going on about being present when the murder had happened at Eliza Fox's holiday party, telling the tale to anyone who would listen.

We spent the rest of the afternoon baking. Olaya moved around the kitchen with grace and composure. No amount of pressure ruffled her feathers. The fabric of her wide-legged palazzo pants hung loose at her feet, her clogs completely hidden. She wore her standard white apron, the simple oval logo on the top left of the bib. Olaya was a minimalist when it came to her marketing efforts. "The shop, it speaks for itself. People come for the bread. I do not need to sell it," she often said.

She was right. Yeast of Eden was a destination for tourists who came just to experience the enchantment of Olaya's breads. Why spend extra time and money when she didn't have to?

No matter how many people worked in the kitchen, the place ran like a well-oiled machine. Felix stood in front of the massive grain mill with its casing made from pine and its high-quality millstone. He'd taken charge of the daily process of turning 350 pounds of heirloom wheat a day into freshly ground flour. He did a weekly grind of rye, spelt, cornmeal, and buckwheat, as well. These Olaya used for the heartier breads she baked, like her Dark Mountain Rye, and now one of the most popular breads she baked, her Black Pepper Parmesan.

The Osttiroler commercial mill—*this* was where Olaya spent her money. "If the bread is not the best, then advertising does not matter. If the bread is the best, that is all the advertising I need," she'd told me more than once.

She used to source her flour from a local mill, but once the Osttiroler had arrived, that was it. I'd done an entire page on the bread shop's website extolling the virtues of a bakery that grinds its own wheat.

I breathed in as Felix worked the machine. The rush of holiday parties meant extra baking, which meant Felix had to grind extra flour. "Wheat is like wine," he said in response to my inhalation. "It has terroir."

I raised my brows in a question.

"Grapes are affected by the soil they're grown in. By the area. By the topography and the climate. Wheat is the same. It has a scent. An aroma that feeds the soul."

Olaya beamed at her protégé.

"Imagine the bread you buy in a grocery store. The wheat used has been sitting around for God knows how long. It's been treated and processed with chemicals. How many nutrients do you think are left after that?"

I made a guess. "Not a lot?"

"Less than that," he said, his dimple materializing as he smiled at the magic of the machine. He was Rumpel-stiltskin, spinning straw into gold. "Flour is an artisan in-gredient, just like cage-free eggs and organic lettuce."

They'd certainly convinced the residents of Santa Sofia that their flour was as good as gold. They'd started bagging it up and selling it in the front of the store. They couldn't keep it on the shelves. "It's amazing," I'd over-heard a customer say. "It's as if, all these years, we've been eating bread in the dark, and now, with this flour, the lights have been turned on. We've gone from black and white to being in living color."

"I am a baker," Olaya often said. "To be in control over the transformation of grain into flour, well, there is simply no other way to fully immerse yourself into the process of baking bread. Flour that is just a few hours old? *That* has become the essence of my artisan bread. It is the core of this bread shop."

Judging by the lines that were sometimes out the door, everyone and their brother agreed.

Apparently, Cordelia Knight preferred her parties to start much later than Eliza's had—which I thought was more typical for the celebrity crowd. I figured many of her guests would have to drive up from Los Angeles. Evening traffic out of the city meant it could take several hours to get to Santa Sofia, so an eight o'clock start time made a lot more sense, especially since it was a Friday night.

Maggie beamed beside me in the white Yeast of Eden van as I drove through the winding roads to the Santa Sofia Hills. "I didn't know Cordelia Knight had a house here, did you?" Maggie asked.

"I didn't."

She fidgeted in her seat, too excited to sit still. "I wonder if she owns it or rents it."

"I feel like we'd know if she owned a house here," I said. Several celebrities did, and it was common knowledge. Sightings happened now and then, but most locals tried to let them have their privacy.

"True," Maggie said. She fell silent, pondering this. "It'd be cool, though, if she really, like, lived here."

As Maggie prattled on about Cordelia Knight's last role, I remembered what those two women from Eliza's party had said about the scandal. Had it been a publicity stunt? The women had said her career had been jeopardized because of it, but if she was hosting an A-list party—assuming A-listers showed up—her career couldn't be completely tanked.

I had a thought. At a stoplight, I pulled out my phone, opened my internet browser, and searched for Cordelia Knight. Her IMBD page came up, of course, and an array of articles about her. I scrolled until I found the story about her beachside canoodling, and there it was. The by-line read "Edward Yentin." The guy had been part journalist, part paparazzi, and it appeared, full-time shyster. I looked at the photo accompanying the article. In it, Cordelia, naked and with her back to the camera, was flanked by two shirtless men, also with their backs to the camera. She glanced over her shoulder, a come-hither smile dusting her lips.

My mind zipped backward to Margarita Lewellyn, the waitress and aspiring actress who went by Rita and who had, I thought, worked with Edward Yentin to stage the photo with Brad McAvoy. Could Cordelia have done the same thing?

I considered this. If Cordelia Knight and Edward Yentin had set up the salacious photo shoot, what would have been the purpose? Cordelia was already a shining star. She didn't need the publicity, and certainly not bad publicity.

Unless . . .

I scanned the article, wondering if someone else had also been involved. Who were the men? Maybe, like Rita, Cordelia had tried to stage the photo in order to draw attention to someone else.

But no one else was named. Only Cordelia's bright star had lost its luster.

I went back to the photo, looking at the unidentified men. What if Cordelia had worked with Yentin to frame one of them—for what, though? I peered at the backs of the men's heads. Could one of them be Brad McAvoy? But no, the hair color was wrong. These two were dark-haired, where Brad was dirty blond.

Someone else, then, with something to lose? What if Yentin had published the photo and article, but had used this photo instead of the one outing one or both of her companions?

I let the idea float away. I was reaching.

I circled back to Cordelia and the negative reaction to the photo. Could the blemish on her career have been motive for murder? There was no evidence she'd been at the party, but the costumes had allowed Brad McAvoy to hide in plain sight. Maybe Cordelia Knight had done the same.

It seemed improbable, but one thing I'd learned over the years was that improbable did not equal impossible, and sometimes what seemed most unlikely turned out to be the truth.

Maggie and I arrived at the gated community in the Santa Sofia Hills. The houses were far, far apart, acre after acre giving plenty of privacy between homes. It was as if each house sat a mile away from the next, and each seemed to sit atop a hill, offering views from the back of each property to the canyon below. I pulled onto Cordelia Knight's property, following the winding drive until we reached the house. I stopped for a moment to gape at the massive structure before us. Maggie's chin dropped wider than mine. "Dang. People actually live like this?"

It appeared they did. The house seemed a million times larger than Eliza Fox's, and hers was plenty big.

The house itself wasn't particularly ostentatious, but it

communicated wealth. It was a simple Spanish two-story with off-white stucco walls and a traditional red-tiled roof, both of which went on and on and on in both directions. Elaborate landscaping, what looked like an expansive courtyard right in front, defined by another stucco wall, and black iron accents, not to mention the size, were awe-inspiring. The place had to be eight or nine, or maybe ten thousand square feet, depending upon how deep the house was.

"Wow," Maggie said, still gaping as we pulled around to the side entrance, just as I'd been directed to do at Eliza Fox's. Apparently, celebrities didn't like the help using the front door.

I parked alongside a Divine Cuisine catering van. So, they'd gotten the last-minute call, too.

Inside, someone on the kitchen staff directed Maggie and me to the library. The house was expansive and wide open inside, with a center room overlooking a manicured backyard with a swimming pool as the focal point. The next room seemed to be an extension of the one before, heavily plastered archways marking the change in space and offering a new set of furniture and decorative touches that flowed from the previous room.

We followed the directions the woman in the kitchen had given and finally found the library at the front of the house. Like Eliza's library, there was a Christmas tree made from stacks of books, but it was twice the size. There was also a pine tree—bigger than Eliza's had been—decorated and standing right next to the fireplace. It was as if Cordelia was one-upping Eliza.

A strange feeling of déjà vu came over me, even without the Dickens theme. The question that rose to the surface, like oil sitting atop water, was: *How did Cordelia know about the tree made of books in Eliza's library, who'd catered that event, and the exact menu?*

The idea that Cordelia *had* been in attendance at Eliza's party circled back into my mind. If Yentin had double-crossed her with the photos and article, she'd have had motive. And if she had been at Eliza's party and seen him, she'd also had the means and the opportunity to murder Edward Yentin.

Maggie and I spent the next hour and a half setting up the bread tables just as we had at Eliza's party. We traipsed back and forth, through the house and kitchen, out to Yeast of Eden's van, then back through to the library. The trays of Star Twisted Bread, the same miniature candied sweetbread shaped like candy canes, and small crescent dough reindeer heads and Santa heads could have been picked up from Eliza's party and relocated here. It was all so similar, which was something Olaya would never do had it not been specially requested.

"It's perfect," a woman said from behind where Maggie and I stood. I turned to see her surveying the tables. It was Cordelia Knight herself, a gown slung over one arm, her bright red lips curved into a satisfied smile. "Absolutely perfect."

The movie star didn't look the same in real life as she did on the screen. She was taller than I'd realized. And thinner. But there was something else I couldn't pinpoint.

From beside me, I heard Maggie's sharp intake of breath. "Ohmygosh, ohmygosh, ohmygosh. Cordelia Knight. I love you. I seriously love you! I mean, *The Corner Shop*? It's one of my all-time favorites," she gushed. "And *The*

Runaway Train, of course. Classic. And I want you to know, I never believed the whole scandal, plus your private life is your private life, am I right? It's a free country."

Olaya had asked me to keep Maggie's fangirl enthusiasm in check, but I couldn't have scripted a better way to broach the very subject I wanted to know about. Way to go, Mags!

"Thanks, honey," Cordelia said as her eyes skimmed over Maggie. "And you're right, but it doesn't work that way." She dropped the garment over the back of a chair. The hem of the dress looked dirty, like it was too long and had dragged on the floor. Surely she wasn't going to wear that tonight? Cordelia's smile faltered. "That reporter is—was—a complete charlatan."

Maggie fisted her hands and pumped her arms overhead as if she'd just gotten the winning answer in *Jeopardy!* "I knew it! He ambushed you, right?"

Cordelia dipped her chin—her version of a nod. I pictured her smile in that photograph, though. She looked as if she'd known she was being photographed, and had posed for the shot. Was Yentin a charlatan because he'd taken the photo, or because he hadn't done with it what he'd promised? "Let's just say I'm not sorry he's gone," she said quietly enough that no one but Maggie and I could hear her. Her voice dripped with derision, as if anyone who thought otherwise could—I'd been about to finish that thought with the words *jump off a cliff.* I bit my lower lip, stopping myself from saying it aloud.

"Did he trick you?" Maggie asked, pure innocence.

But Cordelia was done talking about it. She waved her hand dismissively. "It doesn't matter. It's over now. He didn't hurt me."

"I heard you lost a part over it," I said boldly. I'd consider that harmful.

Cordelia shrugged. "True. But Hollywood has a short memory."

Hollywood might, but did her fans? I shot a glance at Maggie. From her bright eyes and big smile, it seemed that they would, indeed, forgive Cordelia Knight for not always being the girl next door.

"Do you have a special someone, Ms. Knight?" I asked innocently.

Maggie screeched. "Ivy! Cordelia Knight was named the sexiest *single* woman last year by *The Scout*!" She demurred to Cordelia. "Rightly so, of course. Nothing else matters."

Cordelia's smile grew. She basked in the adoration Maggie was blanketing her with. "Thank you. It's such a silly thing to be recognized for," she said, but from the way she stood up a little straighter and held her chin a little higher, I didn't think she actually considered it all that silly. And Yentin's photo certainly supported that part of Cordelia's brand.

Maggie turned to me and lowered her voice. "She was with Greg Nathanson, but they split *years* ago."

Oh! A light bulb went off over my head. Now that she mentioned it, I did remember seeing tabloid photographs of the two of them together. From my recollection, they'd been on-again, off-again. "I thought I saw something about an engagement to a businessman or something."

Once again, Maggie spoke before Cordelia could. "He's a Brit, and after the scand—" Maggie stopped short before putting her foot in her mouth. "Erm, Cordelia didn't want to move to the UK, and, um, he didn't want to live here."

Cordelia's smile tightened. She hadn't missed Maggie's near misstep. She gave a mirthless laugh. "You know more about my life than I do."

Maggie gulped. "Sorry. I'm a fan."

"When you choose a life in Hollywood, you're choosing to live out loud. You have to accept it. I did a long time ago, though I don't always like it."

From where I stood, I thought she not only accepted it, but embraced that part of her celebrity. "You have a nice house," I commented. It was a clunky change of subject, but this woman was hosting a party in a few short hours and we'd soured her mood with talk of old boyfriends and loneliness.

"It's so huge!" Maggie blurted.

"To rattle around in alone," she said, almost too quietly to hear. Her lips curved down into a frown.

I gulped. My hand found Maggie's beside me, and I squeezed it, silently communicating to her that we should stop. "I'm so sorry, Ms. Knight. We didn't mean to dredge up old memories."

She shrugged, as if she had not a care in the world. "It's fine. Fame is a lonely beast. Isn't that a saying? If it's not, it should be."

"Do you know Eliza Fox?" I asked, thinking about how similar they were. I'd played matchmaker with Olaya Solis and Penelope Branford, forging a friendship between them where none had previously existed. Maybe I could do the same for these two lonely starlets—assuming neither were murderers, of course.

"I've met her a few times," Cordelia said. She held one hand out in front of her and picked at a cuticle. She shuffled slightly. Because she was copying Eliza, baked good to baked good?

"She's so sweet!" Maggie said, not picking up on the change in Cordelia. "We catered her Dickens party last week, and, oh my God, it was amazing." Her smile fell, and she looked stricken. "I mean, until they found that man at the bottom of the cliff."

Cordelia's head shot up as Maggie continued, wide-eyed. She wagged a finger between us. "Me and Ivy were both there." She glanced at the table of breads behind us. "We did almost the exact same breads for her as we did for you here."

Neither Olaya or I had mentioned to Maggie that Cordelia Knight had requested the same spread Eliza Fox had had at her party, so to her, it was an innocent obser-vation, but I saw a flicker of something in Cordelia's eyes. *She* knew she was copying Eliza's party spread bread by bread, and she'd requested the same people to serve. The question was still, why? Why did Cordelia Knight feel the need to replicate exactly what Eliza had done?

I noticed something then. Cordelia's hair in the past had been darker. Brown, not blond. Now, though, it was nearly the same shade as Eliza's. "Your hair," I said. "It used to be . . ." I trailed off. Was it uncouth to comment on the appearance of a famous actress?

She gathered up her hair and ran her hand down it. "You know what they say. Gentlemen prefer blondes."

Maggie giggled.

Whether or not it was true—after all, I'd had plenty of fun as a ginger—blond looked good on her.

Cordelia looked us up and down suddenly. "You're not dressed for the party."

I raised my eyebrows—both of them, because raising only one was not in my genetic makeup. "I didn't think we were staying long."

She gasped, instantly tense. "Of course you're staying. Who's going to serve my guests and keep the table looking good? There is more food, right?"

I answered her last question first by lifting the table skirt to reveal the boxes of extras we'd stashed there. "This is everything you ordered. There are extras of everything."

"Good. And you'll both be right here to make sure the food is replenished and the tables remain looking perfect."

A statement, not a question.

"Olaya said we weren't—"

"She must have misunderstood."

A woman glided into the room, quietly clearing her throat to get Cordelia's attention.

Cordelia turned. "Oh! Mary, you're here." She grabbed the dress from the chair and thrust it at the young woman.

"To the dry cleaner's, miss?" Mary asked, letting the garment drape over her arm. I could see now that it was more than just a dress. A hip-length cape of the same color, but with a maroon satin border, was underneath the gown. Mary didn't have a good hold on the bundle, and one corner of the cape dropped toward the floor. The hat pinned to it lay in a heap.

"Be careful, Mary," Cordelia scolded harshly. "It's a rental. It has to be returned."

In a different era, Mary might have curtsied. As it was, she gave a very slight bow of her head, then gathered up the dress and its accoutrements, retreating as quietly as she'd appeared.

Cordelia turned back to Maggie and me. "Go. Go home to change, and I'll see you back here in an hour."

Before either Maggie or I could protest again, she turned on her high heels and hurried out of the room.

Chapter 20

I dropped Maggie off at the bread shop so she could collect her car, then headed home with the plan of reconvening at Yeast of Eden in thirty minutes. The encounter with Cordelia bothered me. I let Agatha outside and grabbed a bite to eat so I wouldn't be famished and tempted by the food at the party—after all, we were meant to serve it, not eat it. Just as I was getting ready to head out again, I wondered if I should bring my camera. Cordelia might like to have a few candids of the partygoers. I was surprised, in fact, that she hadn't hired me to take official photos like Eliza had.

A split second after having that thought, I shifted focus to the dress—not the one Cordelia had been wearing, but the one Mary had gathered up to take to the dry cleaner's.

Three things stuck out to me: 1) the dirty hem of the dress, as if it had been worn outside; 2) the hat, which was really more like a bonnet; and 3) the fact that it had that cape with it. The whole getup was horribly out of style. There was enough fabric that hoops could fit inside of it, and who wore capes like that? Someone like Cordelia would have designer coats to wear.

It was, in fact, less of a couture gown and more like . . . A costume.

My skin pricked because I was pretty sure I'd seen it before.

I took off the harness I'd just put on Agatha. She scampered off with the treat I held out for her, finding a safe place to chew on the treasure where no one—meaning me—could take it from her again. Meanwhile I grabbed my laptop, sat on the couch, and started scrolling through the photos of Eliza's holiday party.

It felt like I'd taken thousands of pictures, when in reality, it was more like a few hundred, but finding one that had captured the dress like the one I'd seen at Cordelia Knight's house felt like searching for a missing AirPod— impossible, even though you knew exactly where you dropped it, and how could it possibly have disappeared?

Finally, after I'd gone through the entire collection twice, I found the elusive photo—or at least I thought I had. The focus of the shot was not the woman wearing the ornate dress, whom I now thought looked like she was dressed as Emily Cratchit, but a couple dressed as carolers, songbooks open in front of them, mouths rounded into *O*s as they sang a snippet from "God Rest Ye Merry, Gentlemen."

The Emily Cratchit figure was turned away from the camera, and the cape over the balloon-skirted dress gave the figure wearing the entire ensemble no shape whatsoever. The bonnet hid the woman's hair. There was no way to know if it was Cordelia Knight, but if it was her in the shimmery gown, she'd left before the sheriff's team had arrived and detained everyone.

After I dropped Agatha at her surrogate human's house, aka Mrs. Branford, and picked up Maggie again, I pictured the dirty hemline of the dress. As soon as we arrived back at Cordelia Knight's house, I snatched up my cell phone and started to text Emmaline. I got as far as typing: *Cordelia's worth investigating. She says she wasn't at Eliza's party, but if I'm right, she definitely was.* And *she was outside.*

I stopped before I hit Send, hemming and hawing. I didn't know if Cordelia was guilty of murder. I hadn't seen her face in the photograph. Did I have the right to throw her name into the mix? I'd done that with Eliza—inadvertently, but still—and it hadn't worked out well.

I grumbled under my breath as I made the decision.

Maggie shot me a side-eye. "Are you okay?"

I shoved the phone back into my bag and nodded. "I'm fine. Come on, let's go."

Back inside Cordelia's house, I no idea how to determine whether the star had been at Eliza's party. My mind reviewed all the things I *didn't* know. Had Cordelia known Yentin would be at the party? If so, how? Was her intent to catch him unawares and lambast him for his public smear job of her—if that's what it had been? Or had she intended to kill him all along? And if so, why?

Besides replenishing the bread on the table, there wasn't much for Maggie and me to do. A young woman manned the Divine Cuisine table on the other side of the room. I made a mental note to check the kitchen and scan the crowd to see if the lovely Rita was here working the party. I hadn't ruled her out as a suspect.

Maggie star gazed, eyes wide and mouth gaping at each celebrity she spotted. I took the opportunity to slip away. "I'm going to find the restroom."

She nodded, not tearing her eyes away from the mingling guests for fear of missing something.

Before I left, I tapped her on the shoulder. "Maggie, bring it down a notch."

She blinked, finally looking at me. "Am I that obvious?"

I tried not to roll my eyes. "A little bit."

"I'll try," she said, her cheeks turning red, "but it's so exciting being here. Seeing all these movie stars and singers! Tae's not *even* going to believe it!"

I suspected that her boyfriend would be hearing about this party for months to come. The second I stepped away from the table, she scanned the room again, a mesmerized expression on her face. I was happy to see her snap out of it, though, as someone came up to the table and perused the breads. Maggie morphed back to her role as an ambassador for Yeast of Eden, telling the guest about everything on the table.

Despite the costumes that had been worn at Eliza's party, I recognized a few people who had been there. The two women I'd overheard talking about Cordelia were here, still glued to each other's sides. Their eyes traveled the room, and their lips were constantly moving. They were gossiping and telling tales, I thought. Hollywood busybodies.

Camera in hand, I wandered. The majority of the party was happening in the wide-open great room. I stood to one side of the wall of windows overlooking the now-pitch-black backyard. It was a little disconcerting know-ing that, just like at Eliza's, anyone outside could see into the house, but if someone lurked out there, none of us in-side would have a clue about it. A shiver danced over my skin at the idea.

I pushed the thought away and started snapping photos. Cordelia held court over by the baby grand piano, a glass of wine in one hand, her other at her throat as she laughed. For someone who'd been shamed by having her naked figure plastered all over the tabloids, she played it off ex-pertly, looking every bit the It Girl she planned to be again. She'd changed into a slinky red dress that shim-mered in the low light of the room, her blond hair styled to look like Marilyn Monroe's. A server, dressed in black and white, glided up to her, stopping long enough for Cordelia to take a fresh glass of wine. She said something to the server, who moved on. I snapped a few more photos, blurring the background so the sole focus was Cordelia.

As if she sensed me looking at her, she stopped sud-denly and stared through the crowd, her eyes meeting mine. Without breaking eye contact, she said something to the people around her, then weaved her way through the guests, heading straight for me.

I quickly slung the camera strap over my head, swing-ing it behind my arm and out of sight.

"What are you doing?" Cordelia demanded.

"What do you mean?"

She pointed to my side. "You look like a paparazzo with that thing. You can't take pictures in here."

I feigned innocence. "I'm so sorry. I just assumed . . ."

"Assumed what?"

"I was hired to take pictures of Eliza Fox's party. I just assumed you'd want the same thing," I said, leaving enough unsaid to make it sound like it was part of the Yeast of Eden service she'd paid for.

The tinge of anger on her face melted into uncertainty. "Oh—"

"I don't have to," I said.

"Eliza hired you to take pictures?" Cordelia asked, needing to hear it again.

"She did. And she bought them all." I watched her face for a reaction, but if she was afraid she'd been photographed, her expression didn't reveal it. *She's an actress*, I reminded myself.

Another server dressed in black slacks and a white button-down shirt appeared in my peripheral vision carrying a tray of appetizers. Cordelia spotted him and flagged him down. I recognized Zac. Directly behind him and staring at Cordelia was Rita, behind Rita was Renee Ransom in her wheelchair, and behind Renee, passing by, head down, was a man who looked an awful lot like Brad McAvoy.

What the . . . Why would Eliza's husband be at Cordelia Knight's holiday party, especially after the estranged couple had just begun mending their relationship?

I peered, trying to get a better look, but he was too far away, and then, *poof!* He was gone—melted into the crowd. "Was that Brad McAvoy?"

Cordelia looked over her shoulder in the general direction I was pointing. She squinted her eyes, then quickly seemed to think better of letting her skin form wrinkles. Her eyes returned to their natural state. She shrugged nonchalantly. "I didn't invite him, but it's certainly possible."

She crooked her index finger, beckoning to Zac.

Zac quickly turned to say something to either Rita or Renee—or both, since they each nodded—then headed toward Cordelia and me. Rita walked past Zac, heading for the library, where the catered food tables were. Renee stayed put and surveyed the room.

"Hors d'oeuvre?" Zac asked. He held the tray out, balanced on the palm of one hand. It wobbled, and he quickly gripped it with his other hand to hold it steady. I didn't blame him for being nervous talking to Cordelia Knight. The woman was beautiful, and even if Zac was madly in love with Rita, Cordelia was in a different league. I suspected she would make any man tongue-tied.

Cordelia plucked a phyllo triangle from the tray. As she took a bite, crumbs from the thin, crispy pastry cascaded over the bodice of the sparkly red dress. She jumped back, bending forward and holding the appetizer out in front of her to avoid any more flakes. "Are you serious? Why do we have these? They're too messy! These were *not* at Eliza's party!"

Zac's eyes opened wide. "Ummm . . ."

Cordelia flung her half-eaten triangle onto the tray. "Take them back to the kitchen and don't serve any more of them," she ordered, shooing him away. To me, she said, "No more pictures," and then she walked away, her anger melting into a practiced plastic smile. She was like Dr. Jekyll and Mr. Hyde, and from what I could tell, her Mr. Hyde temperament was the stronger, more prevalent one.

Zac, the poor guy, made a beeline for Renee. A moment later, he headed back to the kitchen, tray in hand, and Renee Ransom's gaze tracked Cordelia across the room. I did the same, watching her play hostess as she tipped her head back to laugh at someone's joke, or lightly touched another's arm and gave a sweet smile. The woman was a pro.

On my own again, I scanned the guests, starting when I caught sight of Rita Lewellyn watching Cordelia.

The rest of the evening was uneventful. Rita came and went, refilling trays with appetizers and circulating among the guests. She avoided the bread table, giving Maggie and me a cursory nod and a faint smile the first time she passed.

Zac came into the library, his tray filled with rumaki and stuffed mushrooms. Not a phyllo triangle was in sight. I watched his gaze fall on Rita, but instead of the adoration I'd expected to see, he darted his eyes toward me and sidestepped to avoid her.

"Hey," I said.

He turned his back to the room. "Is she gone?" he asked.

"Who?"

"Rita," he said.

I scanned the room. "She's gone. Why? What happened? Are you fighting?"

"She said she needed space," he said, and now I could see that his eyes were red-rimmed and the upbeat personality I'd seen from him in the past had been replaced with a heavy dose of the morose. "I've been trying to give it to her, but it's kinda hard when we're both working the party. I wouldn't have come, but Renee said I had to if I wanted to keep my job. Ms. Knight wanted the same people here who were at Ms. Fox's party."

It was sweet, how deferential he was to the two starlets. Poor guy was a mess, though. "I'm sorry, Zac. If there's anything I can do . . ."

"Yeah, get her to come back to me," he said, with a sad little laugh.

Just then, Rita walked by holding a tray with several glasses of wine. Instead of her normally confident demeanor, she had her head down. She paused long enough to flip her wrist to glance at her watch, prompting me to do the same. Twelve forty-five. It was almost time to call it a night. Rita continued on, stopping and turning the tray so a woman could take one of the glasses of red. Rita didn't give a sideways glance or any indication she'd even seen Zac and me standing there.

We watched her as she took one of the glasses with white wine and handed it to Cordelia. She'd had a drink in her hand the entire evening. The woman could hold her liquor. It was impressive. Rita passed another one to the man next to Cordelia. She stood there for a moment, watching them.

"What's she waiting for?" Zac muttered. "That guy's nobody. I mean, I don't know who he is, but he's definitely not Spielberg or Ron Howard or Scorsese."

Rita must have come to the same conclusion, because she abruptly turned and walked back to the portable bar at the back of the room to refill her tray with fresh glasses of wine. Zac looked up to the ceiling and blinked. An effort to control his heartbreak. "I don't understand. It's like she's a zombie."

Rita definitely seemed like her mind was elsewhere. Poor Zac.

I gave his arm an encouraging squeeze. "Hang in there. Things have a way of working themselves out."

He nodded, but looked doubtful. "Maybe. I thought about getting her a ring, or maybe some flowers. Still thinking about it."

Ah, youth. A ring was so vastly different from a bouquet of flowers, but to Zac, they were equal. I mentally weighed the two options against each other. Would either of them sway Rita?

"What happened?" I asked.

He gave a heavy sigh. "I don't really know. This morning she said that this was it. Her big break was coming." He hung his head. "I shouldn't't have said it."

"Said what?"

"I told her it was a long shot, but Seattle was a sure thing. She totally freaked out on me. Said I didn't support her, but she was going to make it in Hollywood." He pointed toward her. "Doesn't look like the big break happened."

He was right. Rita looked pale and tired.

The next thirty minutes dragged by. Maggie and I were exhausted. We finally started packing up the leftover bread in disposable trays to leave for Cordelia. Across the room, Renee Ranson directed Rita, Zac, and the other servers to do the same. "Take what's left to the kitchen to be boxed up. Come on, let's get it done. I want to be out of here by two."

They did her bidding. Zac and Rita avoided looking at each other, and they were done breaking down the tables at the same time Maggie and I finished our cleanup. We followed them to the kitchen, avoiding the lingering guests and their end-of-the-night chitter chatter.

"Good party," a woman said.

Her companion looked around. "Where's Cordelia?"

The first woman waved her hand. "Sloshed. Said she needed some fresh air."

"I'll wait, then." The women drifted off while a few other people made their way to the front door without waiting to say good night to their hostess.

It was at that moment that the scream shattered the night. Beside me, Maggie screeched in response. "What was that?!"

I had no idea. I ran through the great room, Maggie hot on my heels. Zac trailed behind us. Rita ran toward us from the kitchen, breathless and pale and pointing to the wall of windows overlooking the backyard. It had been dark outside before, but now it was lit up with stringed lights, the perfectly manicured lawn and flower beds dotted with solar lamps.

I looked in the direction Rita pointed—straight at the glowing water of the swimming pool. A cluster of people gathered on one side. The water churned, as first one, then a second person jumped in, both still fully dressed in their party clothes.

"What's happening?" Renee demanded, wheeling herself next to us. "Why is that bin here? It belongs in the kitchen."

I glanced at the abandoned plastic container, recognizing it as one of ours. Starstruck Maggie must have dropped it. I put it out of my mind, though, quickly refocusing on Rita as she stammered. "I . . . she . . ." Rita's face crumpled. Zac's face melted. Without another thought, he walked over to her and draped his arm around her shoulder, whispering something into her ear as he pulled her close.

She looked at him, her eyes wide with what I could only describe as terror.

"It's going to be okay," Zac said.

Then we all watched in horror as the two men who'd plunged into the water resurfaced, dragging something— no, some*one*—from the water. I clapped my hand over my mouth. Even from where I stood, I could see the shimmering red dress and the blond hair.

The body they'd pulled from the swimming pool was Cordelia Knight.

Chapter 21

Emmaline and her team, including Captain York, showed up a short time later. Once again, the remaining party guests were detained, everyone's statement was taken, and I found myself side by side with my best friend as she contemplated another yuletide murder.

Another déjà vu, and one I could definitely have done without.

"Did you see anything suspicious?" Emmaline asked me.

"You mean anything that made me think a murder was about to happen?" I shook my head. "No. Nothing."

Emmaline swung her arm wide, gesturing toward the row of windows. "There's a clear view of the yard, yet no one saw anything."

"The lights weren't on outside earlier," I said, remembering the gooseflesh on my arms as I'd stood with my back to the windows. Someone *had* been out there, waiting for the opportunity to kill Cordelia Knight.

Emmaline mused aloud. "Why would Cordelia leave her own party to go into the dark backyard? And why did the lights get turned on at all?"

"I did that." We turned to the man who'd spoken. "I needed a smoke. I found the light switches by the door, so I turned 'em on." I noticed a smashed pack of cigarettes in one of his hands. "No need to light up in the dark if there are lights."

That was true enough.

"Tell me what happened," Emmaline said after asking for his name, which she wrote on a fresh page in her narrow pad.

The guy shrugged—not with nonchalance or disinterest, but more like he couldn't quite believe what had happened. "I lit a cigarette, and I was heading to one of the chaise lounges. Never made it that far. I saw something in the pool. No idea what it was at first. But then I bent down to get a closer look and—" That head shake again. "I saw that it was a body. A dead body."

Emmaline led the man away to ask him more questions, communicating to York with a mere glance that he was to finish the conversation she'd been having with me.

"When did you last see Ms. Knight?" York asked.

I closed my eyes against the somber atmosphere, thinking. "It was twelve forty-five," I said.

His eyes thinned to slits. "And you know that how?"

I remembered looking at the time on my phone, omitting the part about Zac and Rita's rift.

York watched me. After a few seconds, he glanced at Maggie. For a split second, my anxiety flared. Maggie and I had been present when two murders had taken place. I knew we were both uninvolved in the crimes, and Emmaline knew it, too, but from the perspective of anyone else on the outside looking in—including York—we were both suspicious characters.

Us, along with the Divine Cuisine crew.

"Anything else?" York asked.

"Not that I can think of. Maggie and I started breaking down our tables."

He repeated the questions to Maggie. Halfway through, her hand found mine. I squeezed it, willing my strength into her. "Can you tell me anything else?" York asked her.

Maggie's eyes pooled with tears. Two murders, one of them of a starlet she'd admired. The girl was barely holding it together. When she spoke, her voice was small. "No."

"Let me know if you think of anything."

As York handed her a business card and started to walk away, I did think of something. "I was able to take a few photos of the guests." I glanced over my shoulder, pointing to where I'd left my camera in its bag. "Not a lot, but some. If that helps."

York stopped. "It might. Let's see them."

I nodded and went back to the library, where I'd left my purse and camera bag behind the table. Maggie followed me and sank into a plush chair, her thumbs immediately flying over the keyboard on her phone. Texting Tae with all the evening's events, I supposed.

I pulled my phone from my purse, using my thumb to activate the screen, ready to send my own text to Miguel. I pulled up my texting app as I slung the strap of my purse over my shoulder and picked up the camera bag.

The unusually light camera bag.

My heart stopped.

I dropped my purse, and it hit the floor with a thud. I unzipped the camera bag, knowing what I'd find before I flipped open the flap. No, no, no.

My extra lens was there, but the camera itself was gone.

I spun around. "Maggie! Did you see anyone near my stuff?"

She looked up, mouth agape. "No, I was with you."

I cupped my hand against my forehead, stunned by the idea that whoever had killed Cordelia Knight had risked stealing my camera so the photos I'd taken couldn't be seen by the police. And they'd been bold enough to do it in plain sight.

Emmaline had returned, and in an instant, she and Captain York were by my side. York was a full head taller than Em, and burly compared to her small stature, but Em exuded the strength and power of her position. She was focused. Two homicides in her town in two weeks wasn't something she was taking lightly. The first was big news because it had happened during an Eliza Fox party. This one was even more high profile. Cordelia Knight may have fallen from Hollywood grace, but she was still a celebrity—and a beautiful one at that.

Edward Yentin's life was as valuable as Cordelia's, but I knew, just as Emmaline did, that the media would expend far more energy covering the latter.

"Camera with photos from the party is missing," York said.

"For how long?" Emmaline asked.

I shrugged helplessly. Maggie and I had been in and out of the kitchen packaging the leftovers, and back and forth to the bread shop's van, loading up our empty containers and table décor. "I'm not sure. Five minutes here, ten minutes there."

"And you didn't see anyone hanging around the area?"

"Just the servers were in here toward the end of the night. People started leaving."

Emmaline looked at Maggie, who stood next to me, wide-eyed. "Did you see anyone?"

"Hanging around the table?" She shook her head. "No."

"It'd be hard to walk away with a camera. Too bulky to easily hide," Captain York said, any animosity he felt toward me put aside. "Canon? Nikon? Sony?"

"Canon," I said. "And you're right, it wouldn't be easy to walk away with it unseen." Yet someone had done just that.

By now, the police had taken statements from the party guests who'd still been here when Cordelia's body was discovered, and they'd also gotten a list of everyone who'd been invited to the soirée. There was no doubt in my mind that the camera, along with the murderer, were long gone. Still, Emmaline directed one of her deputies to conduct a search for it. "Just in case," she said, though from the tone of her voice, I could tell she didn't hold out much hope. To me, she said, "Get Maggie home. We'll talk later."

I read between the lines. We'd be talking about the case in the coming days, and nothing else, because Emmaline was going to be burning the candle at both ends until the murders were solved.

Maggie and I were both quiet on the drive back to Yeast of Eden. The town was dark, a winter chill in the air. "You okay to drive home?" I asked her as I pulled into the parking lot behind Yeast of Eden and into the space next to her car.

"Totally. I'm fine. See you Tuesday," she said, but I could see in her eyes that she was still shaken.

Maggie didn't usually work Saturdays unless it was a special event, and the bread shop was closed Sundays and Mondays. "See you Tuesday," I echoed, watching her as she exited my car and got into her own. I waited until she'd pulled out before I heaved a shaky sigh and headed home myself.

As I lay in bed, tossing and turning, I tried to come up with a motive for Cordelia Knight's murder. She'd been on the top of my list of people with a motive to kill Edward Yentin. Now, though, if I assumed the same person killed both Yentin and Cordelia, she was obviously in the clear of the former. I stuck with that theory because it made the most sense. Two murders with two different murderers, within such a short time frame, was too hard to wrap my head around.

As I fell asleep, my subconscious got to work. I awoke with a start. I still didn't have any other answers, but I realized I hadn't yet told Emmaline my theory about Cordelia and her dirty-hemmed dress. I grabbed my phone and dialed her, glancing at the clock after the line was already ringing. I'd managed to get five hours of sleep. I was pretty sure Emmaline got less than that, since she and York had still been working the crime scene when Maggie and I left.

Just as I expected, Em answered with a tired, yet alert, "Hey, Ivy."

"Hey. Listen. I've been thinking about motive, and I came up with an idea."

"I'm listening."

I charged ahead by posing the question we all wanted answered. "Who would want to kill both the reporter and Cordelia Knight?"

"So far, all we have is the spread Yentin did on Cordelia a few months back. That's a motive for *her* to kill *him*, but it has no bearing on someone else wanting to kill *her*. There is no other common denominator . . . that we've found."

"I thought the same thing. But listen. I didn't have a chance to tell you this yesterday, but *Cordelia was definitely* at *Eliza's party*."

It felt like a bomb dropping, but Em didn't respond with the enthusiasm I'd hoped. Then again, I hadn't really expected her to. "You're sure about that?"

"Ninety-five percent sure," I said, and I told her about the gown going to the dry cleaner's and the photo I'd taken at Eliza's party that captured enough of the dress to convince me it was, indeed, Cordelia.

"I see where you're going with this." Em spoke slowly, processing the information I'd just given her.

"The dirty hem of the dress tells me that Cordelia was outside in that outfit. What if Cordelia *saw* what happened to Yentin—?"

She finished the sentence I'd started. "—and was blackmailing whoever pushed him."

"Exactly."

I heard the rapid *clickity-clack* of Em's fingers against her keyboard. After a few seconds, she cleared her throat.

"So, no one noticed Cordelia was there because she was in costume."

"Maybe she didn't want to be recognized," I suggested. "She seemed to have her own little rivalry going with Eliza."

"She sees Yentin's murder . . . and the murderer. She attempts to blackmail him or her. But why? Why would she do that?" I had no hypothetical answer for that. Em went on. "She throws her own party, with many of the same guests who'd been at Eliza's. Which raises the last question: Why so many of the same guests?"

I snapped my fingers. "What if she wasn't entirely sure *who* the murderer was? They were all in costume, right? So what if it was another chimney sweep, or a caroler who pushed Yentin—but she wasn't sure *which* chimney sweep or *which* caroler?"

"That *could* explain why she invited so many of the same people on the guest list," Em said. "Maybe she thought she could somehow convey that she was on to him—or her—making the killer sweat."

"To flush him or her out."

"The killer couldn't take a chance on Cordelia knowing his or her true identity—"

"So the killer lured Cordelia out to the backyard and killed her. No chance it was an accidental drowning?" I asked.

"Uh, no. Someone whacked her on the head pretty good before she went in the water."

A chill swept through me. Yentin's murder might have been a crime of passion or opportunity. But adding Cordelia's murder to the list meant we had a cold-blooded killer on our hands.

"This theory eliminates a few people," Em said.

Oh, wow, she was right. It knocked several people off the suspect list: John Calvin, Nicole Leonard, and Eliza Fox, to start with. None of them were at Cordelia's party, so unless one of them had snuck into the backyard unseen—which was unlikely, given the height of the fence and the gated community—they were in the clear.

I rubbed my eyes, thinking about this theory, and two new questions surfaced. I rattled them off, one after the other. "Why wouldn't Cordelia have told the police if she witnessed a murder? What was in it for her?"

"She already had fame," Em agreed, "but maybe she had money troubles."

Maybe she did. There were a ton of celebrities who'd blown their millions. Maybe Cordelia Knight had been one of them. For all anyone knew, she may have been up to her eyeballs in debt, and with no new movie roles coming in, resorting to blackmail wasn't such an outlandish idea. Em had the resources to investigate Cordelia Knight's finances, which I knew she would.

"Any sign of my camera?" I asked.

"None," she said.

I hung up, bummed that I'd probably never get my camera back. It was a loss I couldn't afford to replace. I went into the kitchen, Agatha on my heels, put on an apron—a blue-and-white-striped stone-washed linen number that had become my favorite—and got my mind off of things with a little baking.

It manifested in the form of a flaky piecrust. I made the filling for chicken potpies, spooned the hot blend of chicken and vegetables into mini blue cocottes, and topped each one with a layer of dough, crimping it around the edges to give it a nice finish. I created a decorative steam hole in the center of each one. I left two of them on the counter so I could freeze them after the filling cooled, and after applying an egg wash to the other two, I placed them in the preheated oven.

A short while later, Miguel and I sat across from one another at my kitchen table for a late lunch, each of us with a steaming cocotte in front of us.

"Ivy, you have to be careful. Whoever is behind this has killed twice now," Miguel said after I told him about the party the night before, filling him in on all the details of Cordelia Knight's murder.

"All the more reason he—or she—has to be stopped."

He tapped the tines of his fork against the crust, breaking into it. A ribbon of steam curled from the potpie. "Does Emmaline have any suspects?"

"I don't think so, but she has people she can eliminate now," I said. "Three people with pretty strong motives, but who weren't at the party."

"Right. Eliza and her parents," he said.

"Exactly. Even though Cordelia was invited—and apparently went—to Eliza's party, she hadn't reciprocated the invitation. I would have seen her. At least I *think* I would have. No way John Calvin could have gotten past security, plus he would have stood out like a sore thumb. Then there's Nicole. She might have been able to blend in a little bit better than the other two, but she's petite, and whoever hit Cordelia on the head and then pushed her into the pool would have been taller, wouldn't they?"

We dug into our potpies, which had cooled down enough to eat. Miguel nodded after the first bite. "Very tasty, Ivy. The crust . . . mmm."

I was pretty sure my smile stretched from one ear to the other. Miguel was a chef and restauranteur, so praise from him was high praise, indeed.

Agatha's nails clicked against the hardwood floor as she ambled into the kitchen. She lifted her head, and her flat little nose wiggled as she sniffed. "You have to wait, Ags," Miguel said, using the nickname he'd taken to calling her. He leaned over to scratch her head. She looked up at him, blinking, her tongue curling as it slipped in and out of her mouth. I never gave Agatha scraps at the table, and Miguel didn't, either, but he'd started giving her a little something when we cleaned up, and Agatha had come to expect it and wait for him. It was kind of sweet, even if it was a bit of a bad habit.

We finished our meal, cleaned up, and went to the living room. We dimmed the lamp, and the lights on the Christmas tree twinkled. Miguel sat on the end of the couch, and I snuggled up against him. He stretched his arm out behind me, letting his hand come to rest on my shoulder. We sat in a contented silence for a few minutes before he broke it. "I worry that you're involved in all this, Ivy."

Him and me both. The danger of chasing a murderer was visceral and intense—especially when the murderer had no problem killing—twice—just outside a room full of people. "I know."

It was only when I was drifting off to sleep that night that I remembered the man I'd glimpsed in Cordelia Knight's living room. The man I thought might have been Brad McAvoy.

Chapter 22

The next morning, Emmaline and I met up at Cuppa, a new coffee shop a block down from Yeast of Eden. I wrapped my hands around my heavy white mug of steaming pumpkin-spiced latte and waited for her to continue. "Johnette Calvin," Emmaline said. "It took some digging, but we found the article Yentin was working on. You were right about the abuse, but if Yentin's article is true, it wasn't at the hands of her father. Yentin interviewed people who knew Johnette. She ran away because of a family friend.

"I checked her alibi for Friday night. Eliza and Nicole, along with Brad McAvoy, are in the clear. Whoever you saw at the party that looked like Brad? It wasn't him. The three of them had dinner out at Palermo's. Plenty of witnesses there. They spent the rest of the evening at home. Security camera footage confirms the time they returned to Eliza's house. None of them left again after that. None of them killed Cordelia Knight."

"What about John Calvin?" I asked.

"He and his friend—" She flipped open her notepad, turning pages until she found what she was looking for. "—Russ Riddleson—spent most of the evening at the Tap Room. Too drunk to drive. Bartender had to get them a ride share back to their motel, well after time of death. So. All their alibis check out."

"Do you think we could be looking at two different murderers?" I asked, not wanting to believe it.

"Anything's possible," Em said, her expression grim. "But I hope not."

"Any suspects from the party?"

"It's a slow process."

I took that to mean that, no, they didn't have a specific person of interest.

Emmaline headed out to the sheriff's department with a to-go cup of coffee while I stayed put, still sipping my latte. I'd brought along a mystery novel—*Hercule Poirot's Christmas*—to distract myself.

Agatha—the author, not my pup—was the queen of the mystery novel. I was amazed at how she managed to write so many books, each time stumping the reader as to whodunit. It was always someone who flew under the radar. Someone who was least expected.

My mind wandered as I read the familiar story. Someone who was least expected. Assuming the two murders had been committed by the same person, we'd already eliminated the people most likely to have done it. That left only a handful of suspects.

Brad McAvoy. He'd been at Eliza's party—uninvited—and I thought maybe I'd seen him at Cordelia's, but he had an alibi. Unless Eliza was covering for him.

He could have snuck off after their dinner out. It was possible. I wasn't ready to discount him quite yet.

The two gossipy women. I didn't even know their names, but they'd definitely been present at both parties and would certainly be unexpected.

A handful of other guests had been at both parties, but no one with a particularly strong motive.

Maggie and me, of course.

It hit me then, like a fifty-pound bag of flour to the head. Both parties had been catered by Yeast of Eden *and* Renee Ranson's Divine Cuisine. Renee had been at both parties. Zac, the wannabe chef, had been at both. And then there was . . . Rita.

Rita, who happened to look over the cliff and spot Yentin's body.

Rita, who'd come on to Brad McAvoy, only to be shut out—one more humiliation at the hands of Yentin.

Rita, who might have been seen by Cordelia Knight.

Rita, who'd shot hate daggers at Cordelia during the party.

Lovely Rita.

It could explain why Cordelia had elected to have her party catered by Divine Cuisine again, specifically requesting the same crew.

Rita Llewelyn had been at Eliza's party. Yentin had screwed her over, promising her the moon as a result of his tabloid reporting. I'd seen Rita talking to a chimney sweep.

Edward Yentin.

He'd walked away. She'd probably been angry. I posed a few *what-ifs*.

What if Rita had followed Yentin outside, catching him alone while everyone else was distracted by Eliza's descent and speech?

What if Cordelia had seen the whole thing happen?

What if Cordelia had insisted the servers at her party be the same so she could confront Rita? To what end, though? Rita was a server and an aspiring actress. My guess was that she didn't have money, so blackmail couldn't have been the motive.

This led to my next *what-ifs*.

What if Rita had something on *Cordelia*—courtesy of Yentin?

What if Rita had been blackmailing *Cordelia*, and this was Cordelia's chance to stop her?

What if this whole hypothetical scenario was way too far-fetched. It sounded like the plot from a bad movie, not real life.

Still, I called Emmaline, finishing the last drop of my latte before she answered. I cut to the chase. "Did you find any dirt about Cordelia Knight on Yentin's computer?"

"Hang on, I just got here." I heard the *tap tap tap* of her fingers on the keyboard. A minute later, she was back with me. "Checking the report." She fell silent again, and I knew she was reading. Another minute passed before she cleared her throat. "He had quite a lot on Cordelia Knight, actually, including some pretty, um, graphic photographs of her with—"

She broke off, leaving me hanging. "With who?"

"You're not going to believe this." She gave me the name of one of Hollywood's most notorious bad boys.

"You're kidding." She'd been trying to survive one

scandal, but those photos were far from explicit. Another scandal might have done her in.

"Afraid not."

That was more motive for Cordelia to kill Yentin, but it still left the question of who killed Cordelia. I went through my *what-ifs* about Rita with Em, ending with, "There isn't a single shred of evidence, though."

Emmaline's fingers stopped tapping against her keyboard. "Two murders, Ivy. No theory is implausible, evidence or not."

We hung up. Talking it through hadn't given either of us any clarity, but Em was right. We had to consider every possibility.

I went back to my *what-if* theory. Yentin having sex photos of Cordelia would be motive for her to kill him. *What if* that's exactly what she'd done, *what if Rita* saw her, and *what if Rita* had been blackmailing *Cordelia* over it?

Before I could even think about what I was doing— and why—I pulled my phone out, searched up the number for Divine Cuisine, and dialed.

A woman answered. "Divine Cuisine. We're here to make your next event special."

I cut to the chase. "Is this Renee?"

"Who wants to know?"

"It's Ivy Culpepper."

She didn't bother to hide her heavy sigh. "Look, I don't know what you want, but we have another party tomorrow, I'm understaffed, and I don't have time for anything—"

"I won't keep you. I just . . . I keep thinking about what happened to Cordelia Knight. And Edward Yentin, of course. Two parties. Two deaths. And we were there for both of them. I'm a little freaked out by it, if I'm being honest, and, well, I thought you'd understand."

Every word of what I'd just said was a hundred percent true. Renee must have sensed my sincerity because her voice softened. "I've got too much to do to think about it, but yeah, there's been too much death."

My goal in calling was to somehow direct the conversation to Rita Llewelyn. Renee Ranson had done me one better by mentioning the event they had coming up. "You have another party tomorrow? Is it the last one you're catering before Christmas?"

"Yes, thank God. If I have to make another peppermint punch or Yule log, they might as well push *me* over a cliff." She fell silent for a weighted beat, then said, "Geez, I'm sorry. That was in poor taste. I guess it's really getting to me."

"I understand," I said. "Who's the party for? Another celebrity crashing our cozy town?"

"God, no. I also hope I never have to cater one of those again. The pressure to get everything just right is great enough as it is. Add celebrity into the mix, and, God, my blood pressure has been through the roof. Never again."

"I hear you."

"Olaya never seems fazed by anything," Renee said, seeming to forget her rush to get off the phone.

"It's her nature," I said. It was true. Olaya Solis was the picture of serenity.

"Well, it'll never be *my* nature, so I guess I'm screwed. And then there's the young people, who are so unreliable. Something conflicts with their work schedule and, *poof!* They're gone. They leave me high and dry. Rita and Zac are handling the party. I need some Valium."

Renee Ranson was difficult to like, but at the same

time, I knew what she'd been through and where her angst came from. Being the victim of a hit-and-run would certainly change your outlook on life, and your general disposition. Losing an employee during the busiest season of the year didn't make things any better.

She'd opened the door for me, though. "Can I help you with anything?" I asked. "We don't have any more parties to cater, so I'm happy to fill in for you."

"Why would you do that?" she asked, clearly suspicious of my motives.

I couldn't tell her my ulterior motive was to get close to Rita, so I spun a tale, which wasn't completely untrue. "It'll be a good distraction for me. And a good deed for the holidays."

"I'd pay you," she said, making it clear she wasn't going to accept charity.

"Oh, well, sure, if you want to, but like I said, I don't have anything else going on, so . . ."

"I'll pay you," she repeated, then she gave me the details. "You can meet us there. Six thirty on the dot."

"You got it," I said. "I'll see you tomorrow."

Chapter 23

Too many people had expressed their concern over me getting involved in yet another mystery, but I had a hunch and I had to follow it. I glossed over what I was doing, omitting the real reason I was working with Divine Cuisine, saying instead that I was just helping out a friend.

Mrs. Branford narrowed her eyes and peered at me in my black slacks and white shirt when I took Agatha over to her. "Since when is Renee Ranson your friend?" she asked.

"Since we were both present at two different murders. Camaraderie," I said.

"*Pshaw*, Ivy Culpepper. You have something up your sleeve."

I glanced at the sleeves of my coat, feigning innocence. "I don't know what you mean."

"I suspect that by filling in tonight, you hope to glean some information from somebody."

It was like Mrs. Branford lived in my mind, privy to my every thought.

"The question is, who?" she mused.

Most of my thoughts, I amended. "Mrs. Branford, are you feeling all right?" I asked, holding the back of my hand to her forehead.

She pulled away and narrowed her eyes. "Be careful, Ivy. Someone who has killed twice won't hesitate to do it again."

Gooseflesh rose on my skin. She was right, of course. I wasn't being cavalier, and I was well aware that a murderer was out there . . . murdering people. All the more reason to try to stop it from happening again.

"I will," I said, offering a reassuring smile. "I'm always careful."

The party Divine Cuisine was catering wasn't being thrown by a Hollywood type at all, but by a business-woman who wanted to give thanks to the employees who had helped make her IT company a success. In an industry woefully bereft of females, Sarah Battel ran a company that tipped the scales toward the feminine gender.

At six thirty on the dot, I stepped from my car, which I'd parked a street down. I tucked my driver's license and the single car key in one of my back pockets, sliding my cell phone into the other. I walked back to the party's address and stopped at the back of the white Divine Cuisine van. The doors were open, the inside stacked with bins and trays. Someone would be back here any second to direct me.

The van was parked on the driveway of the house, which sat on the outskirts of Bungalow Oasis, a stone's throw from Miguel's street. It was refreshing to see a successful person who chose to stay in a modest house, relatively speaking, rather than move to the Santa Sofia Hills, where the houses were mansions, à la Cordelia Knight.

Sarah Battel's bungalow looked bigger than Miguel's, but like all of the homes in this section of Santa Sofia, it was built into a hill, which gave it multiple levels, and like Miguel's, it had a front deck with views of the Pacific Ocean. This was the trade-off: smaller house than those in the hills, but incredible views that were worth their weight in gold.

Compared to both Eliza and Cordelia's parties, the one in Sarah Battel's house would be much cozier, and also more personal.

And hopefully murder-free.

I breathed in the cold, salty air, bracing myself for the evening ahead. Rita spotted me when she came out from the house. Her eyebrows pinched together. "What are *you* doing here?"

She had no reason to be snooty, and frankly, it puzzled me. *I* was the one thinking *she* might be a murderer, so why was *she* getting attitude with *me*? I debated how nice I should be to her. After all, putting aside the potential that she might have killed two people, she'd also broken Zac's heart. She didn't really deserve my kindness, I decided. "Good to see you, too, Rita," I said, making it clear that it wasn't *actually* good to see her. "I'm helping out Renee at the party tonight."

She frowned. "You know Renee?"

"Oh yeah. She and I, we go way back." Only as far back as when I'd discovered the truth about what had happened to my mother, but Rita didn't need to know what my definition of "way back" was.

Her frown deepened, and it left me wondering why she cared whether I was there or not. She didn't know me from Adam. I was nothing to her. Without another word, she grabbed a plastic bin from the back of the van, hauling it into the garage and then into the house, leaving me alone. I grabbed a random bin, figuring they all were going inside. Serving utensils rattled around inside of it. I traced the path Rita had taken, into the garage and through a door that led to stairs going up to the house.

At the top of the stairs, a figure appeared. I'd expected to see Rita again, but instead, it was Zac. He took the steps two at a time, meeting me in the middle. "Switched teams, I hear," he said with a smile.

"What?"

"Working for Renee now, not the bakery? That's what Rita said."

"Oh. Got it. No, no. I'm just helping out tonight." He was a lot happier than the last time I'd seen him. "How's everything going?" I asked, suspicious that the breakup with Rita was a thing of the past.

"Ivy . . . Ivy, right?"

I nodded, thinking how distracted the guy had been over his love life to not be sure about my name at this point. Especially given the fact that he'd told me all about the ups and downs of his love life. "Right."

"We made up, Rita and me. God, what a roller coaster, but it's all good now. All it took was showing her how much I love her. She knows, and . . . yeah. We're moving to Seattle!"

My smile was forced, but he was too giddy to tell. I wondered how many bouquets of flowers he'd had to buy her to prove his love. "That's great, Zac," I managed. "When do you go?"

"We're leaving tonight, right after the party. Can you believe it? You were right. Things have a way of working themselves out."

Had I really said that? "Wow, that's great," I said again. I sounded like a broken record, but mostly because I didn't know what else to say. If Rita was the murderer, I needed to prove she'd killed Yentin and Cordelia before she and Zac left town. "Is Renee up there?" I asked, using my eyes to point to the door at the top of the stairs.

"Nah," he said as he slid past me. "She's not here."

Maybe she'd taken that Valium and checked out for the night. Before I could ask why, he was out at the van. I continued up the stairs, stopping at the top to get my bearings and see where the kitchen was. The house was similar to Miguel's in that it had a front room with big windows leading to a deck, which overlooked the Pacific. While the bedrooms in Miguel's house were on one side, with the kitchen in the middle and a sunroom in the back, in this home, the bedrooms were in the back. A renovation had been done, removing a wall so that the kitchen was part of the main living space in one expansive room. The front windows revealed the stairs leading up to the front door. This place was *not* wheelchair-accessible. That explained Renee's absence—and probably contributed to her angst yesterday.

"Right here," a woman called, waving me over. She was dressed in a pine green wraparound dress, had her dark hair pulled up into a bun, and wore a sparkly Christmas tree pin. Rita was in the living room at a draped table, setting appetizers on structures of varying heights. This was a technique Olaya used, too. Height added interest to the presentation of the food.

"I'm Sarah," the woman said, drawing my attention back to her. "Sarah Battel."

"Ivy Culpepper," I said as I looked around. "You have a beautiful house."

Sarah beamed. "Aw, thank you. It is great. A treasure."

Rita cleared her throat. "Uh, we have a lot to do. Ivy, start on the cheeseball," Rita ordered. "It's in the refrigerator."

In light of Renee's absence, it sounded like Rita was in charge. "Nice to meet you," I said to Sarah before washing my hands and getting to work. The cheeseball in question wasn't a ball at all, but a cheeseball mixture shaped in the form of a Christmas tree. Chopped parsley mimicked the pine needles, cherry tomatoes were the ornaments, slivered almonds created a garland ringing the tree, and a yellow star topper had been cut out of a bell pepper. It was stunning and so festive.

I arranged it on a square tray, laying a variety of crackers around the base of it. Rita told me where to place it, and I waited for further instructions. "You can make the punch," she said, indicating the sleek glass punch bowl sitting on its own small square table. "The recipe's right there."

I spotted the card tucked under one of the heavy footed glasses, the angular shape matching that of the punch bowl. Zac carried a brown box filled with clanking bottles. "Here you go," he said, setting the box on the floor next to the punch table.

He left me to it, going to Rita. "What's next, boss?"

She pointed to another tray of appetizers on the counter in the kitchen. Sarah had disappeared. "Is it just the three of us?" I asked.

Zac carried the tray to Rita, holding it while she transferred the stuffed mushrooms, which must be one of Renee's standard offerings, to the decorative plates. "Yep," Zac responded.

As the one in charge for the evening, that meant Rita would be scurrying to and fro. I hoped I had a chance to finagle some conversation out of her, or better yet, a confession.

Rita jutted her chin toward the box of bottles in front of me. "They're all chilled. We'll add the ice when the first guest arrives." She pulled her phone from her back pocket and checked the time. "Which is in about thirty minutes."

I mixed the ingredients right into the bowl, starting with cranberry juice, two bottles of dry Prosecco, two cups of apple cider, diet ginger ale, and finished with one and a half cups of dark rum. I stirred it all together, feeling halfway drunk just by proximity. I decided I'd save the cranberries and orange slices, which were already cut and waiting in a plastic baggie, until after the ice was added. I put the empty containers back into the box and carried it straight down to the garage, setting it in the back of the Divine Cuisine van. If Renee was anything like Olaya, she would insist that all party trash be disposed of away from the event, which meant back at the dumpster at Divine Cuisine's kitchen.

Zac came up to the van carrying a stack of trays and the utensil bin I'd taken up, now empty. "Anything else to put in here before I move the van?"

"Not that I know of," I said.

He deposited his armload and closed the doors. "Be right back, then," he said, climbing into the driver's seat.

"Zac," I said, stopping him before he closed the door. He looked at me, all wide-eyed and happy. I gulped. I didn't want to be the one to spoil his happiness. "Nothing," I said, and waved him off. "Never mind."

Back upstairs, Rita stood at the sink, cleaning everything up before the guests started arriving. "Can I do anything else?" I asked her, glad to catch her alone.

"It's under control," she said. "Your job is to make sure the plates remain full. We're only doing heavy appetizers, so just be on top of it."

"Got it." I cleared my throat, ready to broach the subject I'd come here to discuss, but I started with an easier topic. "I hear you and Zac are heading to Seattle soon."

She sighed, looking none too pleased with the prospect. Maybe things weren't quite as rosy in Rita's world as they were in Zac's. "That's right."

"Seattle's a beautiful city."

"It rains all the time," she grumbled, "and it's so far from Los Angeles. I said I'd give it a try, but I don't know."

"So, you guys might come back if you don't like it?"

She mashed her thin lips together until her deep red lipstick was a single line slashing across her face, and she shrugged. "I might. We'll see."

Poor Zac. He thought Rita was committed. The truth was, she was anything but. "Hard to be discovered up there," I said. "If you want to be an actor, I mean."

She narrowed her eyes as she looked at me, not an ounce of uncertainty in them. "Oh, I'm *going* to be an actor."

"Good for you. Chase those dreams." Now was as good a time as any. "Did you know Edward Yentin? He would have been a good person to know, I bet."

"A good person? Hardly." She scoffed. "That guy was the worst."

Sarah appeared, her lips freshly painted with cranberry-red lipstick. "Are you talking about that reporter who died?"

"Yes," I said quickly before Rita could try to shut down the conversation. I moved my finger between Rita and me. "We were both there. *And* at Cordelia Knight's when she was . . . *found*."

Rita turned her back to us. Sarah's hand flew to her neck, and she chuckled nervously. "I hope you didn't bring that bad luck with you."

"Oh no. Don't worry. The police are closing in," I said, fudging the truth.

At this, Rita's head shot up, and her posture went rigid. "They are? Who do they think did it?"

Was that guilt causing her to worry? "I'm not part of the police, so I couldn't really say. All I know is that they found some interesting things on the man's computer."

Rita quickly dipped her head, focusing on rearranging the food on one of the trays. "What kind of things?" she asked, trying to sound nonchalant.

Before I could answer, the doorbell rang. Sarah clasped her hands together, her lips spreading into a wide smile. "And so it begins. Let's *icksnay* the *urdermay*, okay? Is everything ready?"

"Ready," Rita said.

"I'll just add the ice to the punch," I said, hurrying to the freezer. I took out a bowl that had been filled with nugget cubes, quickly sliding them into the punch bowl, finishing the whole thing off by pouring in the cranberries and laying the orange slices on the top.

Sarah had been waiting with her hand on the doorknob. I nodded to her, and she opened it, greeting her first guests with hugs and cheek kisses. "Welcome! Come in, come in!"

Rita and I stood in the kitchen, politely out of the way, while Sarah showed her employees the punch table, the soda and beer station next to it, and the appetizers. "Help yourself. There's plenty!" She picked up a remote, and the next second holiday tunes played from invisible speakers.

A party of all women, excepting Zac, had a completely different vibe than a coed event. Sarah's guests had all dressed up, looking ready for the theater or a reception to greet the queen of England, but they were relaxed, less concerned with exuding any sexuality. It was as if the pressure was off them. They sipped their punch. Zac stood at the beer table, pouring Heineken into frosty beer glasses, and cherry sparkling water from a can into a punch glass for one of the teetotalers.

The chatter started low, but as more punch was drunk and more hors d'oeuvres eaten, the laughter and the voices grew louder. Rita and I stayed busy refilling the appetizer trays, picking up discarded plates and napkins, and rinsing off dishes in the kitchen. "Renee likes to have things cleaned as we go," Rita said, her voice low. She rinsed the last plate, and I dried it, setting it onto the stack on the counter. "We'll consolidate the appetizers in a little while, then put out the desserts."

My eyebrows went up, and my stomach grumbled. I hadn't been hungry before coming to the party, but all this food was too tempting, and I could never say no to dessert. When we consolidated, I made a mental plan to sneak a few of the mushrooms and the saucy meatballs to tide me over.

Rita turned and leaned against the counter, wringing a

dish towel between her hands. "Who do the police suspect?" she asked, still trying to sound casual and unconcerned.

"What?" I asked, knowing perfectly well what she was asking, but wanting to make her sweat just a little.

"For the murder of Yentin. Who do the police suspect?"

I looked at her coolly, but felt like I was playing with fire. "Gosh, Rita. I mean, I'm best friends with the sheriff, but I can't really break that confidence."

She tilted her head as she looked at me, like she was trying to read between the lines of what I'd said. The towel still twisted in her grip. "But they have someone."

"What do you mean?" I asked.

"You know. They have someone they think did it."

The smile I gave her was crafty. "They do have someone they think did it."

Her shoulders slumped, and she exhaled, the tension she'd been carrying practically evaporating. "Oh God, good. Good. I'm so glad. It's scary to even walk to your car, you know? Two murders at two parties, and I was at them both. I can't even wrap my head around that."

I studied her, the thought that this wasn't something a killer would say going through my mind. She really *did* seem relieved. Was I completely off base in thinking Rita might be involved in the murders?

My head swam with the possibilities I'd worked through in my head—everything that had led me to believe Rita Llewelyn might have been the one to push Yentin from the cliff, and to clobber Cordelia Knight before shoving her into the pool. But now . . .

She had been planning to go with Zac to Seattle, but she'd backed away from the plan before Cordelia Knight's

party. That led me to the idea that Cordelia had killed
Yentin and Rita was blackmailing her. Now, with Cor-
delia no longer on the hook, Rita had reconciled with
Zac.

Why?

If Cordelia *was* guilty and Rita *had* been blackmailing
her, why would she then turn around and kill Cordelia?
That made no sense. She'd have cut off her blackmail
revenue.

I looked at her again. Her pallid skin, twitchy eyes,
and the shift from her stiff back to her now-hunched
shoulders. She was truly scared, not guilty of murder.
Maybe not even guilty of blackmail. My words came
slowly as I said, "Rita, do you know who killed Edward
Yentin and Cordelia Knight?"

Her brown eyes grew round, and her brows lifted.
"How would *I* know that?" She'd tried to infuse a touch
of indignity into the question, but her chin quivered.

"Did you see something?"

She darted a worried glance over her shoulder. Looking for . . . who? Zac? Oh my God, could *Zac* be behind
this? After all, Yentin had derailed his future with Rita.
Revenge was a pretty good motive for murder. I leaned
forward, laying my hand on her forearm. "Does Zac have
anything—"

She jerked away. "Are you crazy?" Her gaze darted to
the party guests for a second. She lowered her voice. "No
way!"

"Okay, then what?" I asked, surprised at her vehe-
mence. It spoke to her having real feelings for Zac. For
such young people, these two had a complicated relationship.

She looked around again, skittish. "I could get fired."

I drew an *X* across my chest. "I won't tell Renee."

Zac was suddenly behind me. "Won't tell Renee what?"

Rita looked from me to him. "About the note," she whispered.

"Ohhh." Zac skirted around me to stand next to Rita, gently laying his hand on her back. His devotion to her was touching. Maybe her dreams of stardom would fade once they were in Seattle and away from the lure of Hollywood. Maybe her love for Zac would bloom.

"Someone left a note under the windshield wiper of Rita's car the day of Cordelia Knight's party," Zac said.

I hadn't expected this. "What did it say?"

They looked at each other. After Zac gave her a reassuring nod, she retrieved her string backpack from the cupboard where Sarah had told us to stash our things. She dug inside, her hand reemerging with a folded sheet of paper.

I reached for it, but she didn't release her hold on it. One more look at Zac. One more nod of reassurance from him. Only then did she hand it over.

The paper was from a midsized notepad. Unlined. I opened it up and saw the seashell logo for the Sea Shell Inn, one of the motels across from the beach. The one John Calvin and his friend were staying at.

Leave the back gate open, and don't say a word.

"Referring to the back door at Cordelia's house?" I asked. I'd thought it would have been impossible for someone from the outside to have made their way into the party unobserved. They couldn't have been there undetected, unless . . . unless they'd come in through the inaccessible back entrance.

Which, it seemed, was exactly what had happened.

"The police, they don't know about the note?"

Rita shook her head, her hands nervously clasping and unclasping in front of her. "I-I was too scared. I *am* too scared." Her voice dropped to a low whisper. "There's more."

"You can tell me," I said.

Rita sucked in a stabilizing breath before spitting it out. "There was also a baggie with a syringe and directions on a sticky note. It said—" She gulped, closing her eyes against the memory. "It said to put it in a drink and give it to Cordelia at precisely twelve forty-five."

Oh God. "It said that? *Precisely* at twelve forty-five?" The memory of seeing Rita check her watch before handing Cordelia a glass of wine came back to me.

Another memory. I'd overheard the women at the end of the party saying Cordelia was sloshed. From my observations, she'd held her liquor. That meant whatever Rita had given her had to have dulled Cordelia's senses enough that she couldn't fight off her attacker.

Rita wasn't guilty of murder, but she'd been lassoed into being an accomplice. I placed my hand on hers, quieting it, giving it a squeeze. "You need to give that note to the authorities," I said. "And you need to tell them the truth. You're withholding evidence."

Rita's lower lip trembled. "But I gave her something, and she died! Will they send me to jail? I c-can't—"

I squeezed her hands again. "Rita, you have to tell the police what you know."

She looked at me, nothing more than a terrified girl. "I d-did it. I undid the latch on the gate. But I swear, I didn't know someone was going to kill her!"

Sarah poked her head over the wide island. "Everything okay in there?"

Rita turned her back so Sarah wouldn't see her glassy eyes. My mind raced with Rita's bombshell. Only Zac had the wherewithal to answer. "Sorry, yes, ma'am. Everything's fine."

Sarah hesitated for a moment before saying, "Okay, then. Well, that delicious punch needs refilling."

Chapter 24

I left Zac and Rita to finish the cleanup and left, but not before filling a holiday paper plate with the stuffed mushrooms and meatballs I'd been pining for. I pulled my coat tight around me, bracing myself against the chill wind that had picked up. Finally, it was beginning to feel like December.

I ate as I drove, trying, unsuccessfully, not to spill on my white button-down blouse. A bit of spot treatment was definitely going to be necessary. I made three calls on my way, using the Fiat's handsfree system. The first was a message for Miguel, telling him where I was going. The second was to Mrs. Branford, giving her voice mail the same information and letting her know I'd be a little later than I'd planned picking up Agatha. The third, and most important at the moment, was to Emmaline. She *also* didn't answer, so I left a message for her, then decided to make a fourth call, this one to Captain York. Someone in authority needed to know about the note.

The deputy who answered the phone at the sheriff's station informed me that Captain York was not in. She directed me to his voice mail. I was *O* for four with my phone call outreach. "Captain York, hi. It's Ivy. *Erm*, Ivy Culpepper. I have some, uh, new . . ." I trailed off. Did I really want to give him my thought process over voice mail? I decided at the last second that, no, I really didn't. Emmaline trusted me. She'd call me back and want every last detail. York, on the other hand, was a different story. If I told him what I thought had happened, he'd most likely tell me to back off.

"Talk to Rita Llewelyn," I said. "She's one of the servers. She has critical information." One thing about the note left for Rita was the straight arrow it pointed to the Sea Shell Inn. John Calvin had an alibi, though, and surely he wasn't stupid enough to leave a bread crumb leading straight to him.

Was he?

I ate a meatball, catching a dribble of sauce before it dropped onto my shirt, and headed straight for the up-scale motel.

Once I got there, I realized I didn't know what room Calvin was staying in. The Sea Shell Inn was on the very nice end on the motel spectrum, but it was still a motel, which meant the front office was open twenty-four hours a day.

"Hey!" I said, making my voice bubbly and my smile big.

I passed a rack of brochures and information cards on all the touristy things to do in and around Santa Sofia. A vending machine with sodas stood next to one full of sweet and savory snacks ranging from Oreos and Snickers bars to Funyuns and Fritos.

The young man at the front desk looked up from his cell phone as I approached. "Help you?"

I gave a huge sigh. "Oh my gosh, I hope so. I'm looking for my friend. John Calvin? I know he told me he was staying here, but I can't remember his room number."

The man raised his eyebrows. "Oh yeah?"

"Yeah. Is there any way you can look him up and—"

"Nope. Sorry. Can't give out personal information about our guests."

"Oh." My smile faded "That's too bad. I . . . um . . ."

"You can sit here and wait if you want, but I can tell you this. I saw him drive outta here 'bout an hour ago. Two men in a mom-mobile. Can't help but notice 'em. No idea when they'll be back."

The information wasn't exactly helpful. I looked around to see if a random notepad with the motel's branded logo sat around, there for the taking.

I didn't see one.

I thanked the man and left. Back in my car, I considered the options. Where would John Calvin be? At Eliza's house, once again trying to ingratiate himself into her life? Arguing with the mother of his child somewhere? Or would he be back at the Tap Room?

I went with the latter, driving the two miles from the motel to the bar. The parking lot was dotted with only a few vehicles, and right there, front and center, was the minivan John Calvin was tooling around town in. I hit my palm against the steering wheel, victoriously. "Yes!"

Before going inside, I sent another flurry of texts. John Calvin had been at Eliza's party, even if he wasn't at Cordelia's. It was always possible there *were* two murderers, and that he'd done in Edward Yentin. Either way, I wanted people to know where I was.

After hitting Send on the last message, I locked my car, zipped up my jacket, and headed across the dark parking lot. The place definitely needed more lighting for pitch-black nights. I'd never been inside the Tap Room. It was a typical low-rent bar with a long counter running along the left side of the space, bottles of every type of alcohol under the sun on the counter behind the bar, the top-shelf liquor on wood shelves mounted to the wall. Classic rock played in the background, loud enough to hear but not so loud you had to raise your voice to talk over it.

There were more people inside than there were cars in the lot, not surprising since people often came in pairs or groups, but still, for a weekend, it was a slow night. I spotted John Calvin and his friend, Russ Riddleson, right away. They sat at the bar, in the exact same position— forearms resting against the thick beveled edge of the wood counter, hands cupped around bottles of beer, eyes staring blankly at the television set mounted in the corner at the ceiling.

I slid onto the stool next to John. "Hey, Mr. Calvin. Remember me?"

He tore his gaze away from the basketball game to look at me. Recognition landed on his face, and he frowned, not at all pleased to see me. "How could I forget?"

I couldn't blame him for his feelings. I'd kept him from seeing his daughter. If I were him, I wouldn't want to see me, either. "Mr. Calvin, I'm going to come straight out with it. Someone wrote a note on Sea Shell Inn stationery. I think that person killed Cordelia Knight. I'm wondering if you know who it was?"

His gaze flicked to the screen, but there was a commercial break. "What are you talking about?" he asked.

Russ leaned forward enough to look at me. "What note?"

"One of the caterers received a note. It's written on Sea Shell Inn notepaper."

"What's it say?" John asked.

"Doesn't matter," I said, pretty sure Emmaline wouldn't want me spreading around that information. Talking about the note at all was pushing it.

"You think whoever wrote it is a killer. And you're here." John's eyes narrowed as he looked at me. "What, you think because I'm staying there that *I* wrote it? You think *I* killed those people?"

"Captain York said you have an alibi. That you were right here when Cordelia Knight died."

"Damn straight," Russ said. "We were right here drinking Johnny's sorrows away."

We sat in silence for a moment before Russ flagged down the bartender, who sauntered over. "Shot of Cuervo," Russ said.

"Make it two," John said.

Russ flashed John a look that I couldn't read.

The bartender sauntered over, poured the shots, collected the cash from both men, and tapped one of the quarters Calvin slid to the edge of the bar with a nod before wandering away again. Asking the next question in my mind felt bold, but I was here and I couldn't *not* ask it. "Did Edward Yentin come to see you?"

Russ threw back his tequila. John held on to his shot glass with both hands, staring into the gold liquid. For a second, I thought he was blowing me off, our little chat over, but then he spoke. "He showed up one day at my house. Just showed up. He told me he was doing a story on my daughter. I told him to get lost."

"What was the story about?" I asked.

"The life and times of Johnette Calvin," he said with a sneer.

"About why she left?" I pressed.

"Yep, about that. About me. About her mother leaving. About her *assistant*—"

He left the word hanging there, laced with the same derision he'd had when he and Nicole had argued at the beach lot.

"Is that what brought you here? To see Eliza and tell her about the article?" I asked.

John closed his eyes for a beat. "She needed to know the truth. She *needs* to know, but she won't see me."

"What truth, Mr. Calvin?" I asked. "About Nicole?"

He stared at the TV, his lips stretching and twisting with his pent-up emotions. Finally, he said, "She's not who she says she is."

"I know," I said.

At that, he turned to face me. "Then you know I don't trust her. That guy Yentin, he found out who she really is. I'm worried for Johnette."

I felt like the Grinch in that moment, my sympathy for John Calvin growing three sizes, my doubts about him starting to dissolve. He seemed to care about his daughter, and I began to wonder if I'd misinterpreted what Eliza had said about her childhood.

Russ held up his shot glass. Three seconds later, the bartender had poured him another shot of Cuervo. I could see why they'd needed a ride share back to the motel. "Listen," I said. "I know you saw me at the beach the other day. I didn't meant to intrude."

He shrugged, pushing his still-full shot glass away and taking a swig from his beer bottle. He peered at the bottle as if just realizing it was nearly empty. He lifted it up, catching the bartender's eye again. The guy nodded, and two fresh bottles appeared, one for John and one for Russ. "Anything for you?" the man asked me for the first time. About time. I asked for a glass of water, which he promptly gave me—along with a frown—before wandering off again.

John took a healthy drink of his beer.

"Have you seen Eliza's mother since then?"

John blinked as he shifted his gaze from the TV to me. "What?"

"Have you seen her?"

John just shook his head.

Russ scoffed, then took a long swallow from his beer bottle, but John looked curious. Thoughtful, almost. "My mother came up with the name Johnette. She thought it'd be cute. Like John Jr. If she'd been a boy. A girl named for her father, that's what she said." He shook his head sadly. "She passed before Johnette ran away. Thank God for that, because it would have killed her."

"She hasn't been Johnette for a long time," I said softly.

"I know that, but she'll always be Johnette to me."

"How old was she when she ran away?"

"Sixteen," John said.

"Way too young," Russ said with a shake of his head.

"Do you know why she left?" I asked, wanting to know just how attuned to his daughter John had been.

"Do you?" he shot out.

"I have a pretty good idea."

He scrubbed his face with his hand and drew in a breath. "I'm not stupid. She was—*is*—a beautiful girl. She got a lot of unwanted attention, and if you want the ugly truth, it was my fault. I let things happen . . ."

Russ patted John's shoulder. "It's okay, man. You're tryin'."

John shook off Russ's hand. "No man, it's not okay. A father's supposed to take care of his kids. Be their protector. I wasn't that for Johnette."

"You're tryin' to be there now. She just won't let you."

John turned to Russ. "It's still my fault. I don't get a pass because she's still too pissed at me."

They both turned back to the TV, but Russ said, "Maybe not, but you are tryin'. You're going through the steps. Whether or not she wants to hear what you have to say is up to her. You can't control that."

Russ was right. We could only control our own thoughts and actions, not anyone else's.

John had his elbow propped on the bar, his hand cupped over his chin. "I had a drug problem," he confessed.

Hence the steps. His encounter with Edward Yentin was only part of why he was trying to see Eliza. He also wanted to make amends. I eyed his beer bottle, still half full. He hadn't touched his tequila.

"But you're clean now?" I asked, hoping the situation with Nicole and Eliza wasn't driving him to excessive drinking. That could be a slippery slope back to addiction.

He nodded. "I don't touch the hard stuff anymore."

"That's huge," I said. "Congratulations. Really. It's a great accomplishment."

He just grimaced. "It's a pretty hollow victory."

"She's angry," I said. "Whatever happened back then, it affected her."

John peered at the television, but I could tell he wasn't focused on the game. "Of course it did. Things were bad for her."

"It could have been worse," Russ said.

"What do you mean?" I asked.

Russ spun on his stool to face me. "There were some bad people in and out back then. Some of 'em—let's just say they didn't care how old Johnette was. She did the right thing, getting away before it was too late."

"You were there?"

Russ shook his head. "Nah. Not back then."

"Russ helped me get clean," John said.

The two men sat side by side. They didn't look at each other, but I sensed the support one provided the other.

"I did my best with her," John said, "but I was messed up most of the time, so you know, my best wasn't really good enough."

I read between the lines. The unsavory men who'd been in John Calvin's orbit back then had put Eliza at risk. John had never been father of the year to Eliza, but he was here now, trying to make things right. All he could do was ask Eliza—Johnette—for forgiveness. That didn't mean she would forget. It didn't mean she had to tell him what he did was okay. It didn't even mean they could ever have a normal relationship. But if Eliza could forgive her father, it would bring them back to net zero. Maybe that would mean they'd never see each other again. Or maybe it would begin the path to healing, for both of them.

I cupped my hand around my tall glass. "What about Eliza's mother?"

John glanced around the bar, his gaze skimming over each of the other customers there. I expected him to reveal something important about Nicole, but he came back to me and said simply, "What about her?"

"I'm sure there are lots of ill feelings, but for Eliza's sake . . ." I said, remembering both his and Nicole's animosity for one another when I'd last seen them together.

"Ill feelings? You mean like the fact that she left her newborn daughter?"

"Yeah," I said. "Like that."

"She was the cutest little thing, you know?" He kept his eyes straight ahead. "Flyaway blond hair just like her mother's. She *lived* in a blue dress and red sparkly shoes till she was almost ten years old. I couldn't get her out of them." His smile turned melancholy. "About the time she outgrew the Dorothy phase is when she started blaming me, like it was my fault her mother left." He swung his head to look at me. "I didn't push her away. She couldn't handle a newborn. It wasn't like I was ready, either. We didn't plan the pregnancy. Young and stupid. It's a thing. But listen. I might not have been a good father back then, but *I* didn't leave Johnette."

Whether or not he left was debatable. Some people might consider slipping into a drugged-out stupor its own type of abandonment.

I started to get up, but sat back down when John pulled his cell phone from his back pocket. "We were happy once, you know. I didn't push her away." He scrolled until he found what he was looking for, then held the phone out to me. "Tell Johnette—*Eliza*—" he corrected. "Tell her I wanted her mother to stay. I loved her once."

In the photo, John's arm draped around a pregnant woman. His other hand lay on her protruding belly. Her arms hung by her side. It looked like it was taken from across the street. They stood in the shadows of a cluster of tall trees. John's smile split his face, but Eliza's mother wore a frown. I put my hand on John's shoulder. "I'm really sorry," I said again.

"Tell her," he said. "I didn't want her mother to leave us," he said, a tequila-sized dose of emotion tinging his words. "Things might have been different if—" John broke off when Russ turned to look at him. He regrouped. Shoved the shot glass of tequila farther away. "No. I made my own decisions."

If I had the chance to, I'd convey John's regret to Eliza. I believed it to be sincere. A few minutes later, I left John and Russ to their basketball game.

I hadn't even made it to the car when something John said came back to me. I did an about-face and hurried back into the bar. I dropped back onto the stool I'd abandoned a few minutes earlier. "Can I see that photograph again?" I asked.

John didn't question me. He unlocked his phone and with a few swipes, pulled up the picture.

"That's Eliza's . . . er, Johnette's mother?"

He nodded. "She already had doubts. You can see it on her face."

I pinched the screen, letting my fingers splay outward. The quality of the picture was grainy, but I zeroed in on one detail. "You said Eliza has her mother's blond hair."

"That's right."

Which didn't compute. Women often went from brown to blond, but not usually the reverse. Then I noticed something else. The woman stood just a few inches shorter than John. About the same height as Eliza, which raised a red flag. Because Nicole was an inch or two *shorter* than Eliza. My heart climbed to my throat. "About Eliza's mother . . ."

Chapter 25

It's possible to be both surprised and unsurprised by the same thing, I realized. I stared at John as my mind whirled around a new truth.

John stared at me. "What are you saying?"

"Nicole Leonard has been Eliza's assistant for a few years. She just confessed that she's really Eliza's mother."

"Uh-uh. No way." His jaw tightened with anger. "That woman is *not* Belinda."

"You said Edward Yentin showed up on your doorstep. That he knew who Nicole really was. What did you mean?" I asked, flummoxed. Just when I figured one thing out, another question popped up. Nicole Leonard wasn't Eliza's mother. Then, who was she? What had Yentin discovered?

"The guy was a snake. All he said was that he knew who Eliza Fox really was. He said if I paid him, he'd keep the story out of the tabloids." He scoffed. "I don't have that kind of money. If I did, I would have paid. I would have protected Johnette. Better late than never. When I said I couldn't, he said, no problem, that Eliza had been careless, letting some grifter into her inner circle. It didn't take me long to figure out who he meant."

Nicole Leonard.

On my phone, I accessed the photos of Eliza's party that I'd stored in the cloud. I scrolled through them quickly, stopping when I got to the one that showed part of the woman I was sure was Cordelia Knight. It was a strange shot, with reflections from inside showing on the expansive windows overlooking the Pacific. I moved to the next shot, one I'd previously disregarded. A sliver of Cordelia's dress still showed in the corner, but that wasn't what interested me. I enlarged the photo, letting my eyes scan it slowly, looking at every possible detail. In the previous photo, Cordelia's back was turned to the camera. She faced the window, while the few others pictured faced the staircase, where the reflection showed Eliza making her grand entrance.

I tried to focus on the negative space . . . the parts of the dark window that weren't reflecting images from inside. Finally, I saw something. A shadowy figure. That had to be the moment it happened, when everyone was inside and distracted by their hostess descending the stairs and stopping to greet them.

And for whatever reason, possibly so she wasn't recognized, Cordelia Knight had turned the other way, looking out into the darkness.

Looking out at Nicole Leonard. I didn't have proof, but deep down I knew it was. My mind raced. I'd heard the argument between John and Nicole, likening them to divorced parents battling over their shared child. I'd been the one to call Nicole out for her charade. Only her charade wasn't pretending to be Eliza's mother. She'd just glommed on to that because I'd given it to her on a silver platter. No, her charade was being Eliza Fox's right hand, but for what nefarious purpose?

"Did Yentin say anything else?" I asked. "What Nicole was after?"

John scoffed again. "Nope. As soon as he realized I really couldn't pay him, that dude left."

I left John and Russ just as quickly, and a moment later I sped through Santa Sofia, heading straight for Eliza Fox's cliffside house. I tried Emmaline again, expecting to leave another message. Instead, she answered with a clipped, "I got your message. What's going on?"

"Nicole Leonard is not Eliza's mother."

"I know. York's on his way to Eliza's house now."

My exhale shot out like air from a popped balloon. With John Calvin's help, I'd zeroed in on Nicole, and now Emmaline had drawn a heavy black line under the woman's name.

"Ivy, let him handle it," Em said.

I *would* let him handle it, but that didn't mean I couldn't play a part. Emmaline knew that better than anyone. "Eliza could be in trouble," I said, running through the most plausible scenario. If Cordelia had witnessed Nicole shoving Edward Yentin to his death and had tried to blackmail her, *that* was certainly motive for Nicole to get rid of *that* loose end, too. She'd figured out where John Calvin was staying. From there, it couldn't have been too hard to acquire a random sheet of paper from a Sea Shell Inn notepad. If she'd intended to frame John Calvin for

Cordelia's murder, it was a lame attempt. She couldn't scrub away his alibi.

"Ivy."

I heard Em's voice, but my mind was occupied. I moved on to *Nicole's* alibi for the night Cordelia had been killed. She was seen coming home with Eliza, and supposedly stayed there, but Brad had been there, too, which meant it was likely they hadn't been *with* each other the entire time. While Brad and Eliza continued to mend their marriage, Nicole had been on her own. If she'd premeditated Cordelia's murder, which the note left on Rita's car indicated, she also could have stashed her car somewhere accessible by foot from the house. She'd lived there with Eliza long enough to know the property and how to get in and out without being seen. She could have slipped out, crept through the back gate Rita had left open at Cordelia's property, and then what?

"Ivy?"

She had to have been in contact with Cordelia. Em would have to find proof of that through phone records. I assumed the two women had agreed to meet at a certain time outside, away from the party—a rendezvous for one of Nicole's blackmail payments?

At just after twelve forty-five.

"Ivy!"

I snapped back to the moment and to Emmaline's voice in my ear. "Sorry, sorry," I said quickly, then, "I'm sending you a photo. Look past the reflections. I think it's Nicole."

I heard her saying something as I hung up, but I was already pulling over. Pulling up the photo in question, sending it to Emmaline's county email address.

Another thought occurred to me as I sped off again. If she'd been willing to steal my camera, Nicole must have feared I'd unwittingly photographed her at Cordelia's party. I tried to picture the various guests I'd seen throughout the night at Cordelia Knight's house, as well as the ones I'd photographed. If she'd been inside, she'd blended in. The image of a server walking through the library dressed in black and white popped into my head. It hadn't been Rita or Zac, or the other two familiar faces Renee had had working for Divine Cuisine that night. It hadn't occurred to me at the time to wonder who it was. I called up the memory, looking at it frame by frame in my mind. And then I remembered. She'd kept her head down as she'd carried a bin from the library.

The bin.

The abandoned catering bin we'd seen just after Cordelia's body was discovered. Nicole had dressed in black and white, just like the servers. If anyone had seen her in the backyard or the house, she would simply have appeared to be one of Renee's people. Carrying a bin through the house at the end of the evening wouldn't have raised any red flags, either. She was on cleanup duty. She had to have spotted me taking pictures. Getting ahold of my camera was a calculated risk—and one she must have felt was worth taking. She'd used the bin to ferry it out of the library without raising suspicions.

I had to slow down as the road up to Eliza's house started to curve, but my heart hammered in my chest. In my gut, I didn't think Eliza was in any danger, but who was to say what Nicole would or wouldn't do if she felt cornered?

There was no sign of Captain York's county vehicle,

but the gate was wide open—again. Eliza really needed to use her security system, although in this moment, I was glad she didn't. I pulled in and parked in the same spot John Calvin had parked his minivan rental a few days ago. I gripped the steering wheel for a moment and took a deep breath. What was my plan? If I was right, Nicole was a murderer, twice over. She was also a liar. I ached for Eliza. What would it do to her to learn this woman, whoever she was, had been pretending to be someone she wasn't, first as her assistant, and now as her mother? And what would Nicole do when she realized the jig was up?

I didn't have a grand plan, but I went ahead and left the safety of my car. York was on his way—God knows from where—but I knew he'd be here. My only goal, I realized, was to be here for Eliza, because, just as Mrs. Branford had told me, she was going to need a friend when the truth came out.

My knock on the door went unanswered. I tried again, shifting from one foot to the other as I waited. Finally, after the third try, the door flung open. Nicole stood there, her glasses hanging from her beaded lanyard. "Ivy." She glanced down at the daily planner she held, which rested on top of a slim computer. "We weren't expecting you, were we?" Her tone revealed a thread of tension— whether at the precarious situation she was in, or at me, for inadvertently forcing the *mother* card on her, I didn't know.

I smiled. "No, no. I just . . . I was in the neighborhood, so I thought I'd stop by."

"Eliza's busy," she said, probably picking up on the lie. The house was well off the beaten track, so there was no way I'd actually *been* in the neighborhood.

"I won't stay long." And hopefully she wouldn't be staying long, either.

The sound of a car's engine floated down the road. I glanced over my shoulder, hoping to spot Captain York, but the driveway was empty.

"Who is it?" Eliza's voice called from the direction of the kitchen.

I stepped into the entry before Nicole could close the door on me. "It's Ivy!"

"Ooo! Come see what I'm doing!"

"She's in the kitchen," Nicole said, clearly put out.

I followed Nicole, keeping my smile pasted on my face. Eliza wore a navy-blue apron heavily dusted with flour, the marks in front of her hips, precisely where she'd been wiping her hands. She was bent over the counter where she worked, biting her lower lip with concentration as she slowly rolled up one of the two chocolate sponge cakes lying on sheets of parchment paper. She glanced up as we entered the kitchen, and her face split into an excited smile. "I'm baking, can you believe it?"

She spoke with the giddy excitement of a child trying a new hobby.

"What are you making?" I asked.

"A Yule log! I'm going for the gusto my first time out of the gate. When I do something, I give it my all."

I laughed. "You certainly do."

Nicole hadn't responded to Eliza's enthusiasm. I turned to see that she had noiselessly exited the room.

"Put your stuff down. Pull up a stool," Eliza said to me.

Without thinking, I headed to the little hallway off the kitchen where Nicole had first had me leave my things. All I had this time was my purse, which I set on the built-in bench. One of the cupboards behind the bench and at the very top was open. Out of habit, I reached up to push it closed, but stopped when I caught a glimpse of a strap.

A camera strap that had a wildflower design on a white background.

My camera strap.

My heart beat double-time. Instead of closing the cupboard door, I opened it wider, took hold of the strap, and pulled, expecting the camera to come with it. It didn't, and I stumbled off balance, quickly righting myself. I stood on my toes and felt deeper into the cabinet. My fingers brushed something hard. I grabbed hold of it and slid it toward the opening. There it was. My camera. I tucked the loose strap under my arm before checking the camera to see if the memory card was still there.

Oh, thank God. It was!

I put the camera in my purse, laying the strap on top, and brought it with me back to the kitchen. "I'll just leave my bag here," I said with a nonchalant shrug, although my heart was pounding. It had been bold and risky for Nicole to walk out of Cordelia's party with my camera and then leave it barely hidden away, but if you'd committed two murders already, filching a Canon didn't seem like such a big deal.

"Sure. Stick it on a chair at the table," Eliza said without a glance. Her focus was fully on her dough.

I'd done that and had scarcely returned to the island where Eliza worked when Nicole came back in, minus her planner and laptop. "Can I make you some tea, Eliza? Ivy?"

Nicole didn't wait for either of us to respond before turning on the electric kettle and taking three mugs out of one of the kitchen cabinets.

"That'd be perfect." She looked up at me with an exaggerated frown. "My stomach's been unsettled lately.
The tea helps."

A red flag shot up in my mind. Surely Nicole wouldn't
be . . . she couldn't be . . . no. I dismissed the idea of poi-
son. There was no reason for it. She didn't know that I
knew she wasn't Eliza's mother. She also didn't know
that I knew Yentin had discovered her game, whatever it
was. Still, my cynicism was on full tilt. I watched Nicole
like a hawk as she took three herbal tea bags from a tin,
placed one in each mug, and poured in the hot water.

Before she could pick up the mugs to deliver them, I'd
jumped from the stool and scurried over to the counter.
"Let me help," I said.

"Thank you." She stepped back so I could choose my
mug.

I selected a red one with white speckles. It was ceramic but shaped like a tin mug. In cursive, it said *Merry
& Bright*.

For Eliza, I chose a taller, narrower red mug that had a
variety of white *Ho Ho Ho*s all over it in varying fonts
and sizes.

That left Nicole with a green speckled camping mug
that had a line drawing of a Christmas tree.

I let the tea steep before taking a sip, watching as Eliza
finished rolling her first sponge, leaving cracks in it along
the way. "It's not working," she grumbled. "The recipe
said it shouldn't crack, and look, here it is cracking
away."

"It's your first attempt," I said, trying to encourage
her, all the while strategizing about taking Nicole down.
If I timed it right, I could get her to confess just as York
busted in. Of course, I had no idea when that would be,

and if he'd burst through the door, like in my imagination—and the movies—or just ring the doorbell. Of course he'd do the latter, I realized.

"I bet you can do this in your sleep," Eliza said, more as a criticism of her own lack of skills as opposed to an endorsement of mine.

"Olaya can, I'm sure. Me? I've never made a *Bûche de Noël*, so nope, no doing it in my sleep."

"What do you do next, darling?" Nicole had moved next to Eliza. She cradled her mug with both hands, her gaze on her daughter's—

My mind jerked to a stop. No, *not* her daughter. Eliza was nothing but a mark to the woman.

"Nicole," I said, deciding then and there that I wasn't going to wait for Captain York. "Where were you living before you found Eliza again?"

Eliza's tongue had poked out from between her lips as she concentrated on slowly rolling the second chocolate sponge. She stopped abruptly at my question, pulling her tongue back in. "Oh yeah, good question," she asked.

Nicole shrugged. "I don't want to talk about that. It feels like a lifetime ago."

Someone else's lifetime, I thought. I looked at them, side by side. Where Eliza's nose was straight and narrow, Nicole's was a button. Eliza had dazzling eyes the color of a bright cerulean sky, while Nicole's were a muddy brown. A collection of freckles danced across Eliza's face. Nicole had a slightly darker, more olive complexion. There was no likeness between them in any way, shape, or form. We saw what we wanted to see, I thought. I'd believed Nicole was Eliza's mother, so I'd disregarded the differences between them.

So, apparently, had Eliza.

My focus on Nicole was intense. It wouldn't be hard for her to discern that I knew the truth. I tilted my head slightly. "All these years, and you never had other children?"

She held my gaze, her mouth in an unyielding line. Ah, so she did realize. "I was intent on finding my daughter."

"But you knew where she was when she was little. Why didn't you go back to her then?" I asked. "I mean, I talked to John. He never wanted you to leave. He would have welcomed you back."

Eliza swung her attention to me, brows pulled together in puzzlement. "You talked to my father?"

"I did." I directed my tight smile at Nicole. "He showed me a picture of you when you were pregnant."

Her muddy eyes seemed to turn darker. She matched my smile. "It's amazing how different a person can look when they've packed on the pregnancy pounds."

"It really is," I agreed. "But those basic things can't change. You know, like hair color and height."

Nicole's jaw tensed, straining the bands in her neck. I didn't ease up. "And why didn't you go back to see your baby? Or maybe when she was a toddler? Or a preteen? Or any time before she ran away?"

Eliza stared at me, her guard down. "Ivy, what are you doing?"

"Tell her the truth, Nicole," I said, at the same time calling up the photograph I'd asked John Calvin to text me before I'd left him and Russ at the Tap Room. I held it up. "*This* is Eliza's mother, Belinda. Not you. *This* woman."

Eliza stared at me, then back at Nicole. Her eyes pooled instantly with confused tears. "Whaat?"

"I saw your dad, Eliza. He showed me this photograph. Nicole is *not* your moth—"

We jumped when Nicole threw her mug toward the sink. The tea splattered as it hit the counter, bouncing off of it and landing in the sleek black-granite sink, breaking into chunky pieces. She bolted, heading toward the back door that led to the garage and side driveway. I dropped my phone on the counter and ran after Nicole. She jerked the door open and was halfway through, but I caught her by the arm.

"The game's up," I said, feeling a little bit like one of the movie detectives Cordelia Knight had played.

Nicole kicked and growled as I dragged her back to the kitchen. She flung her free hand, catching me on the side of my head, but I held fast, managing to grab hold of her other arm. "Eliza. Get me the strap in the top of my purse," I yelled.

Eliza jumped, skittish, but hurried to the chair where I'd stashed my bag. She pulled out the camera strap, waiting for me to direct her. "Wrap it around her wrists," I said.

Eliza's eyes were wide. Terrified. But she complied. The bulky camera strap wouldn't hold Nicole—the woman was far too crafty—but it would help contain her. I could hold on to it easier than her flailing arms.

"Captain York is on his way," I said to Nicole, close to her ear. "You remember him, right?"

It only took her a split second for recognition to show on her face. She growled like a caged animal and suddenly flung her feet out from under her, nearly knocking my hand free of the strap restraining her arms. I managed to hold on and force her down onto one of the chairs.

Eliza spun in a circle, clawing her fingers against her scalp. She stopped suddenly and took off. I heard her rapid footsteps ascend the staircase. She returned a long minute later with what looked to be the belt to a satin robe. I would have preferred a few rolls of duct tape, but it would work in a pinch—or at least until York arrived.

Which I hoped would be soon.

"Don't listen to her, Eliza. She's crazy. I *am* your mother."

Eliza had started to wrap the belt around Nicole's torso and the chair back, but she hesitated.

"Look at the photo," I told her. "I saw your dad just before I came here. The woman in the photo . . . *that's* your mother. Your father wanted her to come back to you both. She might have, but . . . but . . ."

Eliza let the belt drop and grabbed my phone from the counter. "It's locked."

"Bring it here," I said, angling my thumb so I could hold on to Nicole while pressing the Home button to unlock it.

Eliza gasped as she looked at the photo. She clasped one hand to her forehead. "Oh my God. *This* is my mother." Her breath came fast and furious. She was going to start hyperventilating any second, if she wasn't careful.

"Breathe," I said.

She did, then said, "This *is* my mother. I remember my dad showing me this photo when I was little."

Nicole suddenly jerked. She pressed her feet against the ground and tried to stand, sending the chair backward and smack into my chest. My feet came out from under me, and I started to go down, Nicole and the chair on top. "Eliza!"

Eliza dropped the phone and lunged. She grabbed me around the middle, allowing my feet to make purchase with the floor, then she snatched the belt rope as I forced Nicole back onto the chair seat. Eliza wound the belt around Nicole, fastening it into a knot, then looped the tails around one of the back rails, knotting it again to keep Nicole and the chair connected.

Once Nicole was halfway secure, Eliza scurried around the island, coming back wielding a heavy walnut rolling pin. "Who are you?" she ground out through clenched teeth.

Nicole's face had turned beet red, her eyes dark with fury. She clamped her mouth shut and looked away.

The doorbell rang. York! At long last.

Eliza raced to answer it while Nicole resumed her struggle against her satin binding.

"She asked you a question," I said to her, yanking her back down. "Who are you?"

"Let me answer that." Detective York came into the kitchen on Eliza's heels, taking in the situation with one sweep of his eyes. "Her name is Pamela Davis. Not Nicole Leonard, and not Belinda Monte, your biological mother, Ms. Fox, who, I am sorry to say, passed away from a drug overdose several years ago."

Eliza clapped her hand over her mouth, tears pooling again. The poor girl was getting hit with a lot of information. I hoped Brad was still in the picture and would be here for her when she needed him to be. She charged Nicole, but York stepped in her way, blocking her. Eliza tried to get around him, but he held her back, and now her arms flailed as she struggled to break free. She jabbed her finger at Nicole. "Why? Why would you do this?"

"I can answer that, Ms. Fox," York said. "If you'll calm down now."

Eliza's body went limp. He released her, and she collapsed onto the floor.

York removed a pair of handcuffs, replacing the camera strap with them. "Inventive," he remarked, handing it back to me. He raised an eyebrow at the satin belt holding Nicole to the chair, but it had worked, so he had nothing critical to say. "Pamela Davis, alias Nicole Leonard, you are under arrest for the murders of Edward Yentin and Cordelia Knight."

He went on, but I moved around him, dropping to the floor beside Eliza, cradling her against me. She sobbed into my shoulder. "She . . . she k-killed them b-both?" she asked through her sobs.

York answered. "Yentin dug pretty deep into your life, Ms. Fox. During that process, he discovered Nicole Leonard was an alias. He wrote an article that would reveal that truth." He turned to Nicole, née Pamela. "You couldn't let *that* happen, so you killed him."

Nicole turned her head and spat at him—or at least in his general direction—but missed by a mile. She didn't say a word.

"And you killed Cordelia Knight because she was blackmailing you, wasn't she, Pammy? See, we found her emails to you, and your responses. Seems her laptop is missing, but her mail server synced to her desktop. Deleting the mail application on one end doesn't delete it on her end," he said, speaking to her like she was one of those stupid criminals featured on the radio. Which, apparently, she was.

I snapped my fingers, again. "The laptop! She had one in her hands when I got here."

York looked at Eliza. "With your permission, we'll be conducting a search of the premises."

Eliza's tears had stopped. Now she nodded blankly.

"My missing camera was in a cupboard over there," I said pointing toward the garage. "My guess is it'll show a photo of Nicole, er, Pamela, at Cordelia's party—"

"Placing her at the scene of the crime," York finished. He gave a single satisfied nod and repeated what I'd said just a few minutes ago. "Game over."

Chapter 26

"These are the nails in the coffin," Emmaline said the next day when we debriefed over coffee, referring to the photos on the memory card from my now recovered camera. Sure enough, I'd unwittingly managed to get several photos of Nicole, aka Pamela. She'd been dressed as a server. The photo series was of Cordelia, and I'd blurred backgrounds, but when you looked close enough, there was enough clarity to know it was, in fact, Nicole.

She continued. "Rita left the back gate open, allowing Nicole to slip in, dressed just like the servers who'd been at Eliza's party. She'd blended in, arranged to meet Cordelia in the backyard to discuss their business, then lay in wait for her, clobbering her with something she'd grabbed from inside before shoving her into the swimming pool for good measure."

"With one of Cordelia's own movie awards?" I asked, slack-jawed.

"A People's Choice," Emmaline confirmed. "We couldn't have definitively placed Nicole at the scene without those photos. She was tight-lipped, but as soon as we showed her those, she was done."

An hour later, I sat across from Eliza in her library. "She won't be coming back," I said. Brad was by her side, their shoulders brushing together, thighs touching, hands clasped. I sat in a club chair across from them.

Eliza's lower lip started to tremble. She balled one hand into a fist and pounded it against the top of her thigh. "I couldn't call her *mom,* you know? I suggested Belinda, but she told me she was used to going by Nicole. It never occurred to me that it was all a lie."

"Why would it?" I asked. "You had no reason to suspect she was anyone other than who she'd claimed to be. She was good at her job." I recalled the easy rapport between the two, and the way Nicole had taken care of Eliza. Nicole was as good an actress as Eliza. She'd fooled a lot of people.

"What was her end game?" Brad asked.

Eliza frowned. "Money. It's always money, isn't it? Work her way into my life. She's had access to my bank account almost from the beginning. God, I was so stupid!"

"You're trusting. That's different," I said. It was also a good thing, in my book. After everything she'd been through, I'd have worried she'd come out the other end tarnished, but Eliza was a fighter, and she wanted to believe the best in people.

"I have my accountant going through everything. He's already identified a regular pattern of withdrawals, and she forged my signature and had my car transferred into her name."

Eliza Fox was a long game for Nicole.

Brad's movie star mouth turned down. "So she never intended to play the part of Liza's mother?"

"No. I jumped to the conclusion that Nicole was your mother and the sneaky con woman ran with it. That was my fault. I'm so sorry, Eliza."

"It could have been her plan B," Brad suggested. "If she had to play that card—like if things went south—she would. That way she could worm her way even deeper into your life."

The three of us sat in silence, contemplating this. Nicole was diabolical, any way you looked at it. There was no telling the lengths she'd have gone to milk Eliza dry.

I was here as a friend to Eliza as she processed through everything that had happened, but she'd asked me over as moral support on a different matter. I'd hold her hand if need be. I'd also brought a loaf of cranberry bread that sat on Eliza's kitchen counter, a gift from Olaya. I knew it was infused with all the magic the red berries packed. I hoped it would help Eliza heal just a little bit more.

Brad checked his watch. "Are you sure about this?"

She squeezed his hand tighter but nodded. "I'm sure."

Not a second later, the doorbell rang. "I'll get it." I jumped up, returning to the library a few seconds later, John Calvin at my heels.

"Johnet—"

"*Mph*, no," Eliza said, holding up her hand to stop him. Her voice was shaky, but controlled.

John nodded. He stood awkwardly, twisting his ball cap in his hands. "Eliza. It'll take some time to get used to that. You used to watch that movie over and over and over. Doesn't surprise me you took the name Eliza."

"I reinvented my life, just like she did," Eliza said.

Oh! So Mrs. Branford had been right on the money. I wished I'd put it together. The first time I'd met Eliza, she'd told me she loved classic movies. If she'd wanted to leave Johnette Calvin behind, that meant she had to become someone new—just like Eliza Doolittle. The cockney flower girl had learned elocution from Henry Higgins, transforming herself into a lady. Johnette Calvin, a girl from the Central Valley, hadn't had a Henry Higgins to help her, but she'd transformed herself nonetheless. She'd buried the past and the sixteen-year-old girl she'd been and turned herself into Eliza Fox, a clever and independent new version of herself.

An awkward silence followed. Eliza's hand twisted in Brad's. Finally, John spoke again. "I did my best, baby. I never wanted your mother to leave, but she wouldn't stay. And then it was just you and me—"

At this, Eliza banked her head from side to side. "But it wasn't just you and me. It was you, me, and all your friends. That revolving door—"

He threw his hands up. "I know. I was stupid. Selfish. And the drugs. I put my needs ahead of yours. It's no excuse." His voice lowered, and when he looked at her, I could feel the sincerity. "You deserved better. You deserved to be safe."

"Why now, Dad?" Eliza asked wearily. "Why'd you come now? Do you want money, too?"

John's spine straightened, but he wasn't affronted. He was not aghast. No, he was resigned. His eyes were glassy. "I don't want your money, Joh—baby. You have no idea how many times I wanted to come. How many times I stopped myself. I'm in recovery now. And I'm asking for your forgiveness."

Eliza stayed quiet. John filled the silence. "I looked for you after you took off, you know. Even hired a PI, but the trail went cold. To everyone out there, you were just another runaway. And I sank deeper. Until I was watching TV one night and there you were, big as life. You'd changed your name, and you'd . . . well, you'd grown up . . . but there was no doubt about it. I recognized you immediately."

Tears tracked down Eliza's cheeks. "So, why now?" she asked again.

John scrubbed his face with one hand. "That guy that was killed . . . that reporter? He came knocking on the door one day out of the blue. Said he was doing a story on you and had traced you all the way back to me. I've been clean for five years now. I sent him away, but he sparked something in me. I wanted to warn you about him. And I wanted to see you. To finish my steps. To ask for your forgiveness."

Eliza swiped away the tears and ran the back of her hand under her nose, nodding.

"It's December. Holiday spirit and all. I came here, hoping, but you were having a party. I thought I could maybe talk to you, but then everything happened. I got scared, I'm not gonna lie. Here I was, showing up after that man had visited me, and now he was dead?"

"I trusted the wrong person. I should have let you in when you came back," Eliza said.

He shrugged, because it didn't matter anymore. "You let me in this time."

Eliza propelled herself from the couch, landing in front of him in one swift movement. She flung her arms around him, collapsing into muffled sobs. I didn't need to hear what she said to him to know that their relationship, for all its ups and downs, had a chance to mend.

Brad, with the hard lines of his jaw and his perfect teeth, caught my eye and smiled. "*Thank you*," he mouthed.

I smiled back and left them to their family reunion. The Blackbird Ladies were going to need their tissues when I told them this story.

Chapter 27

The umbrella organization that ran the women's shelter, Crosby House, had hired a new manager recently. Eliza had applied to be a volunteer when I'd first mentioned that I helped out there. She came with me on the very day she was approved—December 23rd. She spent the afternoon reading to some of the children taking shelter there while I baked cookies with some of the women. Once the cookies had cooled, mothers and children gathered together at the large table to spread icing onto the shapes, shake sprinkles onto them, and do their level best piping red and green accents.

"My dad is staying till the first, then he'll head back home. He and Brad have been golfing. Can you believe it?" Eliza laughed as she squeezed a glob of icing from her pastry bag. "I didn't know either of them actually knew how to golf."

"And Russ?"

"He went back home. Apparently, he has a wife and kids he had to get back to."

We parted ways with a hug, Eliza heading back to her husband and father, and me hightailing it to Yeast of Eden for the last party of the season. Until New Year's Eve, anyway.

I parked down the street and walked past the town's Christmas tree, past last-minute shoppers bustling about, their arms laden with gifts, past the shops of my home-town. The bread shop was bursting with activity. This party was one Olaya was holding for her employees, her friends, and her family.

I pushed through the front door, the tinkling of the bell barely audible over the music playing. The people laughed and chattered, cups of Olaya's perfect coffee, or a hand-made latte, or a little spiked punch in one hand, baked delicacies in the other.

Hugs, hugs, and more hugs all around. Martina was livelier than I'd ever seen her. She was the reserved Solis sister, but tonight she was positively gregarious. "Ivy, you are like my little sister," she said, draping her arm around me. Her words were a little slurred from the spiked punch. "Or maybe more like my cousin, but still, you are family."

I raised a brow at Consuelo, who gave a conspiratorial wink. "She's feeling happy.

"I can see that."

Emmaline and Billy sat across from each other at one of the tables. Billy had a candy cane–shaped bread stick clamped between his teeth, his eyes staring intently at his wife. I moved closer to see what was happening, groaning when I saw their hands clasped together, elbows firm against the table, locked in an epic arm-wrestling battle. "Don't say anything, Ivy," Em said, somehow sensing my presence without ever taking her gaze from Billy. "No distractions."

"Enough said." I ambled away, wishing Felix and Janae, Maggie and Tae, Zula, and the rest of Olaya's kitchen crew a merry Christmas, happy Hanukkah, and a happy Kwanza. The group split apart, and there was Olaya, her arm threaded through my father's. They fit together, I decided then and there. She made Owen happy, and my dad could certainly use a little happiness in his life. And for his part, he seemed to bring a glow to Olaya's cheeks.

"Do you approve?" a voice said in my ear.

I turned and smiled at Miguel. "Of Owen and Olaya? One hundred percent."

"Not that they need your approval," said Mrs. Branford with a chuckle. I swiveled my head to see all the Blackbird Ladies sitting at their usual table, Mrs. Branford holding her cane with one hand.

"You're right about that," I said, realizing that Mrs. Branford was actually right about nearly everything.

Miguel pulled me close. "Merry Christmas, Ivy," he said, and he kissed my cheek.

December 24th. I crouched down before Agatha and tightened the little red bow I'd affixed to her collar. I hadn't gone so far as to buy her a holiday dog sweater, tempted though I was. Maybe if we lived in the icy cold of the mountains, but her double coat was just fine for the temperate winter beach climate.

The white lights on the little Christmas tree twinkled,

the sprinkling of ornaments sparse, but enough. We had a few minutes before leaving for my dad's house. I stood, reaching out and letting my fingers flutter over one of the ornaments hanging on the tree. It was an old empty spool of thread, a narrow piece of paper wound around it. On that paper was written: *Ivy's Wish List*. Beneath that was a list of the things I'd wanted from Santa the year I'd been five.

A Scooby-Doo coloring book
Crayons—the box with a sharpener
A bike for Billy
To see Santa
A sleepover with Emmi

I chuckled. I hadn't wanted much, and from what I remembered, Billy had gotten his bike, and I'd proceeded to have untold numbers of sleepovers with Emmaline.

Miguel came up behind me and wrapped his arms around me, his cheek next to mine. "You okay?"

The reunion between Eliza Fox and her father had touched my heart and made me yearn for my mom. Her absence left an ache in me that I knew would never be filled, but I was glad I'd been part of Eliza's and John's reconciliation. I let out the deep breath I'd been holding. "Yeah."

And I was. I was with Miguel.

We gazed at the tree for a minute before Miguel pointed to a shiny silver sphere glinting amidst the pine needles. "Is that a new ornament?"

It wasn't one I recognized. "Mrs. Branford must have brought it over," I said. She was tricky like that. I reached for it, noticing the line dividing the sphere. "It opens."

Miguel moved to my side as I pried the two sides apart. And then I gasped. Tucked inside a pillow of velvet was a shimmering ring. Not just any ring, but the engagement ring my mother had worn for the thirty-nine years she and my dad had been married.

My heart nearly stopped. "What—"

With a gentle nudge, Miguel turned me to face him. "Ivy," he began, "it's taken us a long time to find each other again. I never want to let you go."

I fought back tears, but my eyes welled. This . . . this was happening.

"I love you, Ivy Culpepper, and I want to spend my life with you."

Agatha made a sweet sound at our feet, not wanting to be left out. Miguel looked down at her and nodded. "And with you, Ags."

This. Was. Happening. After my failed marriage, I'd vowed never to do it again unless I was one thousand percent sure.

"Ivy," Miguel said. "Will you spend your life with me?"

A tear slipped down my cheek as I looked first at him, then at my mother's ring cradled in the special silver ornament.

I was completely, totally one thousand percent sure. Ten thousand percent. No, a million percent sure that Miguel and I were meant to be together. That we'd live a happy shared life by each other's side.

"Yes," I tried to say, but the word came out as a croak, my emotions choking me.

"I'll take that as a yes," he said, and I nodded, trying to smile through my ugly tears.

He took the ornament from me and removed the ring.

Then he lifted my left hand and slipped it onto my ring finger.

Finally, the words broke free. "Yes," I said. "I love you, Miguel, and I will be your wife."

He lowered his lips to mine, the white lights on the Christmas tree twinkling in celebration. "The ring," I mumbled. "How . . . ?"

His lips smiled against mine. "Your dad gave me the ring when I asked for his blessing."

And with that, we kissed.

And Agatha barked.

And I said, "Whose house will we live in?"

Recipes

In the olden days in France, the spirit of love drew families together on Christmas Eve, just as it does now. People surrounded the blazing "Yule log" to warm themselves before walking the cobbled streets to midnight mass. The burning ashes of the Yule log, or *BÛCHE DE NOËL*, were said to hold magical properties, protecting newborns from illness and animals from fever.

The log-shaped cake is a symbol of Christmas and a renewal of this belief.

Here's hoping 'yule' have a very happy holiday!

Winnie

YULE LOG (*BÛCHE DE NOËL*)

Ingredients

Chocolate Cake
¾ cup all-purpose flour
⅓ cup cocoa powder
1 tsp baking powder
½ tsp salt
4 large eggs, divided
¾ cup sugar
5 tbsp sour cream
¼ cup butter, melted
1 tsp vanilla extract

Mascarpone Cream Filling
1⅓ cups heavy whipping cream, cold
¾ cups powdered sugar
1 tsp vanilla extract
¼ tsp salt
8 oz mascarpone cheese

Whipped Chocolate Ganache
8 ounces semi-sweet chocolate chips or a block, finely
   chopped
1 cup heavy whipping cream

Instructions
1. Preheat oven to 350°F.
2. Line a 17×12-inch jellyroll sheet pan with parchment

paper, allowing the edges to roll up to cover the lip of the pan.

3. In a medium bowl, blend together the flour, cocoa, baking powder, and salt.

4. In a large bowl, whisk together egg yolks and sugar until light and well blended.

5. Add the sour cream, melted butter, and vanilla extract to the egg/sugar mixture, and blend together well.

6. Add the dry ingredients to the wet mixture. Gently blend until well combined.

7. In a mixing bowl, whip the egg whites until a stiff peak forms when you lift the beaters out.

8. Gently, so as not to break down the beaten egg whites, fold ⅓ of the whites into the chocolate mixture. Add the rest of the beaten whites and fold together until combined.

9. Pour the cake batter into the pan, spreading to make it even. Bake for 10–12 minutes. The top of the cake should spring back when touched. You can also insert a toothpick into the center of the cake. If it comes out clean, it is ready.

10. Once you remove the cake from the oven, carefully lift it from the pan using the edges of the parchment paper.

11. Working while the cake is still hot, use the parchment paper to roll cake into a jellyroll shape, starting on the short side. Allow cake to cool completely.

12. Later, once the cake is cooled all the way, begin the filling. Whip together the cream, powdered sugar, vanilla, and salt until soft peaks form when lifting out the beaters.

13. Add the softened, but still cool, mascarpone cheese and whip again until stiff peaks form.

14. Carefully unfurl the cake roll. Use a spatula or other tool to carefully pull the parchment paper away from the cake, taking care not to break the cake itself.

15. Spread the filling onto the unrolled cake, leaving $\frac{1}{4}$ inch all the way around to allow for spreading. Without the parchment, roll the filled cake back into a roll.

16. Wrap rolled cake in plastic wrap, seam side down, and refrigerate for several hours.

17. After the cooling is complete, make the chocolate ganache by adding the chopped chocolate or the chips to a medium-sized bowl. Heat the cream until it's very hot and on the verge of boiling (in the microwave or on the stove). Pour the hot cream over the chocolate.

18. Once the chocolate starts melting from the cream, whisk together until smooth.

19. Allow the ganache to cool to room temperature, transfer to a large mixer bowl, and whip on high speed until it lightens in color. The consistency should be spreadable.

20. Now to decorate! Start by diagonally cutting off a 3-inch end piece of the log (use a serrated knife), and use ganache to affix the cut section to the side of the larger log. It should appear as a branched piece of wood.

21. Using a spatula, spread the rest of the ganache over the cake. Use the tines of a fork along the length of the log to create "bark" lines.

22. Add fruit such as cranberries and sugared rosemary for a festive touch.
23. Keep refrigerated until ready to serve.

Printed with permission from Life, Love, and Sugar: https://www.lifeloveandsugar.com/yule-log-cake-buche-de-noel/

MRS. BRANFORD'S SPARKLING
PEPPERMINT SWIRL

Ingredients
1½ oz vanilla vodka
1 oz crème de menthe liquor
Splash of grenadine
2½ oz sparkling wine

Instructions
1. Rim a chilled martini glass with crushed candy canes.
2. Fill a shaker with ice. Add vodka, crème de menthe, and grenadine in a shaker. Mix together, then strain into prepared glass.
3. Top with sparkling wine.
4. Garnish with a candy cane (optional).

CHRISTMAS PUNCH

Ingredients

5 cups 100 percent cranberry juice (cranberry juice
  cocktail)
2 bottles very dry sparkling wine (champagne, cava, or
  prosecco)
2 cups apple cider
1½ cups diet ginger ale
1½ cups dark rum or brandy
2 oranges, thinly sliced into rounds
1 cup fresh cranberries

Instructions

1. Chill all ingredients.
2. Fill a large punch bowl with ice. Top with the cranberry juice, sparkling wine, apple cider, ginger ale,
   and rum.
3. Stir to combine. Garnish with the orange slices and
   fresh cranberries.

STAR BREAD

Ingredients

1 package active dry yeast
¼ cup warm water
¾ cup warm milk (low-fat or full fat)
1 large egg, room temperature
¼ cup butter, softened
¼ cup sugar
1 teaspoon salt
3¼ to 3¾ cups all-purpose flour
1 cup seedless raspberry jam
2½ tablespoons butter, melted
Several tablespoons confectioners' sugar

Instructions

1. Dissolve yeast in warm water until foamy.
2. In a separate bowl, combine milk, egg, butter, sugar, and salt.
3. Add yeast mixture and 3 cups flour. Beat on medium speed until dough is smooth and sticky. Stir in enough remaining flour to form a soft dough.
4. Place dough on a floured surface and knead until smooth and elastic.
5. Place dough in a greased bowl, turning it to grease the top. Cover and set aside to rise until doubled.
6. Punch down dough.
7. Turn onto a floured surface and divide into four portions. Roll one portion into a 12-in. circle. Place on a greased 14-in. pizza pan. Spread with one-third of the jam to within ½ in. of edge. Repeat twice, layer-

ing dough and jam, and ending with final portion of dough.

8. Place a 2½-in. round cutter on top of the dough in center of circle as a marker only (don't press through the dough).

9. Using a sharp knife, make 16 evenly spaced cuts from the round marker to the outer edge of dough. This will form a sort of starburst.

10. Remove cutter.

11. Taking hold of two adjacent strips, rotate them together twice outward. Pinch ends together. Repeat with remaining strips.

12. Cover star bread and let rise until almost doubled, approximately 30 minutes.

13. Preheat oven to 375°. Bake until golden brown, 18–22 minutes.

14. Remove from oven and immediately brush with melted butter.

15. Cool completely on a wire rack, then dust with confectioners' sugar.

Don't miss any of the
Bread Shop Mysteries

And keep an eye out for more
coming soon
from
Winnie Archer
and
Kensington Books

Connect with

Visit us online at
KensingtonBooks.com
to read more from your favorite authors, see books
by series, view reading group guides, and more.

for sneak peeks, chances to win books and prize packs,
and to share your thoughts with other readers.

facebook.com/kensingtonpublishing
twitter.com/kensingtonbooks

Tell us what you think!

To share your thoughts, submit a review,
or sign up for our eNewsletters, please visit:
KensingtonBooks.com/TellUs.